PROFESSIONAL
DISTANCE

THORNE & DASH: BOOK I

SILVIA
VIOLET

Professional Distance by Silvia Violet

Chapter One

Thornwell Shipton was not pleased. He'd worked his ass off all week, never getting more than a couple of hours of sleep, and one thing that had kept him going was knowing that on Friday night, he would take a few hours off while his favorite rent boy buried himself balls deep in Thorne's ass. Now he had a message from the escort service telling him there was an issue with his appointment and he should contact them. He was in no mood to deal with more issues. Work had already thrown enough of those his way.

He double-checked that his office door was locked and then tapped his phone to return the call. As it rang, he stared out over the city hundreds of feet below. His office had a lovely view of Atlanta's Olympic Park, but he rarely noticed it these days.

Sheila, the woman who ran the service, answered just when Thorne was sure her voicemail would pick up. "Hello, Mr. Shipton. I'm sorry we had to bother you."

Sheila had a pleasant, soothing voice that probably worked wonders on many of their clients, but Thorne wasn't in the mood to be soothed. "What's the problem?"

"Marc isn't going to be working for us anymore."

"What? Why?" Thorne dropped his head against the window. *No. No. No.* He'd tried a number of escorts before finding Marc, none of whom satisfied

3

Thorne's needs for both dominance and submission, depending on his mood. Marc had been perfect. For the last several months, he'd made Friday night the highlight of Thorne's week.

"He's decided to pursue other interests."

Thorne snorted. That could mean anything. "Fine. I suppose I'll have to cancel the appointment."

"Actually, I have someone else for you."

"I don't think—"

Thorne didn't want to break in someone new. Not this week with him trying to wrap up a report for one of their biggest clients, a report he'd rewritten twice, while prepping to head out bright and early Monday morning to win his firm another multimillion-dollar contract. He'd made a killing as a high-end management consultant, but to keep the money flowing in, he had to be his best every day. There was always someone out there hoping to take his business away.

"Dash is well-suited to serve your needs, and he's available at your usual appointment time." Sheila had been the one to match him with Marc. Maybe... Why couldn't anything go right this week? He really did need a good fuck.

"Fine. Send him then." Thorne hoped he wouldn't regret this.

"Excellent. Do let us know if he meets your expectations. If so, I can book him for your regular appointment."

"I will. Thank you."

"Have a lovely day, sir."

"It's been a shitty one so far." Damn, he sounded bitter and put out.

"Tonight will be better."

It damn well better be. He ended the call.

***

Thorne's intercom buzzed. "A Mr. Dash is here to see you. He says he's expected. Shall I send him up?"

"Yes, Je-Michaels, thank you." Michaels had only been working as a doorman in Thorne's building for a few weeks, yet Thorne had lost count of the number of times he'd almost called the man Jeeves. Michaels' British accent and starched appearance simply begged for it. Years ago he'd loved to watch and re-watch the Masterpiece Theatre version of Wodehouse's Jeeves and Wooster, with Clint, his—boyfriend was certainly not right, even lover didn't fit—boss. His boss whom he'd occasionally fucked. Now, he couldn't remember the last time he'd watched anything but videos of junior consultants' meetings.

Two crisp knocks at the door signaled that Dash had made the long elevator ride to his penthouse apartment.

Thorne's pulse sped up. He resented how very much he needed this respite from work, these moments where he actually let go of all his clients' woes and indulged himself. Yet he kept paying for it, every week that he was in town. He imagined being fucked roughly, hands held down, as Dash whispered dirty words in his ear. By the time Thorne reached the door, he was already hard. Dash damn well better work out; but whether or not Thorne requested him to come back, he was going to get fucked tonight.

He checked the peephole out of habit, although

5

Michaels and the other doormen were quite strict about checking credentials before allowing anyone in the building. The young man standing at Thorne's door appeared to be in his early twenties, as were most of the service's employees. He had dirty-blond hair that curled loosely and was longer than he could have worn it if he'd worked in Thorne's office. His hazel eyes had a mischievous look to them that held promise. His smile, however, wasn't at all what Thorne was expecting. It was fresh and sunny and it reached his eyes, a true smile, like he was meeting a friend, not conducting illicit business.

Quit trying to read so much into him. This isn't a business meeting where you have to size up the clients. It's a fucking hook-up that you paid for.

Thorne opened the door.

"Mr. Shipton?" the boy asked.

Thorne nodded and stepped back so Dash could enter.

"I'm Dash; Sheila told me you were a client of Marc's." Dash lifted the strap of the messenger bag he carried over his head and sat the bag against the wall in the entryway.

"That's right," Thorne answered. "He suited my needs perfectly."

"And you think I won't?"

Fuck. Was he that transparent or was this kid that good? "What I think is that the rapport I had with Marc was hard to find."

"He's a switch and a damn good one." Dash's look said he knew that from personal experience.

"Correct."

"So am I." Dash smiled, and Thorne reacted as if

he'd wrapped his hand around Thorne's dick.

Thorne's gaze moved down Dash's body. He was shorter than Marc, who'd matched Thorne's six feet, maybe five feet nine or five feet ten. His body was lean but not without muscle. If Thorne had to guess, he'd say Dash was a runner. His tight black pants clung to his body, giving the impression he had a rather nice package.

"Shall I make you a drink while we discuss exactly what you'd like tonight?" Dash asked, wandering toward the kitchen.

It took a few seconds for the words to register in Thorne's brain. Dash was…hot, fucking hot. But there was something else about him, something Thorne couldn't define, that had Thorne salivating to get him naked and in bed. If Thorne believed in anything as hokey as "auras," he would've said Dash had a powerful one. Thorne pushed the thought away, disgusted. Too much work and too little sex must have fried his brain. He'd been so busy that week he hadn't even found time to jerk off.

"I don't need a drink, and I don't want to talk."

Dash grinned and propped himself against the bar in the kitchen area, cocking his hip out. The pose was obviously calculated to make Thorne appreciate his slim waist. "That eager, huh?"

"I realize some people hire escorts for companionship. They want to know someone is listening to them. I'm sick of talking: to clients, to employees, to fucking airport desk agents. I don't need you to pretend to be my friend. I need to be fucked."

"Sure of that, are you?" Dash asked, walking

7

around the bar and entering the kitchen.

"Yes."

"In my professional opinion, a bit of relaxing on the couch, talking, easing our way toward fucking would do you some good."

What the fuck? Maybe Dash wasn't right for Thorne after all. Thorne gave the orders here, even if he was the one with a cock up his ass. It was looking less likely that he was going to be in that position. Marc had understood that he didn't want chitchat; that Thorne liked to get down to business right away, blow off some tension and then get back to work.

Dash began to explore Thorne's kitchen. Thorne would have stopped anyone else, should have stopped him. What the hell gave him the right to start messing around in Thorne's apartment? And yet, Thorne simply watched the young man. Dash wasn't like anyone Thorne regularly interacted with. He appeared friendly and easygoing, but he obviously didn't take no for an answer. Maybe he really was a very good switch.

Dash opened Thorne's basically empty fridge and then a door to a closet that was supposed to be a pantry. Thorne used it to store weights and other fitness equipment. He worked out religiously, but he did it at home rather than wasting the time to go to a gym.

"You don't have any food, like none, not even coffee?" Dash looked truly horrified.

"There are some condiments and beer in the fridge." Why did Thorne sound apologetic? He didn't fucking apologize to anyone. *No, you don't talk to them long enough to need to.*

"That's not food."

"I order out. I don't have time for cooking."

"I'd cook for you if you actually had anything here."

He suddenly imagined Dash standing at the stove, wearing nothing but an apron. A nearly crippling shudder of lust shot through Thorne. Damn, he really was a mess.

"I told you I don't want to talk. I don't want to eat either. With what I'm paying you, I know you're not starving, so there's no need to go scouring my apartment for food."

Dash looked hurt for a fraction of a second. Thorne hadn't meant to belittle him. He had no problem with how Dash earned his money, and he hated it when men patronized prostitutes and then degraded them for providing the very service those men obviously needed.

Dash studied him for several seconds. "So you truly want me to just fuck you and then leave."

Did he? He always had with the men he'd hired in the past. "Yes."

"Then your wish is my command."

Chapter Two

Dash began unbuttoning his shirt. Thorne couldn't look away as Dash revealed tanned skin little by little. His chest was waxed smooth, the muscles well defined. Thorne couldn't wait to get a full view. Finally, Dash pulled the two halves of his shirt apart, letting it hang, giving tantalizing glimpses of his pecs and pebbled nipples. One at a time, he undid the buttons at his cuffs. He watched Thorne with heat in his eyes as he brought his arms behind him and let the shirt slip off and to the floor.

Thorne was practically salivating.

"Like what you see?"

Thorne nodded mutely, fully hard now. Dash groaned as he pinched his own nipples. Then he caressed himself, hands moving sinuously down his sides.

Impatience made Thorne find his voice. "Pants off. Now."

"We'll get there." Dash chuckled, but his hands dropped to his waistband.

He dipped a hand in and sucked in his breath. Thorne imagined his fingers teasing his cock.

"Off," Thorne demanded.

"I thought you wanted to be fucked."

"I do. Right fucking now."

"When I'm topping, I'm in charge."

Thorne didn't like for anyone else to have

control. He liked to be fucked, hard, but he didn't like taking orders. So why were Dash's words so fucking hot? Why was he contemplating letting Dash do exactly what Dash wanted?

Dash toed off his shoes. Then he lifted each leg and divested himself of his socks, taking his time, not rushing a single movement. *Fucking bastard.* Finally, he unfastened his pants, pushed them over his ass, and let them drop to the floor.

Thorne realized his mouth was literally hanging open. He shut it quickly, but he couldn't resist licking his lips. Dash's smile said he knew just how stunning he looked standing there in nothing but a pair of bright red and black Andrew Christian briefs that framed his cock and showed off just how sizable it was. Thorne was going to be feeling it for quite some time if Dash used him as thoroughly as Thorne wanted him to.

Dash tugged at his briefs until his cock bobbed free. It was as thick as it had looked tucked inside the stretchy fabric, maybe more so.

"Lube and condoms are in the bag. Get me ready," Dash ordered.

Fuck. Thorne's cock jumped at the command in Dash's voice. But he stood his ground. This was not how things were supposed to go.

"I like to be fucked, but I'm no submissive."

Dash glanced at Thorne's crotch. "Your cock seems to disagree."

"You're gorgeous and naked and sex with you is a sure thing. Of course I'm hard."

Dash raised a brow. "Play along. Say no anytime, but I think you'll like what I'm offering."

He did like it, and he resented Dash for knowing that. Without saying a word, he walked over to where Dash had dropped his bag, opened it, and started to look through it. Wow, Dash had quite an interesting collection of dildos, butt plugs, and…rope, the same bright red shade as his briefs.

"Front pocket," Dash said.

Thorne located the necessary items. Then he walked back to Dash and held them out.

Dash shook his head. "No, I told you to get me ready."

Thorne sank to his knees, giving in to his need to taste Dash first. He could have rolled the condom on, slicked him up, dropped his pants, and offered his ass. That's exactly what he'd have done with Marc. No, with Marc he'd have told him to lube his own damn dick and then get Thorne ready. Why was everything so different with Dash? Thorne hated change, at least he usually did.

Dash sucked in his breath when Thorne wrapped a hand around his cock. Thorne would swear the sound was utterly unaffected, but Dash was a professional—pretending he was as into it was his job. Thorne licked at the broad head of Dash's cock. God, this monster would stretch his ass so good. The taste of Dash's precum had him wanting more, so he dipped his tongue into the slit. Dash's hands came down on his shoulders, his grip tight. Thorne nearly convinced himself Dash was as desperate for more as he was himself. He took Dash's shaft into his mouth, sucking while teasing his balls, rolling them in one hand and using the other to steady himself on Dash's firm thigh.

Dash rocked forward, pushing into Thorne's mouth. Thorne took him deeper, sucking, licking. Fuck, his jaw was going to pop if he took much more. He'd never had a man as thick as Dash.

"Enough," Dash ordered.

Thorne was torn between seeing how far he could push Dash by defying him and obeying because the command in Dash's voice had his dick hard as titanium. They might not have made it very far yet, but Thorne already knew he'd be engaging Dash for another round the following week. Hell, he'd like to have him back the next day. But no, once a week, that's how he did things. Everything in his life had a place, and sex was for Friday nights.

His conscience laughed at him. *You could be fucking someone every night if you'd get over hiding who you are and being afraid of a relationship.*

Fuck off. Things are much better this way.

At least you take that stick out of your ass and put a cock in it on occasion. Or a dildo.

Dash pushed at Thorne's shoulders. "I'm gonna come if you don't stop."

"That good, am I?"

Dash glared at him, but he could see the humor Dash was trying to mask. "You'll do," he responded; then he gestured toward the lube and condom that Thorne had set on the floor.

Thorne ripped the condom pack open and rolled it onto Dash's dick, fighting the urge to rush. Then he drizzled lube over him and stroked him a few times to rub it in.

"Now strip and lube your ass," Dash said.

"I already told you I don't take orders." Thorne's

protest sounded weak even to him. Thank God he spoke to his clients with more authority in his voice.

"You've been doing a damn fine job taking them so far."

He refused to acknowledge that Dash was right, but he stood and did exactly what Dash had told him to do. He didn't take his time like Dash had, though. He pulled his shirt from his pants, made quick work of the buttons, then slipped off his cufflinks and laid them on the coffee table. As soon as he was naked from the waist up, he pushed his pants and boxer briefs to the floor, stepped out of them, and bent to deal with his socks.

"Allow me."

Suddenly, Dash was on his knees in front of Thorne. He hadn't expected that. Not with the I-know-you-want-a-dom attitude. Dash tapped one of Thorne's legs, and he lifted it so Dash could take off his sock. He kissed Thorne on the inside of his ankle, and that mere brush of Dash's lips made him shudder.

Dash grinned. He'd noticed. The fucker. He took off Thorne's other sock, slowly and methodically. He kissed that ankle too and then ran his tongue around the circular bone. Thorne couldn't breathe. Since when was his ankle an erogenous zone? Dash looked up then, his mouth just inches from Thorne's cock, which was hard and flushed and desperate for Dash to kiss it too.

Dash looked up and down Thorne's body. "You're gorgeous," he said, his voice low and sultry.

Thorne didn't know how to reply to that. He kept himself in shape, and he knew he was a nice-looking man, but he didn't expect compliments like that.

Thorne was relieved from the need to speak by Dash taking his cock into his mouth.

Electric current raced through Thorne's body. "Jesus!"

Dash's mouth was so fucking hot, and he sucked so tightly, and oh my fucking God, he took Thorne all the way down, pressing his lips against Thorne's pubic bone.

Dash pulled back. "Enough of that. I don't want things to end too soon."

Thorne wanted to protest, but he'd lost the ability to speak.

Dash grabbed the lube and held it out to Thorne. "Open yourself up. I want to watch."

Thorne's heart pounded. Just how much of him was Dash going to expose? The idea of bending over in front of Dash, showing off his ass, parting it, driving his fingers in deep while Dash watched… Why the hell was that so hot, and how did Dash know he would think so?

He squirted lube onto a few fingers and then moved farther into the living area where he could prop one foot on a stool. He'd never been into performing for his partner, but he sure as hell was now, at least according to his cock, which was so hard he didn't know how he would last once Dash was inside him.

He positioned himself so Dash had a good view.

Dash gave a predatory smile. "You're fucking perfect."

Thorne snorted. "I bet you say that to all your clients."

"I most certainly don't."

More flattery. Thorne should just enjoy it instead of overanalyzing. He pushed a finger into his ass, slowly moving it in and out. He could hear Dash breathing hard, but he kept his eyes closed. He added another finger, working them both deep. Then he held them still and used his leg muscles to move his body up and down like he was riding a cock.

"More." Dash's voice was strangled. Thorne looked at him; his mouth was open and his eyes wide. He'd lost the calculating look he'd had before, and the sweet young man was back, well, a sweet young man who loved ass, anyway.

Thorne added another finger, groaning as he sank down. He'd need to be really open to take Dash's cock.

"Get that beautiful ass of yours to the bed. I want you bent over the end, arms stretched out. I suggest you hold on to something. It's going to be a wild ride."

God, Thorne hoped so. His cock was so hard he wasn't sure he could walk.

"Should we close the blinds, or are you happy to give a show?" Dash asked.

Thorne had floor-to-ceiling windows throughout his apartment and rarely used the blinds. Hardly anyone could see them up so high, especially with the lights dim. Thorne was in the closet. He wasn't willing to risk what coming out would mean to his business, but somehow twenty floors up, he felt distant from such concerns. He liked to take a few risks. "We'll leave them open. Lights low."

The lights dimmed.

"Well fuck me. What other tricks can you do?"

"The system responds to a limited amount of voice commands. I—"

"Like to control things," Dash said.

"Are you always this fucking arrogant with clients?"

Dash laughed. "Only the special ones."

Before Thorne could respond, Dash issued a command. "Get into position. I don't want to wait any longer, and I don't think you do either."

Thorne sure as fuck didn't. His ass felt empty after he'd worked so hard to stretch himself. Just thinking of the look on Dash's face as he'd watched was enough to make him stumble. "Fuck!"

Dash caught him under the arm and supported him the last step of the way. "Thanks." The word slipped out before Thorne could stop it. He hated how vulnerable he sounded.

"Always," Dash said, whispering the word close to his ear.

Thorne turned and cupped Dash's face. He almost never kissed men, especially ones he'd hired, but this time he wanted to. "Do you kiss?"

Dash smiled. "I love to, but I'd figured you for the type who didn't."

"I don't," Thorne said and kissed him.

Dash groaned and opened easily to Thorne's questing tongue. God, his mouth felt good, slick and warm. Their tongues tangled, and the kiss grew wilder, harsher. Dash grabbed Thorne's ass and hauled him up against his body, their cocks sliding along each other.

Thorne thrust against Dash, wanting to feel Dash's cock rub against his. He couldn't help himself; that thick, hard flesh was making him crazy. Dash pulled back and spun him to face the bed. He was so dizzy from the kiss and the sudden movement that he crashed to the bed, managing to catch himself on his arms. Slowly, he stretched out, sinking down, and letting the mattress hold him up.

Dash grabbed his hips and pulled him back. "I can't have you humping the mattress when I'm determined to make this last as long as possible."

"Holy fuck!"

"Yes, it will be."

Thorne worked his hips, but his dick didn't touch anything but air. He doubted he'd survive much longer, but rather than touching himself like he wanted to, he kept his arms stretched out over his head and held the comforter in a death grip. At this rate, he'd rip it to shreds before the night ended. Finally, Dash moved directly behind him and brushed Thorne's hole with the tip of his cock.

Thorne squirmed, wanting to get away and take more at the same time.

"Mmm, so responsive," Dash said. "This is going to be a lot of fun, isn't it?"

"Stop fucking teasing me."

"Oh, you don't like teasing?" Dash teased his hole again. "You want me to give you this?"

"Yes, goddammit!"

Dash pushed in without warning, breaching the tight muscle and making Thorne cry out.

"Fucking bastard!"

Dash held still, he was only a little way inside, but Thorne already felt like he was being split in two.

"Breathe," Dash encouraged.

Thorne wasn't sure his lungs worked anymore, or maybe it was his brain that had gone wonky.

"Relax and breathe." Dash ran his hands up and down Thorne's back on either side of his spine. Eventually, the movement lulled Thorne, and once again, he sank into the mattress.

Dash pulled out and drove in again.

"Oh my fucking God!" Thorne yelled. He'd have sworn Dash was trying to put a telephone pole up his ass. "If that's not all of it, I don't think I can—"

"You'll take it. Don't worry." Dash massaged him again, soothing, lulling. "Just relax and open up."

Fuck that! He was about as open as he could get and not be torn apart.

Dash pulled back and then used slow, tiny strokes, mere pulses. At first it still hurt, but after a few seconds, Thorne needed "more!"

"All of it," Dash said.

He pushed in slow but steady, gripping Thorne's shoulders for leverage. "Push out."

Thorne did, and fuck, fuck, fuck, Dash made it all the way in.

"See? I told you you'd take it all."

"You're killing me." Thorne forced the words out through gritted teeth.

"No, you'll live, but I might just ruin you for other men."

Thorne groaned. "I think you already have."

Dash massaged Thorne's ass, his shoulders, and his back until he was like putty, putty with a pole up its ass.

When he started to move again, Thorne whined, an embarrassing sound. His cock had softened as he'd relaxed, but it hardened again after only a few of Dash's slow strokes.

"Now let's see if I can…" Dash's words trailed off. He tilted Thorne's hips and pushed in deeper.

Thorne's body lit up. "Yes. Right there. Oh my God!"

"I found it."

"Don't you dare stop," Thorne growled.

Dash kept going, fucking Thorne at the perfect angle. Thorne was coming apart. He was so fucking close, but he couldn't get the friction he needed to go over.

"I need…" He couldn't think. Words formed in his brain but didn't reach his mouth. He was floating; the only thing real was Dash's cock.

"What do you need?" Dash asked.

"Please!"

"Tell me, Mr. Shipton."

"Thorne." There. His voice did work. At least for a one-word answer.

"What?"

"Call. Me. Thorne."

"What do you need, *Thorne*?"

Thorne gave up trying to say it. He let go of the comforter. His hand was nearly too cramped to work, but somehow he'd have to force it, because if he didn't get some friction on his cock soon, he was going to lose his fucking mind.

When he reached under his body, Dash grabbed his hand and yanked it out to the side.

"No!" Thorne shouted. "Need to come. Now!"

"Oh, you want to come?"

"Fuck you!" Thorne struggled, trying to free his

hand from Dash's grip.

"No need to be rude. All you have to do is ask." Dash wrapped a hand around Thorne's cock.

Thorne gasped. He was so fucking sensitive now. He gripped the comforter again as Dash worked him. He thrust into Dash's fist and back onto his dick, desperate for release.

"Yes," Dash encouraged him. "Take what you want. Fuck yourself on my cock."

Thorne cried out as he came, the orgasm hitting him so hard the world dimmed. He fought for air as he shot over and over, and Dash kept jerking him off.

When he was done, he collapsed against the comforter, drenched in sweat and utterly exhausted.

Dash let go of his cock and leaned over him, putting his hands on top of Thorne's. "My turn."

He fucked Thorne hard, fast, but still with finesse, keeping his rhythm steady until he cried out Thorne's name. His fucking name. Did he plan that?

Dash jerked his hips against Thorne's as his orgasm seemed to consume him and then it was all over. Thorne would have to go back to the real world where there weren't any brazen rent boys, only fucking demanding clients.

He let out a long breath, deciding a few more minutes wouldn't hurt. He didn't push Dash off like he might have. They lay there, Dash draped over him, their bodies slick against each other, their breathing heavy.

Dash kissed his neck, his back, each vertebra. Then slowly, he rose and pulled out.

Thorne gasped. "Wow, that's…wow." Thank God he wouldn't be sitting on any hard conference room chairs tomorrow.

"All you'd hoped for?"

"More." Thorne immediately wished he could take that back. He felt more exposed with that admission than he had with his ass spread for Dash.

"Good." Dash leaned down and kissed each of his ass cheeks. "I aim to please."

Thorne forced himself to stand. "Whoa." The room spun, and he had to wait a few seconds before he was certain he could make it to the bathroom without crashing to the floor.

"Lie down for a bit if you'd like," he told Dash. "I'm going to grab a shower and then I've got to get back to work."

"You're working on a Friday night?"

Thorne sighed. "I'm always working."

Chapter Three

"So we're done?" Dash asked when Thorne emerged from the bathroom.

"Yes." Thorne had never wanted Marc or any of the other rent boys to stay. But Dash… No. Thorne had work to do. Days' worth of work and he only had until his midday flight on Sunday to finish it. Playtime was over.

Dash didn't say anything else. He simply picked up his clothes and headed into the bathroom. Thorne watched his ass every step of the way, sinking his teeth into his lower lip to keep from calling him back.

When he sat down at his desk, he deliberately shifted in his seat, enjoying how sore he was. Once he heard the shower spray, he turned his attention to his laptop. By the time Dash exited the bathroom, Thorne had written a large chunk of the first report he needed to finish. He glanced at the time. Wow, Dash had been in there for half an hour. Surely he hadn't needed to jack off again. "You do have hot water at home, right?"

"Yes," Dash said. "As you pointed out, I'm well compensated, though my shower is about half that size."

Thorne did like the luxuries his hard work had earned him, and the extra-large shower was one of his favorite indulgences. But was that bitterness in Dash's tone? He hadn't meant to be an ass, again. "I didn't mean—"

Dash held up a hand. "I have sex for money. It's my choice. It's a hell of a lot more fun than other things I could do to save up for school, trust me."

Thorne wouldn't dispute that. Working retail or any service industry job was just a different way of getting screwed. As long as the clients were vetted—and Thorne knew they were—and Dash had a say in whom he worked for… Yeah, it could be much worse.

"You sure you don't want me to stay?" Dash chose that moment to unhook the towel he'd wrapped around his waist and let it drop. Thorne couldn't resist giving him a thorough once-over.

Having him stay was tempting, but Thorne would never finish his work if he did. "I told the service I only needed a few hours of your time. And, as I already told you, I have work to do."

"You have heard of weekends, right?"

"My clients don't care what day of the week it is." He tapped his laptop. "I need to finish this report."

"What you need is to relax."

That was why he scheduled time for sex every Friday. "What the fuck do you think I just did?"

"You came spectacularly, but you're already tense again. Sex is one way to relieve tension, but it's clearly not enough for you."

Where did Dash get the goddamn nerve to lecture him? And why hadn't Thorne kicked him out? "I don't do post-sex cuddling if that's what you're thinking."

Dash grinned. "I would never accuse you of such

a thing."

What the fuck did that mean?

"So what do you do for fun?" Dash asked, ignoring Thorne's wish for him to leave. "Watch TV?" He gestured toward the enormous flat-screen on the wall in front of the couch.

"No." Thorne didn't have time to lie around like that.

"Do you read?"

"Reports for work. Rarely anything else."

Dash sighed and shook his head. "Junk food? Surely you at least eat cake, doughnuts, candy, something?"

Thorne hesitated. Cake used to be a major weakness. Then he hit forty and had to work extra hard to maintain his weight.

Dash grinned. "Ah. Now I got you pegged. You'd love to binge on chocolate cake, wouldn't you? One with a dark ganache on top, maybe a rich cherry filling inside."

Fuck. Cake had never sounded so hot as it did when Dash talked about it. "Okay, you discovered my secret. I have a sweet tooth. But this report still has to get written."

Dash crossed the room and came to stand right by Thorne, still buck naked, of course.

"Surely, the report can wait a little while. Let's have some cake together."

Thorne reached out and skimmed his knuckles over Dash's sleek abs. "Is that a euphemism?"

Dash winked. "It could be, but I think we should have the real thing first."

"Are you always like this?"

25

"Like what?"

Thorne couldn't find the right word to describe what he meant, and that was unsettling because he was rarely at a loss for words. He couldn't afford to be with his clients. "You walk in and just take over. And you're so fucking…happy."

Dash laughed. "I try to see the good in everything."

"How old are you?" Did Thorne really want to know?

"Twenty-two."

Fuck.

"Ah, the optimism of youth."

"You're hardly an old geezer, you know."

Thorne sighed. "I'm forty-two, but sometimes I feel a hundred."

Dash leaned down and nibbled Thorne's neck. Then he ran his tongue around the outer edge of his ear, making Thorne shudder. "You fuck like you're twenty," Dash whispered.

"Jesus, would you stop." No wonder Dash could command top dollar with the most exclusive escort service in town. Thorne grabbed his phone and pulled up the number of Bavaria Haus, a nearby restaurant that made exquisite black forest cake.

His call was answered on the second ring. "Mr. Shipton, how may we help you?" Thorne recognized the voice. Niklas, the front-of-the-house manager.

"Good evening, Niklas."

"It's been too long. I hope you are well."

"Very, thank you. Could you send two pieces of black forest cake and some Viennese coffee to my place?"

"For you, of course. Anything else?"

"Not tonight."

"I'll send Alex. He'll be there in fifteen minutes. No more."

Thorne recognized the name. Alex was one of the waitstaff who often worked the busy weekend nights. Niklas always sent one of the servers since they didn't actually offer delivery. It was a perk for very special customers.

"You have my gratitude."

"Enjoy your dessert."

"I assure you, I will." Thorne ended the call.

"Do you have a bakery on retainer?" Dash asked.

"Not exactly. I'm an excellent customer at Bavaria Haus. When I make special requests, they do their best to fill them."

Dash shook his head. "In other words, they do whatever you say, just like most people."

"That's not—"

"Come on. Everyone does your bidding. That's what you expect."

Thorne would have been offended or at least pretended to be, but Dash looked like Thorne's officious behavior turned him on. Did he get off on topping powerful men? If so, Thorne supposed it was no wonder Sheila had thought they were a match.

"It's true. *Most* people do as I say." *You are an excellent example of an exception.*

"So what are you working on?" Dash asked as he propped his naked ass on Thorne's desk.

"A report. I told you that, and I'd like to get on with it while we wait for the cake."

Dash ignored him, of course. "What kind of

report? What do you do?"

"Aren't you taught not to ask clients personal questions?"

Dash shrugged. "I figure we've been about as personal as two people can be."

"Maybe I'd rather stay fairly anonymous."

"I'm at your apartment."

He was fucking relentless, but Thorne found himself smiling and fighting the urge to laugh.

"Ah, there you go. See? Relaxing a little doesn't hurt."

"Why don't you tell me about yourself?" Thorne said, having no intention of revealing anything else about his personal life, or lack thereof. "What do you do to relax other than fuck, or is that more work than relaxation?"

"That depends on the client." Dash's eyes twinkled as he looked Thorne over.

"Don't even go there," Thorne warned. "No more flattery."

"It's not flattery when it's true."

Thorne sighed.

Dash held his hands up. "Okay. Okay. I like to watch movies, old ones, like from the eighties."

Thorne looked up, horrified. "Eighties movies are oldies now?"

Dash laughed. "Oh yes; I can't believe they had color back then."

Thorne glared at him. "Funny. You do realize I was alive back in those dark times."

"Nothing dark about them; rather sparkly and bright, really. An exciting time for gay fashion."

Thorne made a strangled sound as he fought a

laugh.

"It's working. Some of the tension has left your shoulders, and you're no longer grinding your teeth."

How had Dash known that's what he had been doing? He hadn't realized it himself until Dash mentioned it.

Dash slid off the desk, landing softly on the wood floor. He moved behind Thorne and began massaging his shoulders. "Fuck, when was the last time you had a professional massage?"

"Try never."

Dash tsked. "You've got to do something about this, or you're going to end up with a neck injury."

"I don't have time for nonsense like massages. I—"

"Have to work." Dash's mocking tone should've pissed him off. Instead, he found it adorable. God, he was infuriating.

"You also have to live," Dash insisted.

Thorne lived for his job. When he'd been hired, Symthson had been a mid-range firm, but he'd wowed some very important clients, and the firm's reputation had grown as had his salary. When Mr. Symthson himself had retired, Thorne bought out his shares, making him the owner of 30 percent of the company, 10 percent more than anyone else. Now Symthson Associates was arguably the best at what they did. Relaxing wasn't going to keep that success going. *But can* you *keep going if you don't?*

The doorbell rang then. Thorne stood and waved Dash away.

"Would I shock the poor man at the door?"

Thorne shook his head. "No, but he might try to

steal you." If Alex was the server Thorne thought he was, he was rather flirtatious.

Dash stepped into the bedroom, and Thorne answered the door.

"Good evening, Mr. Shipton. May I say you made an excellent choice? The black forest cake is my favorite of our desserts."

"It's quite delicious," Thorne agreed.

Alex's tongue snaked out, and he wet his lower lip. "Yes, it is."

Thorne had clearly remembered him correctly. He handed Alex a wad of cash. "Keep the change."

His eyes widened. "Thank you. Enjoy your cake."

"I will." Thorne took the carafe and the pastry box and shut the door. The moment it clicked shut, Dash stepped out of the bedroom.

"Forget him stealing me. I think he would have been happy to stay and enjoy you, maybe topped with cake."

"Ha! He just knows his craft, like you."

"Maybe Sheila should hire him away from the restaurant business."

Thorne laughed. "Maybe she should."

Thorne set the food down on the coffee table. "Do you usually eat dessert naked?"

Dash grinned. "I don't really see the need for clothes. They're too confining, but if you'd like me to dress…"

Thorne looked at him. Dash's cock was semi-hard again. What exactly had he been thinking about? "No, I like you the way you are."

"I had a feeling you did."

Thorne got mugs and a few dessert plates, so they wouldn't have to eat out of the containers.

He set them down on the table and opened the box that held two large slices of cake. Dash groaned. "That smells amazing."

Thorne could only agree.

"Here. I'll do that," Dash said, taking the plate from him. "You sit back and relax. This was my idea after all."

Thorne leaned back on his sofa. He didn't mind watching a gorgeous, naked man serve him cake and coffee. Dash plated up the cake and then filled mugs for each of them, moving gracefully through every step, seeming to position himself in a way calculated to show off his many charms. By the time Dash handed him a piece of cake and settled on the sofa next to him, Thorne's cock had let him know that round two with Dash was a necessity.

Thorne took a bite, trying to concentrate on the cake rather than the man in front of him. Not an easy task, at least not until the rich chocolate and tart cherry hit his tongue. "Mmm. Just as good as I remember."

Dash looked ready to come from his sample. He licked his fork and grinned at Thorne. "Perfect. I knew you had to enjoy something other than sex and work."

Thorne took another bite. He closed his eyes and simply enjoyed the pleasure. Why hadn't he ordered this recently? Oh yeah, because he'd have to work it off. But this time, he could work it off with Dash instead of the infernal treadmill.

"What are you thinking?"

"Why?"

"You smiled, and I don't think it's just the cake."

Why not just admit it? *You know you're not letting him go without fucking again.* "I was thinking about all the calories in the cake and then realized I could work them off with you."

"First of all, calories don't look like a major issue for you, and secondly, why not do both."

"Both?"

"Eat and burn it off all at once."

Dash slid off the couch and positioned himself in front of Thorne. He pushed Thorne's legs open, and Thorne gave no resistance. His cock was all for finding out what Dash had in mind.

Dash untied Thorne's robe and pulled it open. Then he dipped a finger in the cake's whipped icing. But instead of licking it off, he rubbed the cream on Thorne's nipple.

Thorne glared at him. "What are you doing?"

"Eating you," Dash said.

He leaned forward and sucked Thorne's nipple into his mouth, stealing the breath Thorne needed to launch a protest. He licked and sucked, cleaning off all the icing. Thorne was now fully hard and fighting the urge to squirm. Dash gave his other nipple the same treatment. "Good?"

Thorne nodded reluctantly. Dash loaded his fork with a bite of cake and fed it to Thorne.

"Tasty?" Dash asked.

"Oh, yes," Thorne said, but it wasn't the cake. It was the way Dash was looking at him. Thorne knew he was far from done with this man. "Don't let me stop you. You seemed to be enjoying your nonconventional eating methods."

"Oh, I am."

Dash scooped up more icing and filling and spread them on Thorne's cock, and Thorne gripped the edge of the couch to keep from pushing Dash's head to his crotch. He wanted to let this play out if he could stand it. How was he so fucking hard when he'd already come once that night?

Dash licked him, barely touching his cock with his tongue. It was torture, but finally Dash had him all cleaned up. That's when he started sucking in earnest.

No, Thorne wasn't going to let things end like this. "Dash. Dash!"

Dash pulled back and looked up.

"I want to fuck you this time."

Dash grinned. "I would like that very much. Don't move. I'll get what we need."

"You want me to fuck you here?"

Dash nodded. "Something about having you on the couch, all cake smeared. It's just perfect."

Thorne loved the idea.

"Grab a blanket from the closet by the door. We'll use it to protect the couch. I have a feeling things will get messy."

Dash grinned. "I'm counting on it."

They spread the blanket out, and Dash reclined against the arm of the couch. He lifted his legs and held them doubled on his chest, showing off his ass, which Thorne now wanted desperately.

Thorne opened Dash up, driving his fingers deep, not being gentle. Dash moaned and squirmed, obviously loving it. "Fuck me, Thorne. Please."

He was so beautiful, and he really did seem as

desperate to be fucked as he had to top Thorne. Thorne's hands shook as he rolled on the condom. He'd intended to play with Dash, to cover him in icing like he'd done to Thorne, but he was too impatient, too desperate to feel that tight hole clasp around his dick.

He teased Dash, pushing a finger just barely inside him. "You ready for my cock?"

"So ready!"

"Good. Because I'm going to give it all to you. Can you take that?"

"I can take anything you want to give me."

He was perfect. Exactly what Thorne wanted. What if… No. Focus on the sex. That's what Dash was here for, what he was paid for.

Thorne lined up his cock and drove in hard.

"Fucking fuck!" Dash shouted. "God, that's—"

Thorne didn't give him a chance to get the words out. He pulled back and thrust again, filling Dash up.

"Bastard!"

Thorne chuckled. He worked Dash's ass, keeping up a steady rhythm, driving deep, until he was begging. "Please. More. Need to come. Please."

Thorne pulled all the way out, sat on the couch, and pulled Dash onto his lap. "Ride me."

Dash grinned. "Tired of doing the work?"

"You did tell me to relax."

Dash rose up and took Thorne's cock in his hand. He stroked him a few times, dragging a groan out of him. Then he positioned himself and started to sink down on him, slowly, so slowly.

"Stop torturing me," Thorne demanded.

"Payback."

Thorne huffed. "I never went slow."

"So now I'm forcing you to for taking me like a beast."

"You said—"

"I loved it, but this is fun."

Dash kept lowering himself at the pace of a snail. How the fuck were his leg muscles holding him for so long without even quivering?

Thorne ran his hands up and down Dash's thighs. "Impressive."

Dash winked. "I try."

Dash finally hit bottom, but he didn't move.

"You'd better fuck me right fucking now."

"Or?"

Thorne dug his fingers into Dash's hips, trying to make him move. "Or I'm going to eat every last bite of cake that's left."

"Ooooh, that's quite a threat."

"And I won't even eat it off you."

Dash rose up and slid down, still slow, but at least he was moving.

"I thought that would disturb you," Thorne taunted.

Dash increased his pace, but somehow Thorne was sure Dash had the upper hand. It didn't matter that Thorne's dick was in Dash's ass and Thorne was the one making threats. Determined to take back more control, he wiggled around until he could get more leverage. He tried to hold Dash still while he thrust up into him.

"Yes," Dash shouted. "Show me how much you need it."

"Damn right I will. I'm going to fill your ass."

"Yes, stuff me fucking full."

"Fuck!" Thorne was so close. One more thrust. Two. And he was coming. He pulled Dash to him and bit down on his shoulder to muffle his shout.

Dash cried out, "Fucking God, I love that. Bite me harder."

He did, and Dash came, shooting sticky fluid between them, looking more fucking hot than Thorne thought possible.

After they'd caught their breaths, Dash rose off Thorne and flopped down on the couch next to him. "I'd say we earned the cake."

"More than," Thorne agreed. Silently, they each polished off the last of their pieces and drained their coffee mugs. Thorne hadn't felt so at peace in ages. He could get used to this.

No, I'm paying him for sex not for dessert. I don't need anyone.

Are you sure? That little voice in his head was dangerous.

Dash is an escort. This isn't a date.

"So I guess you require another shower now," Thorne said, needing to stop the thoughts in his mind.

Dash laughed. "I'll just clean up and go if that's what you want."

"I… Yes, I need to work." He did but… No, he wouldn't ask Dash to stay the night. He didn't do sleepovers.

Dash kissed the top of his head, the gesture sweet and caring. It felt more intimate than anything else that had happened.

Dash picked up his clothes and disappeared into the bathroom. Thorne never should've let him stay.

36

Stick to a schedule, that's how he got so much done. Once a person started deviating, that's when things got fucked up. Expectations change. Slacking off becomes the norm, and everything falls apart.

Or you work yourself to death and die of a heart attack before you hit forty-five. Which is worse?

Thorne used the blanket from the couch to clean himself off and then pulled on some shorts and a T-shirt. He'd shower again later before bed.

Dash is in there. You could join him.

No. Enough is enough. Though if he were honest, Thorne wasn't sure he'd ever have enough of Dash. The man was a whirlwind, and Thorne couldn't say no to him. That should worry Thorne more than it did.

He tried to turn off the part of his brain that had jumped on the Team Dash bandwagon, but he'd barely written a paragraph before Dash exited the bathroom. He didn't speak at first, probably trying not to disturb Thorne. He gathered his things, including the bottle of lube that lay on the floor by the couch.

"So I guess I'll be going," Dash said when his bag was packed up. He lingered in the entryway. Was he hoping Thorne would change his mind and ask him to stay? He looked like he wanted to, but of course he would, since he'd make more money that way.

"Yes, thank you."

"I'd love to see you again."

"Would you now?" Thorne asked.

Dash looked down, submissive again, teeth sunk into his lip.

Fuck, he knows what that does to me. "Next week. Same time. I'll call to confirm the appointment."

"Lovely. See you then."

Dash was gone before Thorne could say anything else. The apartment suddenly seemed very large and very quiet.

Quiet is good. I like quiet.

Chapter Four

"Riley, can you hand me a spatula?"

"Sure," Riley Dashwood searched the counter. Where had he left the spatula? Oh, there it was. He passed it to Susan.

She scraped down the sides of the mixer and added an egg to the Italian-cream-cake batter.

"How are we doing on time?" Riley asked.

"We'll make it."

Riley wasn't as convinced. This was the biggest order Susan's fledging catering business had gotten yet. He was thrilled to have the opportunity to work with her. She'd lived next door to his family when he was a kid, but they'd become close when they took the same cooking class several years ago.

While Riley wasn't ashamed of the work he did as Dash, he didn't intend to fuck men for money much longer. He wanted to get an associate's degree in baking and pastry arts, and he'd been saving so he could finally enroll. If things went well, he'd be able to take some classes after the start of the year. Being an escort beat the hell out of waiting tables or taking whatever crap job he could find in a restaurant kitchen with no training or professional experience.

His job also gave him time during the day to cook and bake; after several friends asked him to make cakes or other desserts for them, he got the idea to start charging. Then Susan had approached him about starting a small catering business, mostly desserts but some savory hors d'oeuvres as well, and he'd loved every minute of it so far. Sure, it was stressful when you knew the food had to be the best, but it gave him almost as much of a thrill as fucking a client he was really into.

He turned off the mixer he was using and tasted the devil's-food-cake batter. "Mmm."

"Good?" Susan asked.

"Heavenly."

Susan had suggested espresso powder and just a touch of red pepper, enough to add interest without heat. The extra ingredients had perked the batter right up.

"You had a new client last weekend, right? How did that go?" Susan asked as Riley started filling the mini muffin tins he was using to make tiny cupcakes.

"You do realize how inappropriate this conversation is, right?"

Susan had never been bothered by Riley's job. In fact, she took glee in embarrassing him by asking about it. Probably, she was just trying to make sure he was staying safe and that he was truly okay with what he was doing.

She laughed. "We're both adults, and I like to check up on you. Besides, it's nice to have you doing something exciting since Lilah's job's so boring. Not many fun stories from her accounting office."

Susan's daughter was a source of consternation. She'd turned out straitlaced and all business despite her mother's rather vivacious personality. But in truth, Riley's job was less exciting than most people imagined.

"Friday night was interesting." Riley continued scooping out batter, trying to keep each muffin cup even without spilling drops on the tray. Mini cupcakes were damn cute, but they were also a pain.

"Interesting good or interesting bad?"

"Good. The new client is an uptight-as-hell businessman, but I like him." Riley tensed as he heard the slightly wistful tone in his voice. He more than liked Thorne. The man intrigued the hell out of Riley. He couldn't wait to go back and see what else he could do to help Thorne let go. He wasn't sure where he'd gotten the nerve to push Thorne so hard the week before, but something about him called to Riley. He'd had uptight clients before, but Thorne seemed desperate for something. The longing in his eyes when he'd looked at Riley after his shower had been so intense. Riley hadn't thought Thorne would give in to the suggestion that he stay longer, but he'd been thrilled when he had. Licking cake off him was one of the hottest things Riley had ever done, and that was saying a lot.

"Uh-oh," Susan said. Damn, she had caught his tone.

"What?" *Play it off.*

"I've never heard you use that tone when talking about a client, or anyone else for that matter."

"I've enjoyed plenty of clients."

"Not like that."

True. He'd jerked off to thoughts of Thorne most nights that week. He'd even imagined Thorne when he was with other clients. He'd often pictured an actor or a porn star, sure, but never another client. Was he getting himself in trouble? Should he cancel their appointment that night?

Riley imagined Thorne sitting at home alone, working, lonely, and tense because he didn't show up. Or what if Sheila sent someone else to fuck him?

No, Thorne was his.

Fuck, that kind of thinking was definitely a bad sign.

It's good money. I'd be crazy to cancel. Thorne had left a mind-boggling tip.

"Riley, are you okay?" Susan asked.

"Yeah, I'm fine."

"This guy must be rather impressive."

"He is. Totally hot."

"Young like you?"

Young clients were rare, in part because of the expense. Riley didn't come cheap, which was why he was going to be able to start culinary school very soon.

"No. He's forty-two."

"Ha! That sounds young to me, but I guess not to you. This old geezer must keep himself in shape."

Riley grinned. "Yes, he does."

"Too bad you can't introduce me."

Riley shook his head.

"I suppose he only goes for men, anyway."

"That's not something I ask."

"I guess not, too personal. Even if you've had your dick in his ass."

Riley made a strangled noise. "Susan!"

She ignored his protest. "The Italian cream is ready to go in the oven. What about the cupcakes?"

Riley slipped the trays of mini cupcakes and the round pans of cake batter in the oven, and Susan set two timers.

"Are you seeing him again tonight?" she asked.

"Yeah; he used to have a regular Friday night thing with Marc. I've taken that over now."

Susan smiled. "How is Marc?"

"He's fine, I guess. I haven't heard from him in a few days." In part because he was avoiding talking about Thorne. "He loves his new apartment, and his first day of work went well." Marc had been the one to get Riley hired at the service. He and Riley had shared an apartment for several years, but Marc had followed his new boyfriend to California, though Riley thought the guy was a dick.

"You can go if you need to," Susan said. "All that's left is icing these and delivering them."

"Are you sure?"

"You were out late last night, and you will be again tonight. Go take a nap."

"Actually, Thorne keeps to a strict schedule. He was writing a report for work when I left last week. I kinda feel sorry for him."

"The man lives in a penthouse apartment and has enough money to hire you? He's probably doing okay."

Riley smiled. "True enough." And yet, he wasn't so sure. "I'm happy to stay and help with the icing. I doubt I could sleep anyway, and I enjoy practicing when I get a chance."

"Okay, we'll have some extra cupcakes. You're welcome to take them."

Riley imagined what Thorne would say if he showed up with cupcakes. "I think I will. They really are awesome with the pepper."

"I knew you'd like that trick."

Maybe one day he'd teach Thorne how to make a cake.

I don't hire men for companionship. Thorne's words echoed in his mind.

Maybe Riley would change that. Maybe he would also get Thorne to admit how much he enjoyed submitting.

Chapter Five

Thorne's workweek was just as bad as he'd expected it to be. At least, the memories of Dash and the anticipation of what was to come once he was back in town on Friday made it bearable, more than bearable actually. He'd jacked off every single night in the hotel, thinking of Dash while he finger-fucked himself and pretended it was Dash's cock inside him.

That afternoon, he'd had a final tedious meeting with the client who claimed to want his advice but argued with him every fucking step of the way. A delay at the airport did nothing to ease Thorne's annoyance. His neck and shoulders ached with tension by the time he landed in Atlanta. He couldn't wait to see Dash. After coaxing, pushing, and manipulating clients all week, he wanted to let go and concentrate on nothing but pleasure. He was so eager to be held down, forced, and used that he had to move his jacket in front of him to hide his hard-on as he stood in the taxi line.

He reached home with barely time to clean up and change before Dash arrived. When he emerged from the shower, he slipped on his plush terry robe, another one of the luxuries he afforded himself. The robe had cost more than some of his colleagues' suits, but he had the money, and he loved the feel of the soft fabric against his skin. He figured there was no need to dress since he hoped to be naked within minutes of Dash arriving. This time he wasn't going to let Dash distract him. He was going to get down to business right away.

The buzzer alerted him to a visitor before he had a chance to pour himself a cocktail, but that was fine—even the best bourbon was no match for Dash.

"Mr. Dash is here to see you, sir. Shall I send him up?" Michaels asked.

"Yes, thank you."

"You're welcome, sir."

Thorne frowned at the agitated state of his stomach. Butterflies. Fucking butterflies. He'd hired this man, and he was—oh fuck, why'd he have to think of that—twenty years younger.

Dash knocked, the same two sharp taps as last week.

Once Thorne let him in, Dash eyed him appreciatively. "Dressed for the occasion?"

"And why shouldn't I be?" Thorne asked as he pushed the door shut.

"It's a good look for you." Dash's gaze traveled down Thorne's body. "You have beautiful feet."

"Is that a thing for you?" Thorne asked, wiggling his toes.

Dash laughed. "So you can be playful after all."

Thorne snorted at his impertinence.

"And my thing is whatever my client wants."

Thorne raised a brow, challenging him.

"It's not a particular fetish of mine—though I appreciate beauty in all forms and places—but I aim to serve my clients' needs."

"Or to tell them what those needs are."

"Is that what you'd like me to do today?" Dash

asked. He seemed to grow a few inches taller as he let the commanding persona settle over him.

Thorne ignored him. Dash had his messenger bag with him again, but he was also carrying a white paper bag that smelled of cake—rich cake.

"What's that?" Thorne reached for the bag.

Dash slapped his hand away. "It's a surprise for later."

Thorne frowned. "Why do I feel like you wanted to tack 'if you're a good boy' on to that sentence?"

Dash laughed. "Maybe I did."

"I told you I—"

"Don't do submissive. And I told you I wasn't so sure you didn't."

Thorne hated how right Dash might be. "Look—"

Dash held up a hand. "I have an idea for tonight. Would you like me to run with it and see where it takes us, or are you going to wrest control?"

Why the fuck did that sound so sexy—grappling with Dash, fighting for who would be on top. "Is both an option?"

Dash grinned. "We'll have to see."

"Worried about an old guy's stamina?"

"You don't seem the least bit old to me."

Dash's statement caught Thorne off guard, because it wasn't made in the same playful tone. It sounded serious, heartfelt. Or maybe Thorne's brain was too clouded by lust to tell. "I'd like to hear your idea."

Dash set the paper bag down on the coffee table and unzipped his satchel. He pulled out a plug—not the giant vibrating one that had caught Thorne's attention the week before—a basic one that was large enough to make a man really feel it but not scare him.

Thorne inclined his head toward the plug. "I like it so far."

"Then turn around."

Thorne almost protested. But he was the one who'd insisted they get right down to business.

"Kneel on the couch and brace yourself on the back."

Damn, his authoritative tone was fucking hot. Thorne's cock was suddenly very much in the game. He positioned himself like Dash had demanded, but he turned so he could see what Dash was doing— rolling a condom onto the plug, then lubing it up.

"So you're just going to shove that up my ass?" Thorne asked.

Dash glared. "I would hope you'd give me credit for a little more finesse than that, but essentially, yes, unless you object."

Fuck, no, he didn't object. He wasn't sure he'd object to anything Dash dreamed up.

Dash knelt by the couch. He pushed Thorne's robe up and out of the way. Then he used both hands to take hold of Thorne's ass and pull his cheeks apart. Thorne groaned. Why was it so fucking hot to be exposed like that? Dash blew against his hole, his breath hot. Thorne couldn't stop the shudder that ran through him.

"Like that, do you?"

"Fuck, yes!"

Dash did it again. Then he brushed the tips of his thumbs over Thorne's hole. He pushed in with one, barely breaching Thorne's defenses. It wasn't enough.

"Stop fucking teasing me." Thorne grabbed Dash's wrist and tried to encourage him to go deeper.

Dash shook off his hold. "We're doing this my way."

"That is not how this is supposed to work." Thorne was the client. And yet, there he was, perched on his couch, ass on display, and loving it.

"Hands on the back of the couch," Dash ordered.

Fucking bastard. But Thorne did what he said.

"Are you going to make me pay later?"

Thorne most certainly was. "Yes. Definitely."

Dash laughed. "Good."

Thorne imagined what they would do when it was his turn. He had to think of a way to make Dash writhe, but his thoughts scattered when Dash pushed a lubed finger into his ass and rapidly added another one.

Thorne pushed back against him, trying to take the digits deeper. "Get on with it."

Dash huffed. "Did you forget everything I told you last week about delaying gratification?"

"I don't fucking believe in waiting for satisfaction," Thorne snarled. "I go after what I want, get it, and move on."

"You're missing out on the deliciousness of anticipation, not to mention basking in the afterglow."

"If I spent time basking, I wouldn't be able to afford you."

Dash tilted his head as if considering that idea. "Possibly not, but wouldn't you be happier?"

"My cock sure as hell wouldn't be."

Dash grinned. "That may well be true. You wanted the best, and here I am."

"Arrogance wasn't one of the traits I requested."

"It's not arrogance when it's a simple fact."

Thorne narrowed his eyes at Dash who chose that moment to push the plug into his ass. "Fucking fuck!"

"For a fancy businessman, you sure as hell cuss like a sailor."

"My grandmother's fault."

"Oh, really?" Dash sounded like he didn't believe him.

"She *was* a sailor, well, a WAVE in WWII. She—"

Dash wiggled the plug, and Thorne stopped. "Go on. Talk all you like. It's not going to stop me."

"I wasn't—"

"That's what you do at work, isn't it? Talk to distract people and then get them to do what you want."

Thorne shook his head. "No, I give them advice."

"I don't need any." Dash pushed the plug deeper.

Thorne squirmed. The fucking thing felt twice as wide as it had looked.

"Just breathe and push against it," Dash instructed.

"Damn it! I fucking know how to take something up my ass."

"Oooh. You're touchy when things don't go your way." Dash chuckled.

"You are seriously trying to get fired."

"No, I'm trying to make you see how much you fight what you need." He pushed deeper before Thorne could respond. A little more and it was all the way in, Thorne's ass tightening around the narrow point before the flange. Thorne took short, ragged breaths as he tried to get used to the sensation of having it deep inside. He fought the urge to move, to twist away from the burn. It fucking hurt, and yet, oh my God, it felt good. His cock was hard as iron. Dash was right: Thorne fucking loved having him in control.

Dash twisted the plug. And Thorne groaned. "Feels good, doesn't it?"

"Yes, damn it."

"Good, now turn around and sit, so we can have some cupcakes."

Thorne must have heard that wrong. "What?"

"Cupcakes. Mini ones. That's what I have in the bag."

"I don't want fucking cupcakes."

"I made them myself." Dash's voice was dripping with sweetness.

Dash had actually made him cupcakes. Why the hell would he do that? "Later. We'll eat them later. Right now, I want to be fucked."

"Won't work while this is in." He thumped the end of the plug, and Thorne jerked. "Cupcakes first. We're building anticipation, remember?"

"Fuck off."

Dash laughed.

"You seriously think I'm going to sit here and eat cupcakes with this thing up my ass?"

"Yes, I do." Still that annoyingly sweet tone.

"You—"

Dash toyed with the plug while using his free hand to stroke Thorne's cock. Whatever Thorne was going to say was lost on a wave of pleasure.

"By the time we're done eating, you'll be so

ready for my cock, I'll bend you right over the couch and drive inside you. But first: We're. Going. To. Eat." He punctuated each word with a pull on Thorne's cock. When he let go, Thorne clamped his lips together to keep from whimpering.

Thorne knew he could stop this anytime. He'd hired Dash to pleasure him, but he couldn't deny that he enjoyed the way Dash took control. He wasn't going to give him the satisfaction of saying so, though. He was going to sit there and eat cupcakes like there wasn't anything unusual going on; at least, he hoped he was.

"I brought coffee too," Dash said, pulling out a thermos.

Thorne stood and pulled his robe together. "I'll get plates."

Dash laid a hand on his thigh. "No, you stay right here. I'll get everything we need."

Thorne started to insist that he could handle it, then realized how it would feel to walk around with the plug in his ass. He eased himself down onto the couch. The plug shifted as he sat. He sucked in his breath, and Dash grinned knowingly.

"You don't want to serve our food naked this time?" Thorne asked, hoping that taunting Dash would get the focus off him.

"Hmmm," Dash said. "Come to think of it, I would like to get out of these restrictive layers."

Why had Thorne asked?

He couldn't help but watch as Dash revealed his beautiful body. With a total lack of self-consciousness, he strutted to the kitchen. How did he move so fluidly?

Dash poured coffee and placed bite-sized cupcakes on plates. "There," he said, settling onto the couch near Thorne. "I think we're ready."

Thorne was ready—ready to be fucked. The faster they ate, the faster they could move on to the mind-numbing orgasm he felt building in his balls. He picked up a cupcake and bit into it. It was so fucking rich and chocolatey that he actually forgot his predicament for a few moments. "You really made these?"

Dash grinned. "Yes, I did. My alter ego is an aspiring pastry chef."

"These are amazing."

"Thank you. I was rather pleased with how they turned out."

"Are they your specialty?"

"No, but they're something I've recently perfected. I'm adding to my repertoire every week. My favorite thing to make right now is cannoli. I finally got some cannoli forms, and I've been experimenting with getting the filling just right. My latest trick is adding a touch of cherry juice. It gives them a sweet/tart punch and… Sorry, I tend to get carried away when I start talking about food."

Thorne shook his head. "Don't apologize. I appreciate food despite being a terrible cook." And he loved seeing Dash all bright-eyed and passionate even when it wasn't about sex.

"I could teach you."

"To cook? I doubt it. I'm a disaster in the kitchen."

"Anyone can learn," Dash insisted.

"The few times I've tried… Well, the building

manager was kind about having to turn off the fire alarm."

Dash snickered, and Thorne couldn't help laughing too. He shifted position to face Dash and froze. He'd forgotten about the plug.

Dash grinned. He had to have seen Thorne's reaction, but he didn't mention it. "What did you burn?"

Thorne groaned. "You're going to laugh at me."

"Tell me anyway."

"Grilled cheese."

Dash did laugh, so hard tears came to his eyes.

"You still think I could make a cake?"

Dash nodded. "I do, but we'd need to work up to it."

"I'll leave it to you. How did you get started cooking?"

"My mom's cooking was not quite as challenged as yours, but it wasn't fantastic. I wanted better food, so I started watching shows on Food Network, and I checked out cookbooks from the library. I went from scrambled eggs to omelets to creating my own quiches, and once I discovered baking, I fell in love."

"So why…never mind."

"Why aren't I a baker instead of a rent boy?"

Thorne nodded. "You don't have to tell me. Like I said, I didn't hire you for—"

"For a man with his ass stuffed full, you look terribly relaxed. That tells me that talking is a good thing for you after all."

Thorne scowled, not wanting to think about how easily Dash turned his world upside down.

"The answer to your question is money. To do

what I want I either need start-up money for a business, or money to get a baking and pastry arts certificate, or ideally both. As you know, I make good money working for Sheila, and I have most of my days free to keep baking. I'm working with a friend who's building a catering business."

Thorne ate another mini cupcake, his third. "I'm glad you have plans because these should be shared with the world. They're even better than the cake we had last week."

Color rose in Dash's cheeks. "I don't know about that. But I'm glad you like them."

"What's something else you learned to make recently?"

"Turnovers. I just learned how to make really good flaky pastry, and I've been trying lots of combinations, even savory ones."

Dash obviously put all of himself into what he did. Thorne understood that. When he had a chance to win a new contract, he fought hard for it. He might occasionally wish he had time for more than work, but he was passionate about helping others make their companies the best they could be. He began spinning a business plan for Dash, excited about all the possibilities.

"You're smiling," Dash said.

"It's the cupcakes." No way was he going to admit what he was really thinking.

"Maybe I'll let you sample my turnovers one day."

"Maybe right now you'll do something about this." Thorne parted his robe and skimmed a hand over his cock.

Dash licked his lips, clearly very interested. "Not yet. Tell me about you. I can't believe you really don't do anything but work. Surely you have other interests."

"I'm on the board at the art museum, and I attend a lot of charity gatherings." Was that it? When had he stopped doing things just for fun? "I used to sail."

"That does sound fun. Do you own a sailboat?" Dash asked.

"I used to. After I got my MBA and started working for Symthson, I bought myself a boat, took lessons, and learned how to sail. It was a gift to myself."

"See? There is another side to you. You lit up when you told me that."

Had he really?

"What got you interested in sailing?"

"When I was a kid, one of my favorite books was *Swallows and Amazons*. Did you ever read that?"

Dash shook his head. "No."

"The four main characters, siblings, are spending the summer at a lake in England, and they have a sailboat. They camp on an island, meet two girls who live on the lake and have their own boat, and all six of them have adventures together."

"Sounds fun. Did you have adventures on your boat?"

Thorne pondered that. "Not too many." He and Clint had taken the boat out frequently. They'd had some wonderful afternoons, but Clint had always had to go back to his wife. Then everything ended. "I sold it when I realized I hadn't taken it out in over a year."

"How long ago was that?"

"Seven, maybe eight years."

Dash frowned. "You should buy another and take it out every weekend."

"I don't really have weekends."

"Which is why you're so tense."

Thorne leaned forward to refill his coffee cup. Once again the plug reminded him that he'd yet to get what he wanted from Dash.

Dash must have noticed because he smiled. "Finish your coffee and then I'll finish you."

"Damn right you will."

He held up another mini cupcake, a white one, and offered it to Thorne. Thorne reached for it, but Dash shook his head. He moved closer and held it up to Thorne's lips. "Taste. This one is Italian cream."

Suddenly, Thorne was aware of the plug again even though he wasn't moving. He took a bite and then licked his lips to capture all the icing. "Delicious."

Dash popped the other half into his own mouth, groaning as he chewed. He looked as lost to pleasure as he had when he was riding Thorne's cock the week before.

"So good," Dash murmured. "I didn't make those. My friend Susan did, but I have her recipe."

"Good." Thorne realized that implied he'd be getting more. But cupcakes were a one-time thing, weren't they? Of course, he could have Dash cater an event for him. Those cupcakes would go a long way to lure in more clients. But it would also be next to impossible for him to hide how much he wanted the man. Mixing Dash and work was a terrible idea.

"I've got more," Dash said.

Thorne slid lower on the couch, dropped his head back, and opened his legs. He shifted around, deliberately making the plug tease him. "Feed me another one."

Dash grinned. "You're fucking hot all spread out for me like that."

"Then get over here," Thorne said.

Dash grabbed the blanket they'd used to protect the couch the week before. He and Thorne spread the blanket out. Then Dash picked up an Italian-cream cupcake, straddled Thorne, and fed it to him.

"Tell me how it feels," he said when Thorne finished chewing.

"The plug?"

"I'd rather you tell me how it feels to wait until *I* decide the time is right. How does it feel knowing I'm going to eventually pull that plug out and fuck you? But until then, all you get is a tease."

"You get off on that, don't you?"

Dash's eyes sparkled. "On what?"

"Making people wait, teasing, working them up."

"I get off on other people's pleasure, and the more things build, the bigger the bang when they go off."

Thorne would have laughed if he hadn't been so horny. "Seriously?"

"Okay, that was really cheesy, but yeah."

"And you want that? You want to see me go off?" Thorne asked.

"I do, but I want it to be the absolute best you've had."

Of course he did and of course he was going to say what Thorne wanted to hear and yet…Thorne was buying into it. And he wanted more. A lot more. But Thorne didn't do relationships, and this one would be doomed from the start.

"Kiss me," Thorne said. He needed that at least.

"My pleasure." Dash licked Thorne's lower lip. "Sweet."

"That's the icing."

Dash sighed. "Icing mixed with you. It's heavenly."

Fuck. This man was too much. Dash kissed Thorne for real then, and Thorne lost himself in it. He tilted his hips, trying to get more full-body contact. Dash yanked his robe open and reached between Thorne's legs to tug on the plug. When he'd freed it from Thorne's body, he laid it on a towel he'd placed on the floor. "You ready?"

"Fuck yes." Thorne turned around and braced himself on the back of the couch; no way was he taking the time to walk to the bedroom. Besides, it was fitting since he'd fucked Dash on the couch the week before.

Dash reached under Thorne and wrapped a hand around his cock. He fought the urge to let Dash bring him to release like that.

"Enough." He pushed at Dash's hand. "I don't want to come before you're in me."

"Are you sure? What if I could make you come again before I did?"

"That's very unlikely."

"We could make a game of it. I make you come twice, and you do something for me. You don't come again, and I owe you whatever you choose."

"I want more of those cupcakes and some cherry

turnovers too."

Dash chuckled. "That sure of yourself, huh?"

"You're not going to win."

"Oh really? Don't you even want to know what I want?"

"No." Thorne could hold out. He was sure of it.

Dash squeezed his cock more firmly and teased his head on the upstroke. "Don't you want me to win? Wouldn't that be better for you?"

"I…" Thorne was no longer sure what he wanted. Dash's hand on his cock was making him crazy. "I don't know."

"If I win, I say what we do next weekend. You can say no if it's a hard limit, but otherwise, you have to agree to try something new."

"Fine, but I really wanted to come with you in my ass."

"Oh, you will."

Thorne shook his head. "No. Can't let…you win."

Dash worked him faster. So close. So close. "Fuuuuck!" He shot, coating Dash's hand in his seed. Dash kept going until the storm of pleasure ceased. Then he lined his cock up and drove into Thorne's ass.

Thorne choked on a shout. He'd forgotten just how fucking big Dash was.

"I love how I just slid right in because the plug opened you up."

"Not…as easy as you…make it sound!" Thorne panted.

Dash didn't slow down. He didn't seem to care that Thorne had never caught his breath after his searing orgasm. He relentlessly pounded Thorne's ass until Thorne was no longer certain he could hold himself up.

Dash yanked on Thorne's hips, and Thorne slipped, pressing his face into the back of the couch. He had no intention of moving and then Dash drove in, jolting and making him rise up. "Oh my fucking God!"

"There we go," Dash said.

As Dash once again slid over his prostate, Thorne realized he just might come again after all. But he no longer thought that would be so bad.

Dash pistoned into him, never seeming to tire, pushing him closer and closer to another orgasm. He'd never come twice that close together, not even in his teens, but now… *Holy God!*

"Dash?" His voice shook.

"You close?"

"I…"

Dash leaned down, his breath warm against Thorne's ear. "Tell me what to do to make you go over."

Did he want to do that? Did he want Dash to win? Fuck, yes he did. "My neck. Bite it. Suck. Mark me."

"Mmm. My pleasure." Dash jacked Thorne's cock as he sank his teeth into the juncture of Thorne's neck and shoulder.

"So close! So…" Dash sucked at the wound on his neck. "Fuck!"

That was all it took. The intensity of his release shocked him, and he shouted loud enough to bring the building down. Dash was right behind him.

The two of them collapsed against the couch, sweaty and spent.

Chapter Six

"God, you're hot," Dash said, breath catching on each word.

Thorne tried to speak but decided it was too much effort.

Dash rose off Thorne's back. "I need to get rid of the condom. Brace yourself."

Thorne winced when Dash pulled out.

"You okay? I got kinda rough."

That was an understatement. "I fucking loved it."

Dash walked away for a few seconds. Thorne hadn't moved when he came back.

Dash skimmed the tips of his fingers over the now throbbing bite on Thorne's shoulder. "That was hot and unexpected."

"So I like to be bitten. It's not all that unusual."

"No, but still unexpected for you."

Thorne forced himself to turn over so he could prop himself against the arm of the couch and look at Dash. "I wear suits. No one's going to see it."

"But you'll feel it. Just like the plug. Anticipation."

"For next week?" Once again, Thorne felt overexposed. He wasn't comfortable with how much he wanted Dash, and he sure as hell didn't want Dash seeing through him.

Dash spread the blanket back out before settling on the couch next to Thorne. "You know, you might

Silvia Violet

consider getting a slip cover for this couch if you enjoy fucking on it so much."

"I've never…" Heat filled Thorne's face. He hadn't wanted to admit that he'd never even been tempted to fuck on the couch with anyone else. He'd always been content to walk the thirty or so feet to the bedroom. "You're right. I should probably order one."

Dash grinned. "You've never fucked on this couch before, have you?"

Why did he always see what Thorne wanted to hide? "No, damn it. You… You make me crazy."

"I aim to please."

"Well, you do. Very much." No point in denying it.

Dash drew Thorne's legs up and over his lap. "I like this side of you. Biting. Fucking on the couch. Eating cupcakes. Being fed cupcakes. Wearing plugs. I want to see more of it."

Thorne didn't like the direction his thoughts were taking. Dash was damn good at pushing Thorne's buttons, and Thorne enjoyed Dash taking charge way more than he wanted to. *But that's why I hire an escort. I want a professional, and Dash knows what he's doing, that's all.*

"You're frowning. What are you thinking about?"

Thorne gave him a wry smile. "My name is Thornwell Shipton, and I'm a control freak."

Dash patted Thorne's thigh. "Very good. Confession is the beginning of healing."

Thorne sighed. "I hate how much I love it when you dominate me."

Dash ran the tips of his fingers over Thorne's abdomen in a soothing caress. "I know you do."

"I don't want you to stop. I…"

"Want more?"

"Yes." Thorne pulled Dash down for a kiss. Dash moved so he could straddle Thorne and deepen the kiss. This time they were gentle, teasing, playful, without the rush of passion that had come before. When Dash pulled back, he laid his head on Thorne's chest, and Thorne wrapped his arms around Dash, holding him there and simply breathing, refusing to let himself think about how out of character this was for him. Dash shifted position to get more comfortable and for a few moments neither of them spoke.

Then Thorne's phone went off, interrupting them. He cut off the ringer. The junior consultant who'd called him despite being told Friday nights were off limits could wait. But he hadn't been able to keep himself from seeing the time. It was already eleven. How the hell had three whole hours passed?

Dash started to pull way, but Thorne stopped him. "Stay."

He could feel Dash smile against his chest. "For someone who doesn't cuddle, you're doing a damn fine job."

"This isn't—"

Dash raised a brow and looked up, his expression clearly telling Thorne to stop bullshitting.

"Fine, but you told me to stop rushing everything."

"That's right. Orgasms should be savored just like cupcakes. In fact, you just might be as tasty as a cupcake."

Thorne scoffed. "I'm no cupcake."

Dash rose off him enough to study him critically as if seriously considering the matter. "If you were, you'd be a dark, rich one, spicy, with a surprise in the center. Maybe Mexican chocolate with a warm cinnamon ganache filling that oozes out when you bite into it, surprising you with its sweetness."

Fucking hell if that didn't turn Thorne on. How did Dash manage it? "If I hadn't just come twice, I'd be hard again after that."

"Ooh. Let me know when you're ready for another round, and I'll describe a full seven-course meal."

Thorne closed his eyes and imagined Dash's smooth voice telling him all about exotic delights. "I might jump you before you finished."

Dash smiled. "Speaking of going another round, I did win our little wager."

"I helped you win, so I'm not sure that counts."

"If a client tells you how to seal a deal, does that contract still count?"

Thorne hated Dash being right. "Fine. You win."

"Trust me, my winning is you winning. Next week we follow my plan."

Thorne didn't like how self-satisfied he looked. "Just what is that plan?"

"I have no intention of spoiling the surprise."

Thorne glared at him. "I hate surprises."

"You're not thinking of reneging, are you?"

"No, I am not."

"You'll love it." Dash shifted off Thorne. "Should I go now?"

Thorne pondered the question. "I should work, but I don't want to."

"Do you always do what you're supposed to?"

"Yes. Well, most of the time. This evening would be an example of not doing as I should."

"Hiring me?"

"Yes. But you are a want not a should."

"I hope so. I'd hate to find out you were being required to pay for a fuck every Friday night."

Thorne laughed. "I wonder who exactly would be giving these orders?"

Dash tilted his head like he was thinking hard. "I'm not sure, but I bet we could create a very hot role play around it."

Thorne considered the idea.

"You look intrigued."

"Maybe."

Dash's grin was positively filthy. "I'll file that away. You want to share anything specific?"

Thorne shook his head. "Not now. I should shower and get back to work."

Instead of moving out of his way, Dash sat back down, straddling Thorne's lap. "What if you didn't work tonight?"

"Look, I—" *For once, just do what you want. Let him stay.* "What would you propose if I said you could stay?"

"More cupcakes and then more of me."

Thorne considered the offer. "Have you had dinner?"

"Wait, you haven't?" Dash looked horrified.

"I'd only been home from the airport for about twenty minutes before you arrived."

"Then you must be starving, even after the cupcakes."

"I am rather hungry," Thorne said. "I'm assuming from your continued needling about my lack of a life that you're free for the rest of the night."

Dash nodded. "I am."

"Then let's go get something to eat."

"I like this plan. How late is the Austrian place open?"

Oh shit, could he take Dash there? Or would their being out together scream desperate man out with his male escort? Why should it? He was being paranoid. "As late as I want it to be, but the atmosphere is rather stuffy and formal despite the waiters' flirtatious attitude."

Dash rolled his eyes. "This isn't *Pretty Woman*. I know all my utensils, and I can even order us a decent wine."

Fuck. He'd just insulted Dash; again. "I didn't mean—"

Dash waved away his apology. "My mother was very into appearances. She even made me do cotillion. They wouldn't let me dance with the other boys, though. It was most disappointing."

Thorne rolled his eyes. "I bet."

WHEN THEY ENTERED the restaurant, Thorne held the door for Dash. It was a simple gesture, but Dash appreciated being treated like a date rather than hired help. Despite how late it was, there were people waiting for tables, but as soon as the hostess saw Thorne, she offered to show them to a private corner table and left them with menus and a wine list.

Dash couldn't resist the urge to tease. He leaned forward and looked at Thorne over his menu. "These napkins are made of actual cloth. How fancy."

"Am I never going to hear the end of this?"

"I might eventually let it go." Or not. Thorne's assumption that he might not be comfortable at a fine-dining restaurant had stung, but not so bad that he couldn't dismiss it. He simply liked keeping Thorne off guard. He glanced at the list of entrees. "What do you recommend?"

Thorne was watching Dash. He'd yet to touch his menu. "I always order the *sauerbraten*."

"Then I challenge you to order something else."

Thorne glared at him, but a waiter approached before he had a chance to reply.

"Hi, I'm Jordan, and I will be assisting you tonight. Would you like to hear about our special?"

"Yes, very much," Dash said, smiling at the waiter in a way he was certain would ingratiate him. He might not have Thorne's money, but he could often use charm to get what he wanted, a great quality to have in his profession.

Dash smiled at Jordan as he described the special—beef rolled with carrots, onions, and bacon. Dash glanced at Thorne just as Jordan finished speaking. He studied Dash, probably not even listening to the server. Thorne didn't approve of him flirting with someone else. Dash rather liked that, and he was also going to use it to his advantage.

"We'll both have the dinner special, and we'll have the *kartoffelpuffer* to start. We haven't chosen a wine yet, but bring us each your best bourbon, neat," Dash said.

The waiter glanced at Thorne who looked stunned. "Mr. Shipton?"

Thorne made a dismissive gesture with his hand. "That's fine. Thank you."

When Jordan walked away, Thorne stared at Dash with what appeared to be a mixture of shock, annoyance, and humor. "You ordered for us."

"I did. I was afraid you wouldn't try something new if I didn't push."

"How do you know I like…whatever it is you ordered."

"You weren't even listening, were you?"

Thorne scowled at him. "I was distracted."

"I do seem to have that effect on you, but you had a chance to change your order and you didn't take it."

"No, I didn't. Dinner will just be a surprise."

Dash studied him. "You told me you hated surprises."

"I do."

EXCEPT WITH DASH, he didn't. That thought terrified Thorne, because it meant that Dash had the power to change him. Dash was a hired companion. No, he was a hired fuck. He'd told Dash he wasn't looking for someone to talk to. What was he doing?

"You know what, I don't think this is a good idea after all. I should go."

He pushed back from the table, but Dash put a hand over his. "Stay. Would it make it easier if this were off the clock?"

God no, that would make it worse. This would be a date, and he'd have to admit… Thorne shook his head. "No. That's got nothing to do with it." That had everything to do with it.

Dash raised a brow. "You should eat. I won't keep you after that."

Thorne sat back down, his heart hammering. Dash was so beautiful, everything he wanted but… He was twenty-two, and he was there because Thorne paid him, no matter how much it seemed otherwise.

He just offered to stay off the clock.

He has to eat, and I'm paying for dinner.

"Do you trust me to know how to pleasure you?" Dash asked, keeping his voice low.

"Yes," Thorne answered automatically.

"Food is just another form of pleasure. It's a sensual experience just like sex. It's fitting that I'm an escort and a chef. The two go together perfectly."

Thorne couldn't take his eyes off Dash. The man had wrapped him in a spell, his voice, the look in his eyes, even the fucking beautiful way his lips moved as he spoke, hot as hell. "Tell me what you ordered for us, in detail."

Thorne could tell by the way Dash's lips curled up in a devious smile that he'd understood Thorne's meaning. Thorne wanted Dash to describe the food in a way that would make Thorne hard, the way he'd talked about cupcakes earlier.

"I ordered the kartoffelpuffer, potato pancakes. They'll be crispy on the outside, but when you bite in, you'll taste the potato. Soft. Smooth. Hot. For our main course, we'll have beef *rouladen*, soft, succulent beef covered with tangy mustard and wrapped around savory bacon and sweet, thinly-sliced onions and carrots. The butteriness of the beef, spice of the mustard, and salt of the bacon will tantalize your mouth. I promise you'll love it."

Dash kept his voice pitched low, and he spoke slowly, dragging out his vowels. By the time he finished, Thorne was half-hard and considering whether to ask for dinner to go and drag Dash back to his apartment.

"LIKED THAT DID you?" Dash asked, well aware of his skill and Thorne's reaction.

"Fuck yes, I did." Thorne's voice was scratchy with need. Would he be asking for another round after dinner?

"Just wait until I order dessert," Dash said.

"We've already had cupcakes."

"We had a lot of things that were sweet, but I"—Dash licked his lips and closed his eyes—"believe you can never have too much."

Dash slipped his foot out of his shoe and lifted his leg, pushing his foot into Thorne's lap. Thorne's eyes widened as Dash pressed against him, discovering that, as he'd expected, Thorne's cock would be more than happy to have dessert.

"Quit that. Our server is headed this way." Thorne looked horrified.

Smiling, Dash lowered his leg and slipped his shoe back on.

Jordan set the kartoffelpuffer and their bourbons on the table. "Did you choose a wine to go with your entree?"

"Yes," Thorne said. "We'll have the Dornfelder."

"Excellent choice. Do you need anything else?"

"No. Thank you."

"Then enjoy." Jordan left them.

Dash used his fork to spear one of the cakes, and Thorne followed suit. Dash tasted his carefully. They were still piping hot. "Mmmm." He closed his eyes to better enjoy the taste. A perfect blend of saltiness and quality-potato flavor. When he finished savoring his bite, he realized Thorne was staring at him; glaring, more like.

"How did you learn to be so…" He waved a hand. "Did you go to seduction school or what?"

Dash laughed. "If there were an Escort Academy, it would be nothing like most people would imagine. Most of us are already quite comfortable with our sexuality when we're hired. It's the unexpected parts of the job—being a therapist, career consultant, personal shopper, companion to a sports enthusiast— most of us could use help with."

"So were you just born knowing how to make men want you?" Thorne looked annoyed that seduction came so easy to Dash.

"Were you born knowing how to swagger around the office and tell people what to do?"

"I don't—"

Dash raised his brows, and Thorne stopped his feeble protest.

"I learned some of that from my dad and the rest from the man who hired me." Thorne looked as though he wanted to add more but ultimately, he didn't.

Thorne finally tasted his kartoffelpuffer then. His response was nearly as dramatic as Dash's had been. "These are amazing."

Dash smiled. "They are." Since Thorne had

answered his earlier question honestly, Dash gave a little more. "Most escorts learn from someone else in the business who thinks we'd make a good candidate and coaches us."

"Did Marc teach you?"

Thorne's expression told Dash he didn't like the idea. Was he jealous? Dash wasn't sure he should analyze how that made him feel. "Yes."

"Were you lovers?" Before Dash could answer Thorne held up a hand. "That was probably out of line."

"Possibly. Marc and I were occasional fuck buddies, but lovers, as in boyfriends, no. Marc's way too much of a prima donna for me."

Thorne laughed. "He is rather particular, but he's good at letting go when he's in the mood to."

"He really knows how to top a reluctant bottom, and he can also surrender beautifully when a client is in the mood. I see why he worked for you." They would have been beautiful together. He'd love to watch Marc pin Thorne down and make him beg the way Dash had.

"That's a sexy smile. What are you thinking about?" Thorne asked.

"A threeway."

Thorne sputtered as if he'd swallowed the wrong way. "With Marc and…"

"You," Dash said.

Thorne stared, looking torn between nervousness and desire.

"Don't worry. Marc's in California, so it won't go beyond fantasy."

THORNE NODDED. "THAT'S probably best." As hot as it would be to see Marc and Dash together, Thorne wanted Dash all to himself. He wanted to cocoon him away from the world and pretend... Pretend what exactly? That they were lovers, boyfriends? That was absurd. "I'm not good at sharing attention."

Dash rolled his eyes. "Of course you're not."

Jordan arrived then with their dinner, and Thorne was glad to have something to focus on other than the lust in Dash's eyes. His entree was exactly as Dash had described, and it smelled amazing.

"Will there be anything else, sir?" The server deliberately looked at Thorne. "Was the appetizer to your liking?"

"Very much so. Dash, do you need anything?"

Dash looked up, surprised. "Oh, no. This is excellent, thank you."

Jordan nodded and backed away.

"They aren't used to me bringing anyone here who's not as old and boring as I am."

Dash studied Thorne like he'd never seen him before. "First of all, you're not old; sure, you're older than me, but—"

Thorne shook his head. "Stop while you're ahead."

"But boring? Not for one second have I thought you were boring."

"I work. That's all I do. Most people find creating business plans to be about as exciting as sitting in an empty room."

"That's what you do? Make business plans?"

Thorne shrugged. "More or less."

"You appreciate good food, you're generous, kind, and did I mention hot? You know how to flirt and how to play when you want to. None of that is boring."

Did Dash really see him that way? "It's hardly in your interest to name your client's faults."

"I already know you're pleased with my work, so I had no reason to contradict you if I didn't mean it."

He had a point.

They ate in silence for the next few moments. The rouladen was possibly even better than the sauerbraten, but it still didn't beat the company. By the end of dinner, Thorne was contemplating asking Dash to spend the night, which told him it was way past time for him to go home, alone. "Should I call you a car?" Thorne asked as they rose from the table.

"No, I can walk."

Thorne frowned. "How far do you have to go?"

Dash bristled. "I can take care of myself."

"Maybe I want to take care of you."

Dash's brow wrinkled in annoyance. Thorne found it ridiculously fetching. "I don't need—"

"It's not about need. I'll call a car, pay the driver, and send you on your way. You don't have to tell me where you live, okay? I'm not going to stalk you." Or not much, anyway. He'd checked Dash out before Dash came to his apartment the first time, the same as he'd done with every escort he'd hired.

Dash smiled. "It's not that. I'm just not used to anyone taking care of me. I've been on my own for a while now."

"You took care of me tonight. I'm just returning the favor."

Dash shook his head, but he was smiling. "Fine. You win. I'll accept the ride."

"You knew I wouldn't stop insisting until you did, right?"

Dash rolled his eyes. "I did, but I actually like that about you, your command mode. I like knowing that you love being in control, but that in bed, I can make you drop that facade. I can take your ass. I can own you."

"Holy fuck, are you trying to make me come in my pants? We are in public, you know." Thorne didn't really care though. Dash had him completely under his spell.

"I wish I could fuck you again tonight," Dash said, voice barely a whisper.

So did Thorne, but before he could respond, Dash continued. "Unfortunately, I have to bake early in the morning; but you'll be thinking about next week when you get home, won't you?"

"Bastard; you know I will."

The car Thorne had ordered arrived then. "The car service bills my account," he told Dash.

Dash nodded. "Next Friday?"

"See you then." Thorne tried to play it cool even though his cock was throbbing and he knew he wouldn't work when he got home. He'd jerk off thinking about Dash and wondering what he had planned for next week.

Chapter Seven

Thorne's office phone lit up. Lauren, his assistant, was paging him. "Yes?"

"Your meeting started at ten."

Thorne glanced at the clock. It was five minutes past the hour. How had he lost track of time? "Thank you, Lauren. Let them know I've been delayed and I'll be there shortly."

"Yes, sir." There was a pause. "Is something wrong?"

"No, I simply need a few minutes to conclude something I started last night. It's…for the meeting."

"Of course, sir." Lauren knew he was lying. She also knew she'd reminded him of the meeting when he'd arrived that morning, but she wasn't about to call him out on either point.

He hadn't actually been working at all. He'd been daydreaming about Dash. He couldn't get the man out of his mind. Thorne had jerked off in the shower, fantasizing about Dash driving his fat cock up his ass, just like he'd done every fucking day since he last saw Dash. It was only Wednesday. Would he make it to Friday with his sanity intact? He could always see if Dash was free later.

No. He shook his head and started gathering the paperwork he needed for his meeting. *Once a week. That's enough.*

He'd always been eager for his Filthy Fridays as

he'd come to think of them. But he'd never obsessed over a man like he was doing with Dash. The intensity of what he felt had to be unhealthy. It was sure as hell unexpected, and he hated the unexpected.

Thorne forced himself to close up his briefcase and head for the elevator, nodding at Lauren as he walked by her desk. He didn't want to go to this meeting. The client who'd called it was a pain in the ass and always had been, the kind who micromanaged the consultation process every step of the way, despite the fact that it was his managers who would implement the changes Thorne suggested, not him. The man's company was a large one though, and he was well connected. Thorne knew better than to risk pissing him off by being even later.

Normally he'd be appalled that he hadn't arrived several minutes early to set up the meeting room. He was terribly critical of tardiness in others. But that morning he couldn't summon the energy to care. Was this burnout? Midlife crisis? Dash tempting him to a life of sin? He wasn't sure he'd mind if it was the latter. The sins Dash came up with were well worth the price of his soul.

But he held more shares than any other partner, so he had to set an example. Friday would come eventually, and he'd have his fun with Dash. Right now, he needed to focus on what was important, not on frivolous pleasures.

***

RILEY'S PHONE STARTED ringing as he walked through the door of his apartment. He'd been baking with Susan for the last six hours. He was exhausted and covered in flour despite the apron he'd worn. All he wanted was a shower. He pulled his phone from his pocket, hoping he could ignore whoever was calling. It was Marc. He'd been avoiding Marc's calls since Friday, texting him back, saying he'd call later.

He had to talk to him eventually. Maybe if he sounded as exhausted as he felt, he could beg off before they got too deep into a conversation about Thorne. Riley knew it was a bad sign that he didn't want to talk about Thorne. But what had happened Friday night with Thorne—the dinner as much as the intense sex—was special and private and the best fucking "date" Dash (and Riley too for that matter) had ever had. If only Thorne wasn't a fucking client.

Riley flopped onto a kitchen chair and accepted the call. "Hey man, what's up?"

"Wow! You actually deigned to answer. Should I be honored?"

"I've been busy. You know I'm working as much as I can to save for school. Between that and baking, I'm worn out." Riley was lying. While that had been his intention, Thorne had tipped him so well, he'd hardly taken any other clients.

"Clients taking it out of you?" Marc asked, his tone lascivious as usual.

"Sucking me dry every time," Riley returned.

"Oh, poor baby. Soooo, tell me about Thorne."

"You already know what he's like." Riley winced. He hadn't meant his comment to sound as snappy as it did.

"Uh-oh." Riley could hear the smirk in Marc's voice.

"What?"

"That tone. What does that mean?"

That I don't like to think about you fucking him; that I'm…in trouble… "Nothing. What tone?"

"That one. I'm supposed to be the one who gets snippy. Dash is all cool and fun and smiling."

Riley snorted. "You know that's not true."

"That's how you are when you're with clients. Right until you nail their asses and have them begging."

As frustrated as he was, Riley had to laugh. "Fine, that's my style, but this is real life. You're not a client."

"I wouldn't mind being one. You're damn good at what you do."

"Likewise."

"So, Thorne…"

"He's a great tipper." That was a safe enough comment.

"And so hot when he gets fucked," Marc practically purred.

Act normal. "Yeah, he's hot, okay? Just like you said."

"What are you hiding?"

He hated how well Marc knew him. "Nothing."

"Riley Dashwood, you like him."

"Of course I like him. You know I can't take clients I don't like. I'm not as good at faking it as you."

"Ouch!"

Riley knew Marc wasn't the least bit hurt.

"I do pride myself on my acting skills, but you know I'm far from indiscriminate," Marc added.

"I'd never accuse you of that. You just don't

mind fucking assholes if they're hot. In fact, I think you like it."

"Thorne can be an ass, trust me."

"Yeah, but it's kinda cute." *Fucking fuck, why did I say that?*

"Cute?" Marc practically cackled. "Oh dear God, you're worse off than I thought."

"What do you mean?" Riley knew he couldn't get away with feigning ignorance, but he had to try.

"You've fallen for him."

Riley refused to think about how accurate Marc's assessment was. "Hardly; I just like how he's all bluster."

Mark sighed. "And such a fun power bottom."

"Did you ever get him to truly surrender?"

"No, I don't think he's capable of that."

Riley was secretly thrilled. He wanted to be the only one who could get that from Thorne. "Did he ever want anything but sex?"

"Nope. It's strictly fucking with him."

Riley wasn't going to reveal that he'd managed conversation and dinner. "Well, the money's good no matter what he wants."

Marc whistled. "His tips are out of this world."

"He's been very good for my tuition fund."

"I thought he would be. But remember this is a job, not a date."

Marc's warning made Riley's stomach flip-flop. "I've managed just fine since I started this job. It's not like I didn't already understand how to enjoy sex for sex's sake." Riley had done his share of one-nighters, club hook-ups, even back-alley blowjobs. He'd met Marc in a club in fact. "Remember how we met?"

"Mmm. I do. I saw you and knew I had to have you."

They'd fucked like wild animals, and it had been hot as hell, but it was just sex. Riley wasn't looking for anything more, so distancing himself from clients hadn't been a problem. Until Thorne. But he could handle it. He only needed to work for a few more months, anyway.

"So how's the baking life?" Marc asked.

"Great." Riley was thankful that Marc's ADD brain never stayed in one place for long. He was like a sparkly hummingbird, but one with a sharp beak that could hold you down and make you do his bidding. He got why Thorne had enjoyed him, but Riley was a better fit to give Thorne what he really needed.

Not that Thorne had asked Riley to "fix" him. Riley shook his head. Maybe he should be a fucking therapist. He couldn't stop himself from wanting to help people. It was his nature, and plenty of clients were looking for a counselor or at least a confessor. With Thorne though, Riley's instincts might just lead him to heartbreak.

***

THORNE WATCHED AS Dash rolled his shoulders, letting his jacket slide down his arms. The garment dropped to the floor. Rather than pick it up, he kept moving toward Thorne, undoing the buttons at his cuffs. "You ready to find out what I've got planned for you?"

Thorne had to swallow before he could speak. "I thought you were all about taking things slow, building anticipation."

Dash unbuttoned his shirt, slowly revealing his smooth, tanned chest. "Who's rushing? I'm just getting comfortable."

"What do you…" Thorne paused to watch Dash remove his shirt.

"Did you forget your question?"

"What question?" Thorne didn't want to talk anymore. He wanted to touch.

Dash unfastened his pants, revealing the gorgeous *V* of skin that pointed toward his cock. It begged for attention, making Thorne want to sink to his knees so he could lick, suck, and nibble.

"Thorne?"

He glanced up. "What?"

Dash had a very satisfied look on his face. "Whatever you were thinking, just do it."

Thorne knelt in front of Dash, took hold of his hips, and yanked him forward so Thorne could bury his face against the opening of Dash's pants, not caring that the sides of Dash's zipper scraped his cheeks. He breathed deep, scenting sweat, the lemony soap Dash always used, and Dash. He'd know the man's smell anywhere. It was part of him, and it made Thorne hard instantly. He wished he could bottle it, spray it all over his sheets, bathe in it. God, he was so far gone.

It's just lust. Dash is young and hot and knows how to hit all your buttons. Focus on what you want. Thorne nibbled the skin that had mesmerized him. Dash sucked in his breath but made no move to stop him.

When Thorne pulled back, Dash slid his hands

into Thorne's hair and pulled him forward again. "More."

Thorne rubbed his face against Dash's cock, which was still trapped behind his pants. Then he rose high on his knees so he could suck Dash's nipples; they were as hard as Dash's cock was now, as hard as Thorne. He wanted to turn around and offer his ass right then, but that would be too easy. What he wanted from Dash was far more complex. He sat back on his heels. "I didn't mean to do this. I was going to talk to you."

Dash shook his head as if trying to clear it. "Neither did I."

Dash sat on the couch and invited Thorne to join him. "Do you remember your question now?"

Question. Thorne had to think. "Yes. I know you're supposed to claim your prize from last week's wager. Could we delay that? I've had a hell of a week, and I have some specific needs tonight." He'd had those needs the week before, but he'd been too much of a coward to admit it. "I have a feeling you're going to enjoy them."

"Watching you come like that, when you didn't think you could, hearing you beg for it while telling me how to get what I wanted, what you wanted too, that was prize enough for me. Tell me what you need."

"I lied to you," he said. That wasn't at all how he'd meant to start.

But rather than looking annoyed, Dash simply inclined his head with a wry smile. "That's not uncommon. Most clients are less than completely forthcoming."

Thorne squeezed his hands into fists to keep them from shaking. Why the fuck was he so nervous? He'd hired Dash, after all. He'd never had any problem telling other escorts about his needs. "Sometimes, I do need a dom, but I'm not into pain, not serious pain, anyway."

"I can work with that." Dash laid a hand on Thorne's thigh, right by his crotch. It was all Thorne could do not to grab it and press Dash's long fingers against his dick.

"You can?" The words came out strangled.

Dash teased Thorne's inner thigh with his fingers, and Thorne spread his legs automatically, giving him better access. "Tell me more about what you need."

Thorne started to speak, but Dash's fingers were driving him crazy. He laid his head back and closed his eyes, enjoying the sensations his teasing created.

Abruptly, Dash stopped and pulled his hand away. "You're not talking."

Thorne pushed himself off the couch. "Did you really expect me to concentrate when you're touching me like that? Would you like a drink?"

Dash smiled. "No, thank you. I never drink when I'm with a client."

Thorne had forgotten that was a policy the service set for the safety of all their escorts. "You had wine at Bavaria Haus."

"I wasn't really working then."

No, he hadn't been. That thought sent Thorne's pulse rate into the danger zone. What if he… No, not an option. "Would you like some water then?"

"Yes, please."

Thorne returned with a bourbon for himself and a glass of water for Dash. "I guess you're thrilled that I'm slowing down to talk."

Dash studied him. "I get the sense that, rather than relaxing, you're stalling."

"Now you're talking like a therapist again."

"Believe me, I've had clients who were convinced I was one, but I'm just here to give you pleasure."

Thorne's hands were shaking so bad now, the ice in his drink rattled. He set it on the table. Never let someone see that you're nervous. That was one of the most basic rules of negotiating, and usually Thorne was damn good at it.

You're not negotiating. You're explaining what you need from an employee.

Why do I feel like my whole life is at stake, then?

"I want you to force me, order me around, make me follow your commands."

Dash sucked in his breath. The reaction was brief, but Thorne saw it before he schooled his face. "I can do that. What else do you want?"

"I want you to tell me what a…what a slut I am." Heat rushed to Thorne's face. He hated the thought of how fiercely he must be blushing.

"Mmm, I can most certainly do that too. How far should I go with force? Do you enjoy being restrained? I have some rope that would look beautiful wrapped around you."

Thorne had seen it. "Wrists only."

Dash inclined his head. "Any other requests, because I have some ideas about how to run with this."

"I want—" Thorne's mouth went dry. Why was this so fucking difficult?

Dash laid a hand on his thigh. "It's not easy to ask for what you want."

"It usually is for me."

"Have you ever made requests like these before?"

Thorne shook his head. But he wasn't being completely truthful. He'd occasionally asked for this sort of play from other escorts, but their opinions hadn't mattered to him.

"Then of course it's not easy. Asking for a business deal is a lot different than asking for something people might judge you for."

Thorne nodded.

"Does it help to know that I won't judge you no matter what you ask for?"

Thorne summoned the courage to look Dash in the eye. He saw nothing there but sincerity. He wasn't mocking Thorne. He wasn't shocked. He was entirely professional. "I want you to face-fuck me, and I don't want you to go easy. I want to choke on your dick." Holy fuck, he'd actually said it.

Dash nodded as if people made such requests of him every day. Maybe they did.

"Have you used a safeword before?" Dash asked.

Thorne shook his head. Marc had suggested it once, on a night when Thorne had wanted to be forced hard and fast with no prep, but Thorne had insisted he didn't need it.

"But you are familiar with the idea?"

"Yes, but—"

"No buts. I won't play around with these

fantasies unless you have a safeword and promise to use it if you want to stop or just slow down."

"I'm not looking to do anything dangerous."

"You want to play around with power. If I'm going to force you and make it good for both of us, then I must have a way to know if your protests are the real thing or just you enjoying the game."

"All right." Thorne felt silly, but then the whole evening was a bit ridiculous. His cock didn't agree though. It was still just as interested in the fantasies as ever, maybe more so with Dash looking at Thorne like a hungry predator.

"Unless you'd rather use another word, red means stop and yellow means you need to slow down or take a break."

"That I can do. I was afraid I'd have to say something ridiculous like tapioca."

Dash grinned. "Only if you want to."

"Hell no."

Dash patted his thigh. "I know this isn't easy for you, but you won't be nervous once you've got my dick down your throat. You won't be able to think at all."

Fuck. How did Dash know exactly when to switch from serious to playful?

He's good at his job. Just like you. So good he makes you believe it's not a job.

Thorne realized Dash was frowning at him.

"What's wrong?"

"Nothing; just nerves."

Dash's look said he knew there was more to it than that, but he didn't push. "Take off your robe and lie down on your back on the bed. You're going to hold your legs up so I can toy with that delightful ass of yours. Remember the plug we used last week?"

How the hell could Thorne forget that? He'd ordered one for himself and spent a serious portion of the previous night with it up his ass. "I do."

"I've got a bigger one that vibrates. Since you enjoyed last week, you're going to wear it while I fuck your mouth. Now get up."

He had to be talking about the plug Thorne had noticed; the one he thought looked like a torture device but also desperately wanted to try out.

"Why aren't you moving?" Dash asked; the condescension in his voice would have served him well in a boardroom.

Thorne glared at him, not ready to give in easily. "Because you haven't made me."

Dash's eyes widened for just a second before he got control of his expression. "You want this to be a fight?"

"I don't surrender easily." Despite knowing what he needed, Thorne had to be pushed to accept it.

"We're starting in the bedroom. If you aren't there in ten seconds, you won't get to come."

Suddenly, Thorne wanted to obey.

Dash grabbed his bag and walked away. Thorne followed, eyes glued to his ass. When they were by the bed, Dash turned and gripped Thorne's chin tightly. He held Thorne's gaze for several seconds, then yanked Thorne to him and kissed him hard enough to bruise. He bit Thorne's lower lip, forcing him to open his mouth.

No, Thorne's mind protested. He wouldn't give in, wouldn't let… He struggled against Dash's hold, fighting to get away. Dash let go and shoved at his chest, and Thorne fell backward onto the bed.

Dash dropped on top of him before he could right himself. He ground their cocks together, the rough friction making Thorne gasp. He dropped his legs open, forgetting to fight. All he could think about was how much he wanted Dash, wanted to be exposed by him, taken by him.

"You want my cock up your ass, don't you? You're a fucking slut for it?"

Holy fucking fuck. Dash's dirty words caught him by surprise. He grabbed the sides of Dash's head and yanked his hair, rolling them as Dash cried out. Thorne had never wanted and not wanted something so keenly.

Thorne straddled Dash. "You think you're man enough to take my ass?"

"Fuck, yes!" Dash bucked, unseating Thorne. They rolled again. This time Dash came out on top. Thank God Thorne's bed was huge. As it was they'd nearly fallen off the edge. Dash grabbed Thorne's wrists, squeezing just the right amount to send a jolt of lust through Thorne. He rubbed his cock against Dash's, hating that Dash still had pants on. He needed flesh-to-flesh contact.

"Your cock knows what it wants," Dash said, his tone mocking. "It's ready to surrender to me; what about the rest of you?"

Thorne glared at Dash, refusing to answer. Dash hung over him, eyes dark with lust, lips full and red from their harsh kiss. He was so fucking gorgeous.

Dash loosened his hold on Thorne's wrists, but didn't let him go. "Do you need to be tied up? Or can

I trust you to stay like this?"

"You want me, you'll have to hold me down." Thorne jerked his arms free, but Dash grabbed him and pinned him again.

Dash gathered his wrists in one hand and reached into his bag, pulling out a coil of red rope.

"You'll stay, and you'll love every minute of it, but this will help you remember who's in charge." He brushed the rope along Thorne's cheek. Thorne hadn't thought his cock could get any harder, but it did.

"Admit that you want this." Dash's voice was low and rough. Thorne wasn't the only one who was horny as hell.

"No." Thorne still wasn't ready to make this easy.

"Admit it. Or things will go a lot worse for you."

"Fuck you!"

Dash shook his head. "That's not what I want to hear."

Dash wound the rope around Thorne's wrists and secured the ends to the headboard, giving Thorne enough play to reposition himself, but not enough to get away. Thorne's heart pounded. This was crazy. He didn't really know Dash, and here he was letting the man tie him up and do God knows what to him. His concern must have shown because Dash leaned down and ran his tongue along the outer edge of his ear. "Remember, say red if you need me to stop. This is all about pleasure. Yours. Mine. I'm here to give you what you want."

Thorne looked into Dash's eyes. "What I want is for you to own me. Do you think you're up for that?"

The evil smile Dash gave him made Thorne's heart skip a beat. "I'm going to wreck your world, then put it back together. You're never going to forget this night." Thorne had no doubt that was true.

Dash reached into his bag again and pulled out the fucking huge plug. "Maybe you won't be so inclined to fight with this up your ass."

"Don't count on that."

Dash leaned down until his lips were almost touching Thorne's. "You won't fight too hard. I know your secret, remember? You love having your ass stretched wide open."

"Fucking bastard!"

"You'll be calling me worse than that before the night is over."

Chapter Eight

Without taking his eyes off Thorne, Dash laid the plug down on the bed. Thorne scowled, but he didn't say anything.

Dash felt around in his bag until he found lube and a condom. He prepped the plug and then slicked his fingers while Thorne watched, eyes wide, chest rising and falling with breaths that were coming fast and harsh. His cock stood at attention, precum dripping from the slit, making a pool on his abdomen.

Thorne needed to be pushed. Dash had seen that from the beginning, had wanted to subdue him and give him what he truly needed. But he hadn't imagined Thorne would admit to what he wanted this soon, or that he would be so blown away by it. The man was too fucking sexy, and Dash's cock was so hard he didn't know if he could hold out long enough to truly torment Thorne.

He brushed a lubed finger over Thorne's hole, and Thorne jerked, twisting away. "Oh no. You're going to stay right there." Dash used his other hand to push Thorne's hips down.

Dash finger-fucked him, keeping a steady rhythm as he stretched him out. Thorne scowled at him but stayed still, though his breaths grew more and more shallow.

"You think that's all it takes?" Thorne challenged. "You think that's going to make me give in to you?"

"No, but this is." Dash pulled his finger out and picked up the plug. He pushed the tip into Thorne's hole, eliciting a gasp. "If you'd been nice, I'd have warmed you up more. Now you're just going to have to take it."

"Fuck!" Thorne shouted when Dash started to push the fat silicone dick in deeper. Dash watched for signs of real distress but saw none. Thorne's cock was hard, his eyes closed. His teeth sunk into his bottom lip, but his ass was trying to take what Dash was giving him. "What's your safeword?"

"Fuck you," Thorne snarled.

"No, that's not right."

"Red. It's fucking red. Now get that thing in me and quit playing around. Are you topping me or babying me?"

Dash pushed harder, and Thorne tensed. "Fuck."

He stopped, waiting for Thorne to adjust. But just as Thorne relaxed, Dash pushed deeper.

"That thing is fucking massive."

"It's not all that long," Dash said, giving Thorne an evil smile.

"Long? My fucking ass doesn't care about long!"

"Ha! This is nothing compared to how your ass will feel after I fuck you."

Thorne tugged on the ropes, like he was testing their strength. "If I weren't tied up, we'd see how easily you could fuck me."

Dash chuckled. Thorne had let him fuck him easily enough the week before. "How long did you feel it after I had my cock in you last week?"

"Not a single fucking second."

Dash pulled the plug out. "I guess you don't want this after all, then."

Thorne continued to struggle, but now he was trying to get exactly what he claimed he didn't want. Dash watched him, loving that he could see the exact moment Thorne realized what he was doing.

"Days. It was days, you bastard!"

"Perfect." Dash pushed the plug back in, all the way this time.

Thorne stared at him, panting, tense.

"I could make you feel it all week this time, but I wouldn't want to damage you. I'll be wanting another round later."

Thorne yanked harder on the ropes, rattling the bed. "Let me loose and we'll talk about damage."

Dash laughed. "I don't think so. You haven't even experienced this yet." He pressed the base of the plug to turn on the vibrations at their lowest setting.

Thorne squirmed, obviously trying to escape the sensation which Dash knew from experience was enough to tease but not really give a man what he wanted.

"Do you want more?" Dash taunted.

Thorne scowled at him. "I don't fucking know."

Dash laughed and turned up the intensity of the vibrations. "Enjoy that for a few minutes then, while I enjoy you."

He settled between Thorne's thighs and took Thorne's cock in one hand. Then he brushed his lips over the tip of Thorne's cock, lapping at the slit, enjoying the bitter taste of Thorne's precum. Since his first try at sixteen, Dash had loved sucking cock, but he didn't think he'd ever craved the taste of a man as much as he did Thorne.

Thorne's hips shot off the bed when Dash took his cock deeper. "Dash, I…" Dash sucked, swallowing him all the way as he shoved Thorne's hips back to the mattress. Thorne fought his hold. "Dash. No. Too fucking much. Dash!"

Dash knew he was overloading Thorne on sensation, but he couldn't stop himself. Thorne's struggles made the headboard rattle so hard, Dash wondered if it would break. He didn't care though. Thorne could afford a new bed.

Dash could tell from the change in the noises Thorne made and the tension in his legs that he was right at the edge. No way in hell was Dash letting him go over yet. He tightened his hand around the base of Thorne's cock and sat back.

"Son of a bitch!"

Dash grinned. "Surely you didn't think I'd make it that easy, did you?"

"Easy? Is that what this was?"

"You want more of a challenge? I can give you that."

He tapped the end of the plug and shut off the vibrations. The tension in Thorne's hips and thighs eased as he sank into the mattress. Dash tugged on the plug.

Thorne glared at him. "What the fuck are you doing?"

"Taking the plug out."

"What? Why?"

"Because that's what I want to do."

Thorne stared at him like he wasn't sure if that was a good thing or not. He winced as it popped free, and Dash simply smiled at him, refusing to give reassurance.

"You feel empty now don't you, empty and wanting. That's just how I want you. It's going to be a while before you have anything else in that beautiful ass."

"Fuck you!"

Dash smiled at his anger. It was exactly what he wanted, Thorne pissed off and ready to prove himself. "I'm going to give you another challenge now. Do you think you're up for it?"

He stripped the condom from the plug and slid off the bed so he could throw the used latex away. When he returned, he straddled Thorne's chest and took hold of the headboard, rising over him. He braced himself on one hand and used the other to stroke his cock. "You think you can take all of me down your throat?"

Thorne's eyes widened. "I—"

Dash watched the action of his throat as he swallowed.

"Yes, damn it."

"Good. You're going to open up, and I'm going to fuck your mouth. If you make it good, maybe I'll fill your ass back up."

He teased Thorne's lips with his cock. Thorne licked at the tip, eyes never leaving Dash. God, this was hot. Dash wanted to drive right in and watch Thorne, but no matter how into the fantasy they both were, Thorne needed an out. He reached down and untied the knot binding Thorne's wrists.

"I don't think you're going to go anywhere now, are you?"

Thorne didn't say anything as Dash unwound the rope and rubbed the reddened flesh underneath. "Press your hands against the headboard and keep them there."

"I'm not intimidated by you."

Dash loved the lust mixed with fury in his eyes, loved that Thorne felt comfortable playing with him like this. "Let's see what you say after I feed you my cock."

Dash repositioned himself, and Thorne dropped his head back and opened his mouth, looking way more fucking eager than his words implied. Dash wrapped a hand around his throat and squeezed lightly. "You want this, don't you? You want me to use you?"

"Just fucking do it," Thorne snarled.

"Tap my thigh three times if you want to stop."

Thorne nodded, and Dash pushed in deep. Thorne swallowed around him, raising his head and encouraging Dash to go farther. God, he felt so good, hot and slick. Dash drove in harder, making Thorne gag. Thorne shoved at his thighs, pushing him back.

"Okay?" Dash asked.

"I fucking love it, you bastard."

Dash saw the truth of that in the flash of lust in Thorne's eyes. "I want you to keep your eyes on me while I take you."

Thorne glared at him, clearly as fucking turned on as Dash even if he was also pissed off.

Dash thrust into his mouth, gently at first and then harder until he was truly fucking his mouth like he'd take his ass. He'd never face-fucked a guy that roughly. It was fucking incredible, and Thorne was so into it. He didn't even struggle when Dash pulled his head up, forcing him to take every inch, pressing his face into Dash's crotch. He didn't hold on to the headboard though. Dash could hear Thorne's hand sliding up and down his cock, but he didn't care because Thorne kept watching him, just as he'd been told to do.

Fuck, he's hot! Dash was going to come any second. He couldn't stop. He hadn't meant to...

He let go of Thorne's head and tried to pull back, hoping he could stop the tide of orgasm, but it was too late. Without warning Thorne, he came, the intensity threatening to knock him out. Thorne eagerly swallowed every drop he had to give. When Dash was finally wrung dry, he pulled back and tried to catch his breath as he stared down at Thorne's cum-stained, swollen lips. "Wow."

Thorne licked his lips and then smiled as he caressed Dash's thigh with a firm touch. "Did I just make you lose control?"

He had. He'd never forgotten himself like that when he was working. "Asshole," he muttered.

"Oh, I like this," Thorne said. He slid his hands along the back of Dash's thighs, encouraging him to rise up so he could cup his ass and knead it. Dash bit back a moan. He wasn't used to being caressed like that. Usually he was the one doing the touching. Most men were only interested in getting their hands on his cock.

He realized Thorne was speaking, but he'd been too lost in sensation to comprehend.

He opened his eyes and looked down again. "What?"

"I really did throw you off your game, didn't I?"

"Things got a little more…intense than usual."

Thorne nodded. "You're not the only one who lost control."

Dash glanced over his shoulder. Thorne's abdomen was covered in streaks of cum, his cock softening against his body. "Fuck."

"A damn good one."

"Yes, it was," Dash said, his voice soft, more honest that he'd meant to be. It was probably the best damn sex he'd ever had.

Thorne was studying him, and Dash was revealing way too much. What if Thorne realized how deep Dash's feelings went? The last thing he wanted was for Thorne to think he couldn't be professional, especially considering how he'd pushed to stay, to talk, to make this more than sex. Thorne didn't pay for sex because he wanted a man to fall for him.

"Are you okay?" Thorne asked.

"I'm fine." But he wasn't. He slid from the bed and practically ran for the bathroom.

After a few deep breaths, Dash stared at his pale face in the mirror and tried to convince himself that his reaction was ridiculous.

Go back out there. Act normal. You're the fucking dom. You just went at him like he existed to serve you.

He's fine.

What if he's not? Get it together and go check on him.

Dash didn't listen to his conscience. Instead, he turned on the shower. Thorne really had seemed fine, more fine than Dash, anyway. The warm water would

101

clear his mind and then he could face Thorne. He just needed a little time. He'd lost control. That was why he was wigging out. It had nothing to do with falling for Thorne. "Don't fall for clients" was the first rule in this job, and he had no intention of breaking it.

THORNE USED THE edge of the sheet to wipe himself down. Then he lay there studying the ceiling and wondering what the hell was going on. Had he done something to upset Dash, and if so, what? Was Dash just concerned he'd screwed up because he'd come when he hadn't meant to? Did he think Thorne wouldn't hire him again because of that?

If so, he was fucking nuts. That was the best sex Thorne had ever had. He'd told men not to be gentle, but no one had ever driven their cock into his mouth like Dash had. Thorne had always been good at deep throating. When Clint had discovered his natural talent, they'd both enjoyed putting it to use, but even Clint had never let go with him like Dash had. It wasn't simply that Dash was a professional. No other rent boy had gone at him that hard, even when he'd offered. Was it because Dash knew Thorne had a way out if he wanted to stop? Or was it…something else?

He heard the shower turn on, but Dash didn't come out to invite Thorne to join him. After a few seconds, Thorne peeled himself away from the sweaty sheets. To hell with waiting for him, Thorne was going to go in there and make sure Dash was okay.

Steam rolled out as he stepped into the bathroom as if Dash had turned the hot water all the way to cook-a-lobster. Thorne pulled the curtain aside, but for several seconds he couldn't say anything because

Dash's beauty—eyes closed, head tilted back, water streaming down his sculpted body—took his breath away. He wanted to lap at the water pooling in his collar bones. Hell, he wanted to give him an all-over tongue bath. And most of all, he didn't want Dash to leave. Ever.

Dash opened his eyes as if he finally sensed that Thorne was there.

"May I join you?" Thorne asked.

Dash smiled. "Yes."

"You didn't come back," he said in Dash's ear as he spun him to face the water and pulled him close. "I got lonely."

"Sorry. I…"

"Did you think I'd care that you lost it? Because I don't. You just made me eager for round two. I loved watching you let go, feeling you shoot down my throat. I loved how you used me, that you took me at my word and believed I could take it that hard."

Dash shuddered in his arms, and Thorne tightened his grip.

"You're fucking perfect. You know that?"

"I…" Dash turned and kissed him. It wasn't what Thorne was expecting. A light brush of lips might not have surprised him, but this was a full-on attack. Dash moved them until Thorne hit the wall at the back of the shower. He didn't have time to be cold out of the water spray because Dash was all over him, thrusting against him, sucking at his neck, toying with his nipples. He gripped Thorne's right thigh and lifted his leg, hooking it over Dash's hip as if trying to get them as close as possible. His hand swept over Thorne's ass, and Thorne jerked. He was overly sensitized and still feeling the loss of the plug.

"Turn around," Dash growled against his ear.

Thorne didn't consider protesting. He let Dash press him to the wall as he thrust against his ass, sliding his cock in the crack, the water making his movements easy.

"I want to be inside you right now."

"Fuck." The word was more groan than speech.

"I want to bend you over and wreck your ass. And I want you to beg for it."

Holy shit. Whatever had unsettled Dash was gone, and the hot, dominating man Thorne had been crazy about was back.

Dash worked Thorne, his cock dragging over Thorne's ass as he stretched Thorne's arms up and pinned his hands. Suddenly he stepped back. "Fuck!" Dash's voice was angry rather than sultry. "No condoms in here."

Before Thorne could say there were some in the drawer of the vanity, Dash shut the water off. He grabbed Thorne's arm and dragged him, out of the shower, dripping wet. "Bed. Now."

Thorne couldn't get there fast enough. "On your knees. Hands behind your back. I want to see you tied up again."

"Yes, God yes." Thorne wasn't sure what had happened with Dash, but he didn't care. Dash's mood was way too hot to bother analyzing.

Thorne must not have moved fast enough, because Dash yanked his arms behind his back and wrapped the soft rope around his wrists. He didn't tie it tight. It was more for show, but just the feel of it against his wrists had Thorne ready to beg. He couldn't wait to have Dash fuck him hard, like it was punishment. He imagined Dash looking down at him, eyes wide, mouth hanging open, loving the sight of Thorne's bound hands lying against the top of his ass.

"Fuck me, Dash. Fuck me like you mean it."

"I do mean it. I'm going to fuck you so hard you'll feel it all week."

"Do it. I'm ready for you. I don't need anything but your cock."

He was glad Dash had used the plug on him earlier, because he was way too impatient for prep. He needed Dash's cock as fast as he could get it.

He heard Dash ripping open a condom. Seconds later, Dash was there, the tip of his cock brushing Thorne's hole. With no warning, he pushed in, hard and fast, not stopping until his balls slapped Thorne's ass.

"Bastard!" Thorne shouted. He was too full. He was going to come apart. He struggled, trying to escape, but Dash pinned him down, lacing his fingers through Thorne's and driving his hands back down.

"Take it," Dash demanded.

He pulled out, then thrust deep again. His cock went in easier this time. After a few more strokes, pleasure surpassed pain, and Thorne quit fighting. Instead, he pushed back against Dash until their bodies were slamming together. It was all Thorne could do to keep his feet under him.

Dash knew just what he needed, driving in at the perfect angle to stimulate his prostate, but Dash wouldn't let go of him so he could jerk himself off. He was going fucking insane without any friction on his dick. He bucked, trying to throw Dash off him.

"Goddamn it, let me go or wrap your fucking hand around my cock right fucking now."

Dash laughed. "No touching. You're going to come without it."

"I can't. I've never—"

"You will tonight."

"The fuck I will." Thorne worked his way out of the ropes and tried to elbow Dash in the ribs, but Dash held on. He was even stronger than he looked.

"I made you come twice last week when you thought you couldn't."

"This is not the same."

"No, it's not. I'm going to fuck you, and you're gonna come because you're a slut for my cock. Because all you need to make you come is me stretching your ass."

Thorne reached under himself and grabbed his cock. He wasn't waiting another second.

Dash slapped his ass. Hard. Thorne gasped.

"Ah, is that what you need? A spanking?"

"No!" Thorne wasn't about to admit how fucking good it had felt, how the sting made his cock even harder. He stretched his arms up and gripped the sheets. "I'm so fucking close. Just put your fucking hand on my cock."

"No." Dash's voice was obnoxiously calm. Thorne wanted to punch him, but he wanted to come even more.

"Dash! I'm—"

"Give yourself a chance. Concentrate on how good my cock feels."

Fighting wasn't working. Well, maybe it was. If anything his balls were even tighter now. His cock even more painfully hard. He focused on the sensations Dash was sending through his body.

"Your ass is so hot, so tight around me. I could fuck you like this all night, over and over. But I want your mouth again too. I want to feel your throat close around my cock. You loved giving yourself to me, letting me gag you with my cock, because you want me to own you."

Thorne gasped. Searing heat raced down his spine.

"You're so dirty. You love being taken like this, used like this, don't you?"

"Fuck! I'm right there. I just can't…"

"Does anyone else know what a cock slut you are?"

"Oh my fucking God!" Thorne's orgasm seized his muscles, stole his ability to breathe as darkness closed in at the edges of his vision.

Dash kept driving into him, but he'd lost his steady rhythm. "Thorne. Oh, fuck. Thooooooorne!" Dash bucked against him, making Thorne's body jerk one last time before he closed his eyes and all tension drained from him. He wondered if he could sink through the bed right to the floor.

Thorne whimpered when Dash pulled out and climbed off the bed, too exhausted to make a louder protest.

"Whoa." Something in Dash's voice made Thorne look over his shoulder. Dash swayed on his feet and had to grab the bed for support.

"Drop the damn condom on the floor and get in bed before you fall over."

Dash did as he said and flopped down on his

side. "I think I'm going to die. But I don't care."

"*You're* dying? I'm fucking twice your age. I may actually be dead already."

"You're in great shape as far as I can see."

Thorne pushed his sweaty hair off his face. "No one's in good enough shape for what you just did to me."

"That may be. I can't even move."

"You don't need to. We're never getting up again."

Thorne pulled Dash to him, and Dash snuggled against his chest. "If you say one fucking word about how you thought I didn't cuddle, I'll put that plug up your ass next."

"Ha!"

Thorne caressed Dash's neck and the curve of his shoulder, and Dash let out a sleepy sigh.

"Stay the night?" Thorne asked.

Dash nodded, or at least Thorne thought he did. He was fading into sleep almost as fast as Dash was.

The next time Thorne became aware of his surroundings he realized he was sticky, stinky, and tangled up with another man. "Dash?"

Dash stretched and turned over. "What time is it?"

Thorne rolled onto his back and reached out blindly, slapping his hand down until he found his phone on the nightstand. He clicked it on, the light from the screen like a needle to his eye. When he managed to read the numbers, they inexplicably said 7:10 a.m. Had they slept all night? "It's after seven."

"Well, fuck me."

"Not now. I'm going back to sleep."

Dash glared at him. "What have you done with the real Thorne?"

"Hmmm?"

"You didn't work last night, and now you're going to sleep in?"

"Shut up and let me sleep."

"Oooh, is Mr. Workaholic not a morning person?"

"No." Thorne pulled the covers over his head. The mattress dipped, and he heard footsteps as he drifted back to sleep.

***

Thorne had no idea how much time had passed since he'd last woken, but someone was shaking him. "Go the fuck away," he mumbled.

"Do you want coffee? I'm going to get some." Coffee? "Oh God, yes."

"I'd make breakfast, but there isn't any food."

Thorne reached for the nightstand again and found his wallet. He pulled out a stack of bills and tossed them in the direction of Dash's voice. "Go get some fucking groceries and let me sleep."

"As you wish, sir."

Later, he'd do something about that snarky tone. He pulled out his key card and tossed it in the same direction. "Here's my key. Take that too."

Chapter Nine

Dash stared at the key in his hand, surprised Thorne trusted him with it. Maybe he was just too sleepy to care. If so, Dash hoped he didn't make a habit of having random men over. Marc said Thorne never slept with anyone but escorts at least as far as he could tell. Dash hoped that was true.

"Why are you still here?"

Dash laughed as he pulled on the clothes he'd worn last night. "Because I can't go out there naked."

Dash scurried through the lobby, waving to the doorman as he exited. It was a different man from the one who usually let him in. He must have the day shift. This man gave Dash a look of disdain instead of returning his greeting. Dash glanced down at himself and realized his pants were wrinkled and he'd missed a button on his shirt. Oh well, so much for first impressions.

He pulled out his phone and used it to find the closest market. Twenty minutes later, he was back with ingredients for omelets and carrot muffins. But when he reached the door, the unknown doorman blocked his way. "This is a private building, sir."

"Yes, I know. I just came out a few minutes ago."

"Who are you here to see?"

Dash's heart was pounding. Would Thorne want this man to know Dash was with him? Dash didn't usually feel like a common prostitute despite the fact that men hired him for sex. But this man was making him feel cheap. Who the fuck was he to do that? "I don't believe that is any of your business. I have a key."

The man jerked it out of Dash's hands. "Only residents of this building or guests they've listed with us should have keys."

"Look, I understand that you don't know me. But I'm supposed to deliver these groceries."

"Those can be sent up. We have a—"

"No. I'm delivering them and then making breakfast which I can't do if you don't let me in." Dash held out his hand for Thorne's key.

"I'm sorry, sir, until I verify—"

"You mean to tell me that people always register friends before giving them a key? That—"

"I know everyone in the building, and I've not seen you here before, therefore—"

"Fine." Dash turned and walked down the street until he found a bench where he could set the groceries. Hand shaking, he pulled out his phone and dialed Thorne's number. He didn't expect an answer. Thorne was probably still asleep with his ringer off.

But he was in luck. Thorne answered on the first ring. "Dash?"

"You're up."

"Technically no, but I'm awake enough to check e-mail and to be very impatient for coffee."

Dash grinned despite his predicament. Have-everything-his-way Thorne was back. "You'd have it now, but the doorman won't let me in."

"I thought I gave you my key."

"You did. He took it from me."

"What?" Dash had never heard such anger in Thorne's voice.

"He said he knew everyone who should have a key and—"

"I'll be down as soon as I find some pants."

"Thorne, if you don't want him to know I'm with you, then I—"

"Are you kidding me? That man is an ass, and if I have my way—and I usually do—he won't have a job after today."

"Thank you." Dash didn't know what else to day. He almost felt sorry for the man.

"Should I be insulted that you doubted I'd handle this?" Thorne asked.

Dash decided not to answer that. He shouldn't have doubted, but he had. He heard muttering and sounds that indicated Thorne was moving around. "Why the fuck are there no clean pants here?"

"Laundress on strike?"

"Very funny."

Dash laughed. "I thought so. I'll see you in a minute."

Dash ended the call and walked back to the door.

"Didn't I tell you that I have to verify your identity before you can enter?" the doorman said.

"And I told you that I have someone waiting on groceries and breakfast. He's angry, and he's on his way down." Dash smiled and stood by the door, holding his bag.

He dramatically drew in a breath of the fragrant summer air. "Nice weather," he observed as the elevator doors opened into the lobby.

Thorne stepped out in a crisp, dark suit that was likely worth more than Dash's car.

The doorman scowled at Dash.

"Good thing it's not terribly hot this morning. I have a feeling my friend gets even crankier when his food goes bad. He's not good with disappointment." Thorne glided toward them, moving soundlessly, like a cat stalking its prey.

Dash leaned in closer and spoke in a stage whisper. "He's a little spoiled."

"Am I now?"

The doorman jumped and turned. "Good morning, Mr. Shipton." The man's voice no longer held the arrogance it had when he'd spoken to Dash.

Thorne ignored him and gestured to Dash to step inside.

"This young man is here to see *you*?" The color drained from the doorman's face.

"He is. I was in bed, waiting for my breakfast. Thanks to you, I'm now dressed and in the lobby, and I've not even had coffee yet. I've decided to call a meeting with the building manager, no point in being dressed for business if I'm not going to conduct some. Misconduct of building employees is at the top of the agenda."

"Sir, I didn't realize... I thought—"

"That he'd broken in, stolen my key, and come back to what, murder me with..." Thorne rose on tiptoe and peered into the grocery bag Dash held. "These?" He lifted out an egg carton. "Or these?" He pulled out a bundle of scallions.

"I'm not supposed to let anyone in who isn't on the list of approved guests." The man's voice quavered.

Thorne glared at him. "He had my key, and you saw him exit, unless you weren't paying such assiduous attention when he left."

"No, sir. I mean, yes, sir. I saw him exit."

"Then why didn't you let him return?" Thorne's tone had Dash on edge, and he wasn't the focus of Thorne's anger.

"He's not on the list."

Thorne turned when the elevator dinged. A lean man exited.

"Mr. Garnet, lovely morning, isn't it?" Thorne asked.

Mr. Garnet was probably fifty-five. He was dressed in khakis and a rumpled button-down, and he did not look at all awake. "Yes, sir. It is."

"Too bad we're going to have to spend it on business."

Mr. Garnet looked like he was bracing for a storm. Dash wondered how often Thorne demanded his presence. He hadn't been kidding when he said the man was spoiled. "What's wrong, Mr. Shipton?"

Thorne looked back at the doorman. "We need to discuss employees and how they handle their jobs."

Mr. Garnet looked like he'd be happy to forget he'd ever seen Thorne or the doorman. "Did something happen?"

"Something hasn't happened. I don't have breakfast or coffee because this man would not let my—" Thorne paused there, obviously not at all sure how to describe Dash.

Dash wondered what he'd come up with.

"Personal chef into the building."

Dash pressed his lips together in an effort not to laugh.

"I was following policy," the doorman protested. "And the young man didn't say he was here to see Mr. Shipton."

Mr. Garnet looked at Dash and then at the doorman. "I'm confused."

"Don't be," Thorne said, taking over again. "I sent Mr. Dashwood out for…"

Dash didn't hear the rest of what Thorne said because he was stuck on the fact that Thorne knew his real name. Sheila never revealed anything personal about the men and women who worked for her. Thorne had stalked him; fucking stalked him. And yet, here he was defending Dash, angry at the doorman's treatment of him. Thorne had always treated him with respect, even apologizing when he joked about paying him.

"I'm going to leave you to handle this now," Thorne said to Mr. Garnet. "I hope I won't have to get involved in such matters again."

"Thank you for calling this to my attention, sir. I'll make sure you never have this problem again."

"I sincerely hope so. I'd hate to have to call my realtor."

"No sir," Mr. Garnet said. "I will brief all our employees on this issue of guests with keys."

Thorne smiled. "Thank you."

Angry as he was, Dash had to stifle a laugh when he saw the expression on the doorman's face. Thorne was so delightfully officious. No wonder he was good at his job.

THORNE TURNED WITHOUT another word and started toward the elevators. After a few steps, he realized Dash wasn't following him. "I'm ready for breakfast now," he called over his shoulder.

"Oh, right." Dash unfroze and followed him to the elevators. Thorne keyed into the one for the upper floors.

When the doors shut, Thorne turned to face Dash. "I'm very sorry about that. There have been some incidents recently in the adjacent building. I know Garnet wanted to up security, but he's taken it too far."

Dash didn't say a word. Was he pissed off that Thorne had rescued him?

"What's wrong?" Thorne asked.

"How the fuck did you know my name?"

Oh, right. He'd let that little secret out. "Do you honestly think I'd give my key to someone I hadn't vetted?"

"And here I thought you respected me."

Thorne frowned. Where was this going? "I do."

"I didn't ask to have your key. I didn't ask for anything other than our basic business arrangement."

"I have my people check out all the men I hire."

"*All* of them. Do you keep a stable of us now?" Dash turned away, color rising in his cheeks.

"Did you want me to just ignore how that asshole treated you?"

"No. I don't know what I wanted."

Thorne had really been looking forward to the morning. How could he get them back on track? "I'm sorry."

Dash's eyes widened. He opened his mouth like

he was going to say something, then closed it and simply stared.

"Yes, I'm a privileged asshole, but I can apologize. I invaded your privacy. It's the only way I can bring myself to allow a stranger into my home."

Dash considered Thorne's words for several tense seconds. Finally, he nodded. "Okay. I can accept that."

"Truly, it has nothing to do with your profession."

"Personal chef or my usual one?"

Thorne smiled. At least Dash appeared less tense now. "You'd make an excellent chef. I'd hire you."

"Good to know."

Thorne wondered if Dash would consider doing exactly that, working for Thorne as a chef, among other things.

"You know my real name now too," Thorne pointed out.

"Mr. Shipton?"

"Bradford Thornwell Shipton. I went by Thorne in school because there were several Brads and I wanted to be different."

Dash looked him up and down. "Trust me. No matter what you call yourself, you'll always be different."

Thorne hoped that was a compliment. "Thank you."

"You're welcome."

The elevator dinged and the doors slid open, but Thorne didn't move. "At work, I'm B.T. Shipton, but I like to be Thorne again when I can."

Dash smiled then, and Thorne realized he'd been

forgiven. "It suits you. You're all prickly, but your defenses hide something rather lovely."

Dash walked out of the elevator. This time, Thorne was the one who stood frozen, because at that moment he knew without a doubt that he'd fallen for Dash and fallen hard.

Chapter Ten

Dash had breakfast ready by the time Thorne was out of the shower and dressed again—this time in cargo shorts and a T-shirt. Dash hadn't even realized he owned any normal-people clothes.

"What?" Thorne asked, catching Dash staring at him.

"Nothing."

"You're staring."

"You're hot."

Thorne narrowed his eyes.

"You're wearing casual clothes like the rest of us peasants."

"Ha. I don't wear suits all the time."

"No," Dash agreed, "sometimes you go naked."

"Would you prefer that?"

Dash considered the offer. "You know I would. But then we might not actually eat breakfast, and I'm starving."

"Me too. It smells fantastic."

"Thank you." Dash gestured toward the dining table. "This way, sir."

Dash had set two places with glasses of orange juice, coffee cups, and cloth napkins he'd found in a drawer in the dining area. "Have a seat. There's coffee in the carafe. Might I ask why you own a thousand-dollar coffee machine if you don't make your own coffee?"

119

"I make it sometimes. I'm not utterly helpless, you know."

Dash studied him. "Hmmm… Maybe."

Thorne rolled his eyes.

Dash prepared two plates and brought them to the table. "Veggie omelets and morning-glory muffins."

Thorne eyed the muffins. "Those look suspiciously healthy."

"They're delicious. Something tells me healthy is not a normal part of your diet."

Thorne frowned. "You said I was in perfectly good shape."

"That's irrelevant. You can have a nice body and still not eat properly. I doubt you eat as often as you should either."

Thorne looked like he was going to protest, but then he smiled instead. "Thank you for making breakfast."

"It's my pleasure." Dash loved cooking for other people and, based on his reaction to the cupcakes, he'd decided Thorne would be an appreciative audience.

Dash sat down just as Thorne took a bite of omelet. "This is amazing. What did you do to it?"

"Nothing special. It's just an omelet."

Thorne shook his head. "I've had plenty of omelets. This is on another plane of existence."

Dash laughed. "I took my time. I sautéed the vegetables, seasoned them, cooked the eggs slowly, but there's no big secret."

Thorne studied him for a moment. "You're hiding something."

"I'm not. I swear."

Still watching him carefully, Thorne took a bite of muffin. His face lit up as he chewed. "Wow, this is so good I don't even care if it's healthy."

"It's not that healthy, but it does have carrot and zucchini in it."

"Trying to get all my veggies in me at once?" Thorne asked.

"Something like that."

After breakfast, Thorne helped Dash load the dishwasher, something Dash hadn't expected. "You cooked for me," Thorne said, obviously thinking that was explanation enough.

"Doesn't the personal chef usually do the cooking and the cleaning up?"

Thorne shook his head. "I'd have the maid do the cleaning, but since mine's not coming today, I'll just have to get my hands dirty."

When they finished, Thorne stood at the counter, sipping coffee. Dash came up behind him and circled his waist. "Have you got time for some distraction?"

Thorne glanced at the clock on the stove. "I wish, but I really need to tackle some work. Although…"

"What's that dirty mind of yours cooking up?" Dash stepped closer and palmed Thorne's cock.

Thorne groaned and placed a hand on top of Dash's. "I need to send some information off by noon. How much of the day do you have free?"

"I don't have to be anywhere until three."

"Stay. Watch TV or whatever while I work and then…"

"And then?" Dash asked, wanting to hear him say it.

"And then I'm going to fuck you."

Dash shivered. "That's exactly what I hoped you were going to say."

"I know I'll need to pay for the day. I'm good with that."

"Sheila will bill you. I'll send her a message."

"Okay. I've got about five hundred channels if you want to chill by the TV or—"

"TV sounds good. I should rest up for later."

"Yes, you should."

THORNE GLANCED UP from his laptop every few minutes. He couldn't stop watching Dash. How did he manage to look so damn hot lying on the couch watching television?

A flaw in the open floorplan of Thorne's apartment—which wasn't usually a problem since he rarely had anyone there—was that he couldn't avoid Dash unless he went into the bedroom and shut the rarely-used door. But he didn't have that kind of self-discipline. How could he deny himself the view? Dash was wearing a truly tiny pair of shorts and a white T-shirt that clung to his shoulders and pecs. He appeared utterly relaxed as if he'd become one with the couch.

"You need to relax."

Dash's words echoed in his head. He wasn't sure he was capable of just lying around like Dash could, except right after Dash fucked the hell out of him.

He's good for you. That obnoxious voice inside again, the one that fought the rigid schedule Thorne usually enforced on himself.

He's dangerous for me. He makes me want

things.

Are those things so bad?

Maybe not. But Dash was twenty-two. No matter how much he enjoyed the sex, he wasn't likely to be interested in a relationship with a man as old as Thorne. He's doing a job. One he's good at. Thorne was arrogant enough to believe Dash truly enjoyed their time together, but it couldn't be anything more than erotic enjoyment.

He forced himself to focus on work long enough to get his report sent off by eleven forty-five. As soon as he received a reply confirming that the team leader of the project had all the information he needed, Thorne closed his laptop and stood. As he stretched, he watched a few seconds of Dash's movie. Based on the hairstyles and clothing, Thorne guessed it was from the eighties. "What are you watching?"

"You're kidding, right?" Dash looked over the back of the couch at him like he was nuts.

"What do you mean?"

"You've never seen this?"

Thorne studied the movie for several more seconds. "Oh, it's that John Cusack one."

Dash picked up the remote and hit pause. "*Say Anything.* It's a classic. Come here right now and watch the rest with me." Dash spread his legs, making room for Thorne to settle between them. Thorne was powerless to resist the offer.

At first he was too busy tracing patterns on Dash's firm thighs and enjoying the feel of Dash's hard chest behind his back to pay much attention to the movie, but by the time John Cusack held up his boom box, blasting Peter Gabriel at his girlfriend's house, Thorne could see the appeal, at least if you were overly romantic.

"I still can't believe you hadn't seen this," Dash said as the credits rolled. "I love all these old movies."

"*Casablanca* or *Breakfast at Tiffany's* are old movies, not the Brat Pack."

Dash waved off his comment as if it shouldn't matter.

"I didn't watch a lot of movies as a…" Thorne's words trailed off in horror. "Fuck, how old were you when this came out?"

"Not born."

"Wow. Now I feel ancient."

"After last night? Don't be ridiculous. You've got life in you yet."

Thorne shook his head. Dash was born in the '90s; that was mind-boggling.

"So what about *The Breakfast Club*, have you seen that one?"

Thorne nodded.

"*Sixteen Candles*? *Some Kind of Wonderful*?"

"Nope."

Dash sighed. "You were so deprived."

He had been, deprived of a social life anyway, not of other things, education included. "I was busy."

"Studying?" Dash asked.

"You guessed it."

"I wouldn't have thought you'd have needed to study too much in school. You seem like the naturally smart type."

Thorne sighed. If only that had been the case. "I'm dyslexic. I've learned to deal with it, but it kept me from reading well when I was a kid and that affected my grades. My parents got me a tutor, and while I'm thankful for a lot of what I learned from her, they weren't okay with me simply improving my skills. I had to be the best in school. No kid of theirs was going to let a disability cause them to make anything other than straight A's. I spent *a lot* of time with my tutor. And a lot of time on my schoolwork."

Dash shook his head. "That sucks."

"Yeah, it did, but look at me now. I'm the success story my father wanted me to be. By the time I was in high school I was thriving academically, but my parents, my father especially, could never believe I'd succeed if he let up the pressure even a tiny bit. I graduated top of my class, exactly like he wanted, but I did it for me, not him. I see my parents for major holidays or if I can't avoid it. Otherwise, I only talk to my sister."

"Are you two close?"

He nodded. "As much as an arrogant ass and his popular married sister with a perfect house, golden retriever, and 2.5 kids can be."

Dash glanced around. "Your house looks pretty damn perfect to me."

He snorted. "No wife, no kids, no letting my parents tell me what and where to buy."

"Ah. Did they pick out your sister's house?"

"No, but they approved of her choices."

"Is that why you work all the time?" Dash asked. "To make sure you stay a success story?"

"That used to be why. Now I think I'm just used to it. I don't know how to do anything else. I tried having a life outside work for a while when I was first

125

hired at Symthson, but it didn't last."

"What did you do for fun back then?"

Fucked my married boss. Had a fucking midlife crisis at twenty-eight. "That was when I was sailing. I actually spent time outside, not just at a desk or on a treadmill, but now…I spend all my time looking for the next client and figuring out how to hold the ones I've got."

Dash watched him, seeming to know there was more Thorne wasn't telling him. "If you lost a client or two, would that be the worst thing ever?"

"No." Thorne needed to change the subject. "You know what would be?"

"What?"

"If you had to leave before I had a chance to fuck you."

Thorne didn't miss Dash's quick intake of breath.

"Is that right?" Dash asked.

Thorne nodded. Dash rose onto his knees and pushed at Thorne's chest until he lay back against the end of the couch. Dash reached for the fastenings of Thorne's shorts. "Let's see what we can do to get this party started, then."

When Dash had freed Thorne's cock, he sucked at the head, gently, no more than a tease. Thorne groaned, enjoying the warmth of Dash's tongue and the sensual, barely there touches. By the time he took Thorne deep into his mouth, Thorne was starving for him, but still, he didn't fight the pace. There was something incredibly erotic about the way Dash was taking his time. Eventually though, Thorne felt the need for more, the need to drive into Dash's ass and make him beg. He gripped Dash's shoulders.

"Enough."

Dash looked up at him. "Really?"

"Yes, I want your ass, and I'm not letting you distract me anymore."

Dash smiled and shifted position so he was leaning over Thorne. Thorne looked up at him. The lust in Dash's eyes stole his breath. "Fuck," he said, more an exhale than a word. "Kiss me."

Dash did. Thorne let him take the lead, a long, thorough exploration, warm, soft lips pressing against Thorne's, Dash's tongue sliding over his, tasting, licking the roof of his mouth. Thorne sucked at Dash's lower lip. He loved how soft it was.

By the time Dash pulled back, his breathing was ragged, and he stared down at Thorne, wide-eyed, shock on his face.

"You feel that too?" A dangerous question, but Thorne was feeling dangerous, feeling like he was on the edge of something, and he wanted to jump.

For a moment Thorne was sure Dash did and he was going to admit it; then Dash schooled his expression. "Shut up and fuck me."

Yeah, that was what he needed to do. No more foolish fantasies. "Bedroom."

Dash scrambled up, slipped, and caught himself on the coffee table. He stumbled drunkenly toward the bed, and Thorne followed, pausing only to grab lube and a condom from Dash's bag. Dash settled on his back on the bed, legs spread open for Thorne. Fucking him face-to-face was a bad idea. It was only going to make the ache in his chest worse if he watched Dash's face as he moved inside him. But no way in hell was he going to give up the chance. This "relationship" could all come crashing down at any moment. If Dash realized what he was feeling, surely he'd run.

He squirted lube on his fingers, dropped the bottle on the bed, and sat on his knees between Dash's legs. "So fucking hot," he murmured as he toyed with Dash's ass, running his finger around the edge of his entrance, giving him nothing more than a little pressure.

Dash moved his hips almost imperceptibly, obviously trying to stay still, to keep Thorne from seeing how desperate he was.

"You want this?" Thorne asked as he entered Dash with a finger, slowly working his way deeper.

Dash gasped and tilted his head back, eyes closed. "So fucking much." God, he was beautiful, and this all seemed so unreal.

"Do you really want this, me fucking you?" He was hanging over the cliff now.

Dash opened his eyes and looked at Thorne. There was fear there and uncertainty. "Thorne?"

"I know I shouldn't ask that. I know that's not what this is."

"I do. I want it." Dash closed his eyes as if he couldn't look at Thorne after his confession.

Thorne pulled his finger out and grabbed the condom, so worked up, physically and emotionally, he could barely roll it on. He slicked his cock and then he was there, pushing into Dash, moving slowly, giving Dash a chance to adjust, though he thought he would die if he didn't bury himself immediately. He needed to be balls deep in Dash, to be as close to him as he could. What was his problem? Insanity? Stress sending him over the edge?

Dash was panting, his leg muscles hard as rock where they lay over Thorne's shoulders. "You okay?"

Dash nodded frantically. "Yes! Just…need more!"

Thorne needed more too. He thrust, finally going in all the way.

"Fuck!" Dash cried.

Thorne hung over Dash, trying to breathe, trying not to fucking come before he even got started, because the hot clasp of Dash's ass—having him there, begging, need so plain on his face, body spread out for Thorne—was almost more than he could take.

Thorne wasn't going to rush this. He kept his rhythm slow and steady. Dash writhed beneath him. "You're killing me. Get on with it."

Thorne cupped the back of Dash's neck, raising his head so they could kiss again. He'd forgotten how good kissing could be. Their tongues fought, shoving their way past one another. Thorne slid his lips along Dash's throat and sucked at the spot where his neck and shoulder met, wanting to mark him, knowing he shouldn't.

"Do it!" Dash demanded.

He bit again, harder this time. Dash cried out and hot cum splattered on Thorne's chest. He let go of Dash's shoulder and drove in hard. No more slow, no more careful. He had to come. Right fucking then. Release hit like a punch, and he was flying, shouting Dash's name, his real name, Riley.

Thorne lay there, knowing his blunder might be unforgivable, but he couldn't move, couldn't apologize. He buried his face in Ri-Dash's neck.

Dash's hands stroked his back; he didn't pull away, didn't tense with anger. Maybe Thorne hadn't ruined everything after all.

When Thorne thought he could sit up without passing out, he rose off Dash, but he didn't look him in the eye. He was too much of a coward. He fumbled his way to the bathroom, disposed of the condom, and splashed cold water on his face. His reflection showed every one of his forty-two years. Twenty more than Dash. Twenty. What the fuck was he thinking? He cleaned himself up, wet a washcloth, and brought it to Dash. Thorne wasn't ready to face him, but he couldn't put it off any longer.

"I'm sorry." More words piled up behind those, but he shut his mouth, locking them in.

Dash watched him.

After a few seconds, Thorne couldn't stand the silence. He sorted through the things he wanted to say and found something appropriate. "Does it help to know I've apologized more to you in a few weeks than I have to anyone in years?"

Dash smiled then. "Maybe. I'd like to think I bring out the good in you."

Thorne's chest tightened. He finally looked into Dash's eyes. Thorne didn't see what he'd expected. Dash didn't appear angry; wary maybe, but not angry.

"I crossed a line, and I shouldn't have," Thorne said.

Dash nodded. "I actually kind of liked it. But please don't do it again."

"I won't." Thorne's heart was beating impossibly fast. He should be thrilled by Dash's response, but he was terrified. Anger would have been better because now he had hope that Dash felt more than lust for him.

"Thanks. I've never been with anyone who called me by my real name."

"You mean any clients?"

"No. Not just clients. You're not the only one who's fucked up about relationships."

Thorne was having a difficult time processing that. "Why would a gorgeous young man like you have such a problem?"

"I could ask the same thing. You're hot as fuck, in great shape for an old guy, and—" Thorne threw a pillow at him.

Dash laughed as he caught it and tossed it to the floor. "You're rich, successful."

"Yes. Most people see those attributes," Thorne agreed.

Dash nodded, obviously getting it then. "But they don't see you?"

"I have a hard time letting anyone in, but I would've thought you'd have it easy."

Dash shook his head. "I tried dating before I took this job. None of the men I went out with wanted what I wanted."

"And what is that?" Thorne asked. "What do you want?"

Dash blushed, which Thorne found ridiculously endearing. "It's dumb."

Thorne hooked a finger under Dash's chin and raised his head so Dash had to look at him. "No, it's what you want. Don't let anyone tell you it's dumb."

"It will sound crazy considering what I do now."

"Who cares what you do? What you are is a

beautiful, kind, talented young man whose job involves making closed-off, arrogant assholes like me understand that there is pleasure in the world and that letting go of their stuffy schedules on occasion is a good thing."

Dash's eyes widened. "Really? That's what you see?"

Thorne nodded. "It is. So tell me. What do you want?"

"I want romance. True love. A fairy tale. I want to have a house. I want to cook for my husband. I want to build things together." He shook his head. "God, I sound like a dork."

"No, you don't." Thorne had dreamed of those things once himself. He'd dreamed of Clint leaving his wife, making a new life with Thorne. Then Clint had died, and Thorne had given up that dream.

"There's someone out there who can build that dream with you," Thorne said. Then he laughed at himself. "Wow. Now I sound like a fucking sap."

Dash grinned. "Don't worry. Your secret is safe with me."

But Thorne had so many secrets, and the place inside where he used to keep them locked up was threatening to break apart.

Chapter Eleven

"Thanks, Drew. I'll get that report back to you tomorrow so you can take a look at it." Thank God the tedious weekly wrap-up meeting was over. Thorne had thought some of the junior consultants were never going to shut up. At least now there were only a few hours left before he'd see Dash.

Drew frowned. "I'm spending the weekend at the lake. It's my family reunion. We don't have internet there, but I'll be on it first thing Monday. We've got another week before we need it finalized."

Thorne's initial reaction was annoyance. His employees knew this wasn't a nine-to-five job. Then he thought about telling Dash he didn't take weekends off. Was he the only one who didn't have a life? "That will work. Just make it a priority on Monday."

"Yes, sir. I will. See you next week." Drew grabbed his suit jacket from the back of his chair and turned to leave. Everyone else had left the room, except Sandra, one of the senior consultants. She and Drew nearly collided in their rush to get out the door. Apparently, Thorne wasn't the only one ready to wrap up the day.

"You first." Drew stepped out of Sandra's way.

"Thank you. Have fun at the lake. Wish I could be there this weekend."

"My mother-in-law will be with us, so it could be

interesting. Hopefully I can spend most of Saturday on a raft with a beer."

Sandra laughed. "I hope so."

"What are you up to this weekend?" Drew asked as he followed Sandra out the door. Thorne was right behind them.

"I've got a date tonight, actually. And tomorrow I'm spending the day at the aquarium with some business-school friends who are in town."

Thorne had been certain Sandra would be working. She often e-mailed him with questions and comments on weekends.

"First date?" Drew asked.

"Second."

"Well, have a nice night."

Sandra smiled. "I will."

Thorne repressed a sigh. His weekend wouldn't be completely lonely. He had a date that night too. Well, sort of. Did he really want that? A relationship? Since he hired Dash, he could ask him to leave anytime if he needed privacy or a quiet place to work. If they were dating, there would be different expectations. Not that he'd be dating Dash if he were dating.

"What about you, Mr. Shipton?" Drew asked, looking behind him. "Have you got plans for the weekend?"

Thorne fought the urge to scowl. Drew was being friendly. "Not really. Just catching up on work."

Sandra frowned. "You should get out more."

"You're not the only one who thinks so." Usually Thorne blew off comments like that, said something about working all weekend being a price he was

Professional Distance

willing to pay, but right then he wanted more weekend plans. He wanted to be like Drew and Sandra.

As soon as he reached his office, Thorne closed and locked the door. Then he pulled out his phone—his personal one, the one very few people had the number to—and called Dash.

"Hello, Thorne."

Fucking hell. Dash said two words to him, and he was already horny. "I want you to stay the whole weekend."

Silence.

"Dash?"

"I… I can't do that."

"Do you have other clients?" Thorne didn't like the thought of Dash going from him to another man, which was absurd. He'd never been possessive about other men he'd hired.

"Not that it's any of your business, but yes." Dash's tone was clipped, but Thorne didn't care. He was determined to get what he wanted.

Maybe that's why you can't do relationships.

"Tell them you're not available."

"Thorrrrrne." At least now Dash sounded more exasperated than angry.

"I'll pay double."

"That's not the point."

Dash made a sound like a growl. Rather than deterring Thorne, it turned him on.

"You're a businessman; profit should be the point."

"I can't blow off my commitments. It's not just clients."

135

"Do you have a catering engagement? We can work around that."

"Thorne, you cannot just call and demand my time. That's not how this works. Other people may jump to do your bidding, but you didn't hire me for that."

"No." He lowered his voice to the barest whisper. "I hired you to make me do your bidding."

"Fuck, Thorne." Dash's voice had gone all husky.

"At least tell me you'll think about it and call me back."

Dash exhaled. "Fine."

Thorne was reeling him in. He was sure of it. "I'll relax. Watch movies with you. Let you cook for me."

"*Let* me cook for you?"

"You said you enjoy it."

Dash laughed, the sound rich and sensual. "Yeah, I did, didn't I?"

"Think about it and think yes."

"Go back to work, Thorne."

Thorne ended the call. If Dash said no, he'd find some way to persuade him once he was at Thorne's apartment.

RILEY STUFFED HIS phone back in his pocket, heart pounding. He'd stepped onto Susan's porch to take Thorne's call. Now he didn't want to go back into the house. Thorne had rattled him, and Susan would see through him in a minute.

He racked his brain for an excuse to leave, but even if he came up with one, he couldn't stick Susan with the rest of the work when he'd promised to help. He needed to call Marc. It would suck to admit that Marc had been right, that Riley had fallen for Thorne. He should have backed away as soon as he realized it, but no, he'd gone in for more, encouraging Thorne to let him stay longer, drawing him in by offering more than sex. Then the weekend had ended with that slow, thorough fucking from Thorne, and Thorne using his real name. Riley had nearly come apart.

He should've been angry. He should have told Thorne he wasn't coming back. No matter how much Thorne seemed to truly like him, this was a business transaction to Thorne, nothing more. Thorne was an arrogant ass who wanted everyone to do his bidding. Riley believed he had a kind heart underneath the bluster, but even under the best circumstances, he'd be a bitch to deal with in a relationship. Besides, Riley was way too young to be on Thorne's radar as an actual partner.

He'd stayed outside as long as he could. Taking a deep breath, he pulled back the screen door. *Look calm. Look unconcerned.*

"What's wrong?" Susan asked as soon as he stepped back into the kitchen. He didn't think she'd even looked at him.

"Nothing. Just a client call."

"Is he giving you trouble?"

Riley shook his head. "No. Not really, not like you probably mean."

"Riley?"

Her look said he better fess up. "He's not harassing me or anything. In most ways, he's an ideal client, considerate, respectful of me as a person, but

137

he's rich and spoiled and wants his way."

Susan nodded like she knew the type. "And what way is that?"

"He wants to hire me for the whole weekend."

"Hmmm. Sounds lucrative, but I'm guessing you have other plans."

"Helping you with cupcakes for one."

Susan waved that off. "I can handle that or get Lilah to help me."

Her daughter, Lilah, hated baking, especially the more tedious jobs. "No, she won't—"

"She'll help if I need her to." Susan's tone said he wasn't going to win that argument.

"I'm not going to break my commitments at the last minute just so my client can have his way."

"I see." Susan nodded. "There's more to this than a change of schedule, isn't there?"

Why am I so fucking transparent? When he was really into a client that transparency paid off, but the rest of the time it was fucking annoying.

"Riley?" She wasn't letting this go.

"I like him."

"That ought to make it easier. Or is a whole weekend too long to have to be 'Dash' instead of 'Riley'?"

If only she knew how little of "Dash" he was with Thorne these days. "I mean I really like him."

"Oh." Her eyes widened. "Ohhhhhh. That's a different problem."

Riley sighed. *It's a problem all right.*

"So you turned him down?"

"I told him I'd think about it, but I'm an idiot to think this could go anywhere, right?"

"I don't know, are you?" Susan asked as she placed a pan of cheese straws in the oven.

"He's forty-two."

Susan dusted her hands on her apron. "Wow. Practically ancient."

Riley remembered that Thorne was probably ten years younger than Susan. "No offense, but yeah."

"That is quite an age gap." She handed Riley a cookie press loaded with cheese-straw dough. "Here, prepare another pan of those, and I'll get started on the spinach dip."

"He's also rich as fuck." Riley said as he concentrated on making the cheese straws all the same length.

"I'm not sure I see the problem with that."

Riley raised his brows, and she tried, unsuccessfully, to snap him with the towel she was holding. "We have nothing in common except…"

"Sex."

Heat crept into his face. They were moving into uncomfortable territory. "Right."

"Are you sure?" Susan asked. "Isn't this the guy you went out to dinner with?"

"Yes, but—"

"Didn't you say you enjoyed talking to him?"

"Sure, but that's just the fascination of getting to know someone. It's not sustainable."

Susan shrugged. "Maybe not."

"What do I do?"

"Whatever your heart tells you."

"That is bullshit."

She laughed. "Maybe, but I can't tell you."

Riley wanted an easy answer but admired Susan

for not giving him one. He stepped behind Susan and caught her in a hug, not caring how messy they both were. "You're awesome, you know that?"

"I try."

When Riley finished helping Susan clean up, he hung up his apron and brushed the flour out of his hair. How did it always manage to get everywhere?

"Let me know what you decide and take care of yourself," she called as he headed out the door.

"Will do."

Once he was in his car, he called Marc who answered almost immediately. "Riley, it's been too long. What's up?"

"You were right." He braced himself for Marc's crowing.

"About what?"

"Thorne."

Marc laughed. "Of course I was."

"He wants me to stay for the whole weekend."

Marc whistled. "Sounds lucrative."

"Marc." Riley's tone was sharp.

"Sorry. Tell me what happened."

"Not much to tell except that it finally happened. I fell for a client."

"Like really, truly, your heart is totally in this, or 'wow, this is the best sex of my life, I hope he keeps on hiring me' fell for him?"

Riley sighed. "I wish it was the latter."

"Fuck."

"Yeah. You called it."

"I was teasing."

Riley knew Marc was lying, but he appreciated that he wanted to make Riley feel better. "No, you were serious."

"I thought you were moony over him, riding the waves of really hot sex with a compatible partner, not truly falling in love."

"What the fuck do I do?"

"What do you want to do?"

How was he supposed to answer that? What he wanted was impossible. "If I knew, I wouldn't have called you."

"I guess not, but seriously, have you thought this through? You're coming to me for relationship advice?"

Marc had a point. He had a knack for picking the worst men ever. "I'm coming to you for advice from a fellow escort. This isn't a relationship."

"You want it to be."

"No. Yes. I'm crazy, aren't I? You know what Thorne is like." Riley had come to resent just how well Marc knew Thorne. That alone should have set off warning signals.

"He's a good man," Marc said. "Despite his idiosyncrasies."

"He is, but can you see us in a relationship?" The last word dripped with so much bitterness Riley wondered if it would burn the phone.

"Riley, how much do you want this?"

"'This' being Thorne?"

"No, a ride to the fucking moon. Of course I mean Thorne."

"I don't know." He did though. He wanted it with all his heart in a way he'd never wanted a man before.

"That's what you have to figure out, then. You've got two choices. You can walk away now, or you can work for what you want and risk it destroying you."

Riley sighed. "That's what I'm afraid of. Destruction."

"You'll survive whatever happens. But unless you want it bad enough to see where it leads and damn the consequences, the sooner you end it, the better."

Riley's chest felt tight as if someone were squeezing the air out of him. "It's not going to lead anywhere."

"That does not sound like the Riley I know. When have you ever been a pessimist?"

"I'm trying to be a realist."

Marc sniffed. "It doesn't look good on you."

Riley wanted to reach through the phone and shake him. "You're giving me mixed signals."

"It's not my decision to make, so I see the benefits of both choices."

"If I try and it doesn't work, then…"

"You'll be hurt. It will tear you apart, but you'll have tried."

Marc sounded almost wistful. He was clearly in a strange mood that evening. "So you think I should stay?"

"I think you should decide how much you want this."

He'd known neither Marc nor Susan would tell him what to do, but he hated having to make this decision on his own. "Okay. I'll think about it."

"Do the weekend if you're undecided. Make the cash. You must have nearly enough for school by now if you've been fucking Mr. Moneybags for over a month."

"God, Marc, you make it sound so—"

Mark tsked. "Baby, you're his rent boy. You can't forget that."

"You just told me to—"

"I told you to use your assets and work for what you want because you just might get it."

Did Marc truly believe that? "You've never been an idealist, Marc."

"No, but *you* are. It's adorable and probably one of the things Thorne likes best about you."

"How do you know he likes me?"

"You wouldn't be having this conversation with me if you didn't think he felt something more than lust for your hot-as-hell body."

There were hints, Riley had to admit that. Like the way Thorne had touched him so reverently last Saturday morning. And the way he'd asked if he felt the connection between them. And he did, but he didn't trust it. "This is crazy."

"Sure it is, as crazy as moving all the way across the country with someone you've dated two weeks."

"I miss you, you know."

"I do know. Let me know what you decide." He sounded sad, not like his usual animated self. Were things okay with him? He doubted Marc would tell him the truth if he asked.

"I will." Riley ended the call. A few minutes later, he arrived home, glad, despite the expense, that he hadn't found a new roommate. He wanted to be alone with his thoughts.

How much do I want this? Way too much. He'd never met anyone like Thorne, never felt a fraction of what he felt when he was with Thorne. He'd only known the man a month, a fucking month, and he was already this far gone. Walk away. That's what he should do.

He imagined never seeing Thorne again, never feeling Thorne's hands sliding up his back, never hearing Thorne beg when Riley was buried deep inside him, never kissing him again like they'd kissed last week—long and sweet and like they had all day. They would have all day if he spent the weekend.

He'd lied to Thorne. He didn't actually have any other clients lined up. He'd intended to be on call for Sheila on Saturday night. But why do that when Thorne was a sure thing?

He'd promised Susan to help her on Saturday afternoon, but Thorne wouldn't mind if he took a few hours to do that. He could even bake at Thorne's place and then take the food to Susan if he needed to. Why was he even pretending he wasn't going to stay?

He picked up his phone and twirled it in his hands for a few seconds, heart pounding. Should he call Thorne? He could do that, or he could turn spending the weekend together into a game, a game that could prove fun for both of them. Instead of calling, he typed out a text.

Still undecided but willing to negotiate. Be prepared to submit to my demands when I arrive.

Thorne replied: *That's hot as fuck.*

Riley smiled and tossed his phone on the bed followed by his T-shirt. Time to shower and get ready for the night. He'd need to pack a bag, because there was almost no chance that Thorne wouldn't do everything he asked.

Chapter Twelve

"What do you want?" Thorne asked, his voice low and sexy, making Dash want to kiss him, but he held back, because he wanted something very particular.

"I want to do something to you that no one's ever done before." Dash craved that, to be Thorne's first in some way. He didn't dare ask Thorne to make their arrangement exclusive, and they were far from virgins, but he wanted something just for them.

Thorne toyed with the cuffs of his perfectly-tailored dress shirt, a sign that Dash had made him uneasy. Dash wanted Thorne relaxed, open, willing. He took one of Thorne's hands in his and kissed the inside of his wrist, feeling the rapid pulse there. He traced a line across Thorne's palm with the tip of his tongue. When Dash pulled Thorne's index finger into his mouth and sucked, he looked up. Thorne's eyes were wide, his pupils dilated. His tongue slid out, and he licked his lips. Dash used his teeth, sliding them along the digit. He had no doubt Thorne was now rock hard in his pants, but he kept going, licking and sucking until he had Thorne right where he wanted him.

"Last week, when I smacked your ass, you pretended not to like it, but your reaction told me you wanted more."

Thorne didn't say anything. He simply watched

145

Dash warily, looking both terrified and desperately turned on.

Dash sucked on Thorne's middle finger for a few seconds. "Have you ever been spanked by a lover, Thorne?"

"I…"

Dash nibbled the pad of Thorne's thumb. "Tell me."

"No."

"Would you like to find out how it feels? Would you like me to bend you over the bed and redden your ass before I fuck you?"

Thorne's breath was fast, harsh. He'd closed his eyes, and his teeth gripped his lower lip. There were droplets of sweat on his brow. "Tell me." Dash made his voice more demanding.

Thorne jerked in response, opening his eyes. "Yes." The word seemed to have been dragged out of him by a force he couldn't control.

"I'll stop anytime if it's not what you want."

"If I do this, you'll stay all weekend?" Thorne asked, gathering back a little of his control.

Dash nodded. "Yes, I'll stay all weekend."

"Until Monday morning?" Thorne asked.

"Sunday night."

Thorne frowned.

"If I stay until Monday, you won't be in any shape to go to work. Don't push it."

Thorne licked his lips. "I'm willing to take the risk."

The look on Thorne's face was so lust-filled, it made Dash dizzy with need of his own. "Sunday night. That's all I can give."

Thorne stared him down for a few more seconds, but ultimately gave in. "We can always renegotiate later."

"I doubt you'll be capable of speech later. Now strip. I'm ready to have you naked."

Thorne's brows rose. "What happened to slow, to anticipation? We do have all weekend."

"I promise there will be plenty of anticipation. I'll have you so revved up by the time I fuck you, you'll be certain you're losing your mind."

"I think I already have."

"We don't have to do this. I can stay the one night instead."

Thorne glared at him. "No."

"Then I expect payment up front."

Thorne looked away and played with his cuff again. "This isn't easy for me."

Dash moved closer and stroked his arm. "I know. I'll go slow. I won't do anything you're not okay with. Do you trust me?"

Thorne still didn't look at Dash. "Yes."

Dash teased the back of Thorne's neck with his fingertips. "If we wait, you'll just worry more."

Thorne turned then and nodded. "You're right."

As he discarded his shirt Thorne asked, "Aren't you going to undress too?"

Dash leaned against the doorframe, watching him. "No. I'm not."

"I thought you loved being naked." Thorne used his arrogant-asshole tone. But it wasn't working. Dash wasn't intimidated, and he could tell how nervous Thorne was by the stiff way he carried himself. He'd fix that though.

"I do, but tonight I want to be dressed while you're spread out naked for me. I want to unzip my pants, take my cock out, and fuck your red, welted ass while you writhe under me."

"Holy fuck." Thorne swayed on his feet like he was dizzy from the thought of it.

"Bend over the bed. Now."

Thorne shoved his briefs down, kicked them off, and did as he was told. Dash spent a few moments taking in the sight of him. He was fucking beautiful.

THORNE HAD FANTASIZED about Dash spanking him several times during the week, but now he lay there, sweaty and scared, as he anticipated Dash's hand on his ass. Dash would stop if he needed him to, Thorne knew that, but he hated how vulnerable he felt—most of him did, anyway. Apparently his cock was all for Dash beating his ass.

Dash stepped up behind him, the smooth fabric of his pants cool against Thorne's leg. Dash was right. It was hot as hell for him to stay fully dressed. It made everything dirtier and emphasized how fucking dominant he could be. Thorne wanted to give himself to Dash, wanted to be taken. If only he could relax enough to enjoy it.

Dash wrapped a hand around Thorne's aching cock. Thorne tried not to react, to stay still so Dash wouldn't know how desperate he already was. But when Dash started stroking him, Thorne thrust into the circle of his hand, unable to help himself.

Dash chuckled. "Like that, do you?"

"Fuck off," Thorne snarled.

Dash released Thorne's cock and rubbed his

hands over Thorne's ass, kneading his buttocks, spreading them, then bending down, so fucking close that his warm breath tickled Thorne's hole.

"Fuck," Thorne whispered.

"Mmmm. This is going to be so fun."

"Fun? It's going to fucking hurt." Was he insane to agree to this?

"You're going to love it," Dash purred.

"Just get on with it."

Dash slid his hands over Thorne's ass again, up and down, warming the flesh. The friction was amazingly erotic. Thorne jumped in surprise when soft caresses turned to the scratch of nails across his flesh. Dash hadn't really hurt him, but now his ass tingled, making him so fucking aware of it.

"Get ready," Dash warned.

Seconds ticked by with nothing, no touching, no words. Thorne's heart raced. When would the first blow come?

"Anticipation," Dash whispered. "It's so sweet."

"Bastard."

Crack! Dash slapped Thorne's ass, not a playful tap but a hard blow that stung.

Dash caressed him. "So sensitive. I love it."

"Of course I'm—"

Smack! Another hit on the opposite cheek.

"That fucking hurt!" It had and yet…Thorne was harder than ever.

"Relax." Dash rubbed his back, hands sliding along the sides of his spine. "Let go. Melt into the mattress and just feel."

"I do feel, and it fucking hurts."

"Feel it here." Dash circled his cock again,

jacking him off for a few seconds, just long enough for Thorne to get really into it before stopping abruptly, leaving Thorne trying to fuck the air.

"How the hell can I—"

Dash cut him off with an assault on his ass. Smacks, sometimes soft, sometimes hard. Thorne wasn't sure what to expect next. His ass grew hot, the burn almost overwhelming, but holy fuck, it was erotic. Pleasure, pain, Thorne wasn't sure what he was feeling, but his balls were high and tight, and he was going to come if Dash didn't stop.

"I knew you'd like it." Dash sounded so fucking satisfied with himself.

"Bastard!" But Dash was right. Thorne loved it. It wasn't the pain exactly. It was mostly knowing that Dash was in control, and Thorne was completely willing for him to be. That and the fact that Dash was getting off on his reactions.

Dash stopped spanking him, taking time to rub and knead Thorne's aching flesh. "You're nicely reddened. Do you think you can take more?"

"Yes." He wanted to if that was what Dash wanted.

"Of course you can. You'll do anything for me, won't you?"

That was true, and it terrified Thorne, but he forced out a ragged "yes." Dash remained still, not giving him any more. He needed to come. "Damn it, take what you want. I promised to pay you, and you're going to get your weekend's worth."

"Fuck, Thorne. I…"

Thorne glanced over his shoulder and looked Dash up and down. Dash's hard cock strained against his pants.

"What is it? Tell me," Thorne demanded, not that he could put much authority into his voice when his ass was on fire and he was bent over the bed.

"You're even more perfect like this than I imagined. Watching you realize how much you love me smacking your ass is just so... I need you."

Thorne smiled. "Then take me."

"I said I'd fuck you but..."

"What do you want?" Thorne asked, because whatever it was, he wanted to do it. Pleasing Dash made him so fucking happy, maybe happier than he'd ever been.

Dash smacked his ass a final time, and he let out an undignified yelp. "Up on the bed. On your back. I want to suck you off while your sore ass squirms against the sheets."

"Fuck yes." Dash's mouth around his cock was suddenly the very thing he needed most.

Thorne managed to pull his legs up onto the bed, wincing at how stiff they were and how fucking much his ass hurt now that he was no longer in the heat of the moment.

"You okay?" Dash asked, his voice filled with concern that made Thorne's chest tighten. He was such a good man. He deserved better than a boring, arrogant asshole.

Thorne turned over and lay on his back, managing not to groan when his ass made contact with the sheets. "I'm fine. Just a little stiff."

Dash grinned at him. "I'll loosen you up."

"I bet you will."

Dash stretched out by his side and drew circles

on his abdomen with his fingertip. "Close your eyes and relax."

"Do you see this?" Thorne pointed to his cock. "There's no relaxing with that."

Dash adjusted his position so his mouth was poised over the tip of Thorne's cock. "Give it a shot."

"I'll give you a shot," Thorne grumbled. "Of cum right down your throat."

Dash laughed before swallowing him down. Thorne wanted it to last, but every scrape of his sore ass against the sheets as he thrust up into Dash's willing mouth sent him closer, and too soon he was shouting, groaning, giving Dash exactly what he'd wanted.

"Fuck," Dash muttered as he laid his head against Thorne's hip. "That… You…"

"Yeah. Yeah. You were right again. I like being spanked."

Dash chuckled, his breath tickling Thorne's sensitized skin. "Of course I was."

"I'd even let you do it again." Thorne didn't like how readily he'd confessed that, but it was true.

"I *will* do it again."

"Come up here. Let me take care of you." Thorne didn't want to leave Dash hanging, not after that amazing blowjob.

"No need," Dash said. He rolled over on his back, and Thorne saw the wet spot on the front of his trousers.

Thorne couldn't help but smile. This was the second time Dash had come before he'd meant to. Thorne loved that he affected Dash so strongly.

"Don't you laugh at me." Dash lifted his hips and

pushed his pants over his legs before dropping them on the floor.

"It's adorable."

Dash scowled as he finished undressing. "Don't patronize me either. I'm fucking annoyed."

"I'm not."

Dash looked at him. He seemed uncertain, not like himself.

"I love that you're really into this, into fucking me, getting me off."

Dash's concern seemed to fade. "Good, because I'm going to get you off again."

"No rush. We have all weekend." Clearly he wasn't as worn out as Thorne was.

Dash continued to study him with an unreadable expression.

"Don't even try to back out."

"I couldn't possibly; you gave more than I ever expected."

Thorne raised a brow. "You're the one who was so sure I'd like it."

"Like it yes, grudgingly admit it wasn't so bad, but…"

Heat rushed to Thorne's face. "You're very good at what you do."

"I don't usually… What we just did…"

Dash looked…embarrassed? That didn't seem right. Thorne stroked Dash's chest, then toyed with his soft cock, feeling it grow just a bit, not serious yet, but letting Thorne know there would be more later. He brushed his hand over Dash's balls and then let the coarse hair on Dash's thighs tickle his hand.

"Don't stop," Dash said, voice barely there.

Thorne could feel Dash's pulse racing under his fingers.

Dash closed his eyes, and Thorne continued exploring his body, running his hands over Dash's calves and shins and then massaging his feet. Dash groaned with pleasure as Thorne sank his thumbs into the arches of Dash's feet, but he kept his eyes closed. He gave Dash's arms and hands the same treatment. Then he leaned down and kissed him gently on the lips.

Dash finally opened his eyes. "Thank you."

Thorne still wasn't sure what was happening. "Are you okay?"

Dash nodded. "Yeah. It's just…no one ever…" He turned away. "Forget it."

"No," Thorne insisted. "Tell me."

"I touch men. I pleasure them. I make sure they come like they never have before, and I'm good at it. But no one touches me like that, like they care how I feel or like they want their hands on me. I know this is a job, and you're a client. I shouldn't be saying these things."

"Yes, you should. It's true that I hired you because I wanted sex. I even told you that's all I paid for, that I didn't want anything else, but I was wrong."

Dash gave Thorne a soft smile. "I have the impression you rarely admit that."

"Almost never. And yet with you, I find myself saying it every time we're together."

Dash nodded.

"With you I don't have to be right." Of course if they were actually in a relationship rather than a professional arrangement, that would probably change. "I love touching you, watching your expression, learning what feels good to you. I get off on knowing you're enjoying it. That was partly why I liked…"

"Me spanking your ass?"

Thorne smiled. Dash was acting like himself again. "Yes."

Dash reached up and traced Thorne's jawline. He looked like he was about to say something, but then he lowered his hand, rolled to his side, and stood. "Let's get cleaned up. Then I'll make you dinner."

"How do you know I haven't eaten?"

"If you have, it was something from a food truck and not worth your time."

"Do you want to be my personal chef?" Thorne realized he wasn't joking. He would hire Dash. He would hire him for anything as long as he got to see him.

"Personal chef with benefits?"

Thorne smiled. "Yes. That."

Dash frowned, looking nervous again. "I want to enjoy the weekend and not think beyond that."

***

Dash made chicken with a blackberry balsamic sauce, sautéed green beans, and saffron rice for dinner. He referred to it as a simple meal, though it looked like complex magic to Thorne.

"So what plans do you have for us for the weekend?" Dash asked when they'd both nearly finished eating.

"Plans? I thought we'd fuck and then nap and then fuck some more."

155

Dash raised his brows. "I'm proud of my stamina, and you—"

"If you say I have good recovery for an old guy, I'm kicking you out."

"You're the one who begged me to stay, and that's not all you begged me to—"

"Enough." Thorne scowled at him, though he wasn't the least bit angry.

Dash looked so perfect sitting across the table from Thorne. He really could spend the whole weekend in bed with Dash, but he'd also realized sex wasn't the only thing he liked doing with him. "We could watch another of your 'old' movies, and you can arrogantly order for me at another of my favorite restaurants."

"My favorite this time."

"Okay," Thorne said. "See, I'm easy."

"Actually, you're a fuckload of work, but once you open up, it is so worth it."

Thorne's cock stirred, something he would have thought impossible so soon after Dash had wrung him dry. "Why don't you tell me what fun people do on the weekend?"

Dash tilted his head as though thinking. "We could rent a boat, and you could take me sailing, maybe play a little pirate and captive."

Thorne's pulse accelerated. Taking Dash out on a boat would be a big step, one that might make it impossible for him to keep a professional distance. He'd never taken anyone sailing except Clint.

"It's been ages since I sailed."

"Have you forgotten how?"

"No, but can we wait on that?"

"Sure," Dash said. He looked perplexed, but he didn't ask any questions.

What else could they do? "What about the art museum?"

"No, you already go there. I need to get you out of your comfort zone. How about the aquarium?"

"I've never been there."

Dash eyes widened. "Really? You've never seen the whale sharks?"

"Never."

"Then we're going. I'll take you to my favorite breakfast spot, give you my personal tour of the aquarium and then teach you more about the movies of your own childhood."

Thorne frowned. "Doesn't sound like enough time in bed to me."

"I promise you'll get plenty of that. By the time we're done tonight, your poor ass will need a rest."

"My cock won't." Thorne ran a hand over his cock, showing Dash how hard he was.

"Beast!" Dash slapped at him playfully. "You'll shock me with your animal lusts."

Thorne rolled his eyes.

"You need to get out more. Do things. And I don't mean client dinners or charity balls."

Thorne sighed. "Fine. Food. Aquarium. Movie. And then fucking."

"Perfect," Dash said, beaming at getting his way.

Chapter Thirteen

Thorne woke to Dash licking his ear. He tried to push him off, but Dash had a firm grip on his shoulder. "Get up. Get dressed. I'm taking you to breakfast."

Thorne turned over and scowled at him, blinking in the bright morning light. "What time is it?"

"Time to be up and awake."

As Thorne stretched, he felt every overused muscle in his body. His ass was still sore as hell from being spanked—fucking spanked—by a sassy little shit who was trying to make him wake up far too early after fucking him two—or was it three?—times, including once in the middle of the night.

"I'm not getting up."

"I have ways of making you get out of this bed that you won't like."

Thorne snarled. "Don't even think about it."

"It's nine thirty, and I'm starving."

"Nine thirty?" Thorne couldn't remember when he'd last slept that late. "Fuck."

"Not before breakfast. You would've had to wake up earlier for that."

Thorne sighed. "It would've killed me, anyway."

Dash patted his leg. "See, it's in your best interest to go out with me and recover a bit."

Thorne looked at Dash, his impish grin, his ruffled hair, the T-shirt that was too tight or rather just perfect to show off his body. "I'm willing to risk it."

Dash shook his head. "Get in the shower. We're going to breakfast and then I'm going to show you my favorite animals at the aquarium."

Surprisingly, Thorne wanted Dash to show him around the aquarium even more than he wanted to drag Dash back to bed.

***

An hour later Thorne and Dash were seated in a vinyl booth with duct tape placed over several cracks in the seat. "Are you sure about this place?" Thorne sure as hell wasn't.

"Relax."

He scowled at Dash. "You say that a lot."

"You're tense a lot."

Thorne looked around. The diner might look decrepit, but it was packed with a wide-range of clientele: men in business suits, women in tennis skirts, families, people of all skin colors, and only a few patrons whose appearance was as ragged as the surroundings. He and Dash had waited twenty minutes for a table.

A thin, dark-haired waitress who looked about Thorne's age approached their table a few minutes after they were seated. "Riley," she said, her face lighting up. "It's been too long since I've seen you."

"I've had a busy few weeks," Dash/Riley said. "Sally, this is my friend Thorne."

Sally gave Thorne an appreciative glance. "Good morning, Thorne. What can I get you?"

"Coffee, please, a lot of it."

"Can do. Same for you, Riley?"

"Yes, and go ahead and bring us some biscuits and gravy while we decide what else we want."

Sally grinned. "Good choice. And may I say you are looking particularly fine this morning."

Dash blushed, actually blushed. "Thank you."

Thorne grinned at him after she walked away. "If you ask me, you look damn fine every morning."

"You've only seen me in the morning twice."

"And both times I wanted to drag you right back to bed."

Sally returned swiftly with coffee and biscuits. The coffee was good, much better than Thorne expected, and the biscuits were absolutely divine.

"Good, huh?" Dash asked after they'd each eaten a few bites.

Thorne nodded. "Very."

"I'll never get tired of you agreeing with me."

Thorne kicked his ankle under the table. "Cheeky bastard."

"You love it."

"Yeah, I do." That was the problem.

Dash perused the menu. "Hmmm. What to order next?"

"Next? Isn't this enough?" Considering Thorne usually had nothing but coffee for breakfast—maybe a muffin or croissant from a street cart if he was feeling extravagant—he'd already eaten three times his usual amount.

"Of course it's not enough. I'd order one of everything, but they'd have to roll us out of here and we'd never manage to walk around the aquarium."

"I'm not sure—"

"How spicy do you like things?" Dash asked,

160

completely ignoring his attempt to be sensible.

Thorne narrowed his eyes. "Don't you already know?"

"Ha. Just for that I'll order the habanero grits, and you can fucking deal."

"I'd love those," Thorne said, voice overly sweet.

Sally returned, and Dash made sure Thorne had no chance to interrupt. "Thorne will have blackberry-glazed bacon, two eggs over easy, and the habanero grits. I'll take the Midtown Benedict."

"You got it." Sally winked at Thorne. "Those grits are my favorite. You've got a keeper here." She jerked her thumb toward Dash.

"Oh, we're not—"

She gave him a look that made him feel like an unruly schoolboy and sauntered away.

He looked back at Dash expecting to see more mocking laughter, but Dash looked worried. "I'm not trying to out you."

Thorne should've cared, but he didn't. "It's fine. I'm not at work, and… Anyway, it's fine." Was he ready to give in, to let everyone know that he was gay? He'd been hiding for so long. Could he make that kind of change? For Dash, maybe he could. But that was stupid because Dash wasn't his, not really. He had no hold on him beyond the time he paid for. "Just don't ask me to bend over the table or anything."

Dash laughed. "I think I can control myself."

***

By the time they'd seen whale sharks, belugas, sea otters, and a host of other underwater creatures, Thorne felt like they'd walked for miles, and maybe they had. But throbbing feet was a price worth paying for Dash's companionship.

"Can we see the whale sharks one more time?" Dash asked.

The exhibit had been packed when they'd first arrived, but now the crowds were thinning. Thorne was more than ready to head home, but Dash looked so eager, he couldn't say no. "Come on."

He pulled Dash in the direction of the Ocean Voyager exhibit. They spent at least fifteen minutes watching the whale sharks, sawfish, rays, and other animals in the enormous tank. Or at least Dash did. As intriguing as the exhibit was, Thorne spent a lot of that time watching Dash.

"You ready?" Dash asked, finally turning away from the tank.

"Yes. Shall we head home?"

Dash nodded, and they made their way through the gift store to the exit.

When they came out into the adjacent park, Dash pointed at the small cafe located between the aquarium and the World of Coke. "Let's get ice cream." He was bouncing like a five-year-old.

"After that breakfast I don't think I should ever eat again."

"If that was breakfast, then we'll call this lunch."

"Says your twenty-year-old metabolism."

Dash turned to face him, but kept moving backward toward the cafe. "We've been walking for hours, plus we'll need energy tonight."

"Fine. I may as well give in now, or you'll pester me until I do." Thorne couldn't wait to use up Dash's energy in bed, but this had been, by far, the best day

Thorne could remember having had in years. "I'm ordering this time."

Dash grinned. "Go for it."

The cafe sold soft-serve ice cream in vanilla, chocolate, or a twist of both. "I'd like a cone of the combo with sprinkles and a cone of chocolate."

The little boy in Dash bounced again when Thorne handed him his ice cream.

"Did I guess right?" Thorne asked.

"Perfect." Dash radiated joy. He must really like ice cream and maybe also the fact that Thorne knew him so well. If only every day could be like this one. But it couldn't. Thorne was living inside a fantasy, secluded from the real world, despite being in a crowded public place. Monday would come, and his fantasy would dissolve.

Dash licked the curled top off his ice cream and gave an exaggerated moan of pleasure.

Thorne's cock liked that a little too much. "Let's find a shady place so we can eat these before they melt."

They found a nearby bench and sank down onto it. Without warning Dash leaned over and licked Thorne's ice cream.

"Hey! You've got your own."

"Stolen ice cream tastes better. Don't you know that?"

Thorne raised his brows. "My sister used to say the same thing."

"She's wise." Dash held out his cone. "Here, taste mine."

Thorne frowned. "It has sprinkles on it."

"Yeah. You asked for them."

"For you."

Dash rolled his eyes. "Just taste it."

Thorne did; the sugar punch of the sprinkles wasn't as unpleasant as he'd expected.

"See, sweet things aren't the enemy," Dash said.

"No, they're not." Somehow Thorne didn't think they were talking about ice cream.

***

Back at his apartment a few hours later, Thorne sank gratefully onto the couch, thrilled to be off his feet. "Movie now?" Dash asked.

"Sure." Thorne closed his eyes and rested his head on the back of the couch.

"Are you going to fall asleep on me?"

"No, old men like me don't fall asleep when we sit down, we rest our eyes."

"Ha!" Dash slapped his thigh and encouraged him to scoot over. "I bet I can find a way to keep you awake."

Thorne scrubbed a hand over his eyes. "Where do you get this stamina?"

"It's a job requirement."

The silence that followed was suffocating. Thorne didn't know how to respond. From the look on Dash's face, his words had startled him back to reality like they had Thorne. Had they really forgotten that Dash was there because Thorne had hired him?

Dash grabbed the remote and turned on the TV. "You do have a Netflix subscription, right?"

Thorne nodded. "I don't know why. I hardly ever use it."

"Let's put it to good use now."

Thorne lay back against the arm of the couch,

and Dash stretched half on top of him, using his chest as a pillow. Thorne let his eyes drift shut again as Dash scrolled through movie choices.

"Oooh, *Footloose*. What about that one? I've been wanting to see it again ever since watching *Guardians of the Galaxy*."

"What? Why?"

Dash sighed and shook his head. "Does this mean you haven't seen *Guardians of the Galaxy*?"

"Um…I don't even know what it is."

"Where have you been? Groot? Rocket? Beefed-up Chris Pratt? Seriously?"

"Is it on Netflix?"

"No."

"We'll rent it then." Thorne grabbed the remote. He exited Netflix and clicked on iTunes. He could feel Dash's impatience as he painstakingly typed in the letters to search for the title.

"You can do that on your phone, you know."

"Whatever." The movie popped up on the screen. "See, there it is. Back in the olden days, we had to drive to a video store to get a movie. You kids have it easy."

"Quit with the old jokes. Anyone that can do what you did last night is nowhere near old."

Suddenly Thorne didn't feel quite so tired. "Maybe when this is over, I'll do it again."

"Mmm. I like that plan."

They started the movie. Dash gave a brief explanation, most of which Thorne failed to understand, but eventually he started to get into it. And yeah, Chris Pratt was surely looking fine. But Thorne was more entertained by Dash's ability to quote the lines and his emotive reactions to everything whether it was sad, funny, or worthy of whoops and cheers.

After an intense scene, Dash caught Thorne staring. "What?"

"You. You're so…fun to watch."

"Are you laughing at me?" Dash pouted.

"No, I'm enjoying you."

"Good. But what about the movie?"

"It's fine. You're better." Thorne slid his hand into Dash's hair and pulled him down for a kiss.

BY THE TIME Dash pulled back for air, his breath was ragged. "Whoa." He grabbed the remote and clicked off the movie.

"We didn't see the end," Thorne teased.

"We'll see it later. I don't care about movies now." He tugged at the hem of Thorne's T-shirt. "Off."

Thorne grinned as he sat up and yanked the garment over his head. Before he could say or do anything else, Dash shoved him back down, hands skimming over his chest.

"You're so fucking hot," Dash murmured. He replaced his hands with lips and tongue. He teased Thorne's nipples and then nibbled at his collarbone. "Bed?"

"Not sure I can move," Thorne answered.

Dash stood, pulled off his own shirt and then shucked the rest of his clothing. He wrapped a hand around his cock and stroked himself. "Would you move for this?"

Thorne smiled up at him. "I'm starting to feel a

little inspired."

Dash kept going, his hand moving faster, his grip tightening. Thorne sat up and reached for him, but Dash backed away. "Come with me."

Thorne did, and the next few hours passed in a tangle of rough thrusting and sweaty flesh.

"What next?" Dash asked as he lay on his back, recovering from his second orgasm.

"A nap," Thorne suggested.

Dash started to protest, but he could tell Thorne was already drifting off. So he rolled over and spooned him. "This has been a great day."

"The best."

"Any withdrawal symptoms from not working?"

Thorne laughed. "Not a fucking one."

"Surprised?"

"I would be if I wasn't with you."

Dash's heart skipped a beat, the words sinking into his skin, warming him. He was tired, too tired to fight what he was feeling. "Earlier when I said that about my job, I—"

"Don't." Thorne's tone was firm.

Dash didn't say any more. Had he read things wrong?

Thorne put a hand on top of Dash's. "It's enough that you're here."

Okay, maybe he'd read Thorne right after all.

Thinking the best response was simply to hold Thorne tight against him, he did just that and fell asleep to thoughts of a day spent like this one, except Thorne wasn't paying him; they were on a date.

Don't get your hopes up, his conscience tried to scold him.

He told it to shut the fuck up.

Chapter Fourteen

Riley's phone rang as he was making himself a late breakfast. After his weekend with Thorne, he'd needed to sleep in. He glanced at the screen. It was Marc. He must be up early unless he hadn't gone to bed yet. It was just after six a.m. on the west coast.

Riley accepted the call. "Good morning."

"Not before coffee," Marc answered. "Did you decide what to do about Thorne?"

"I spent the weekend," was Riley's noncommittal answer.

Marc muttered something.

"What was that?"

"I'm worried about you."

Why was Marc so infuriating? "But you said—"

"To consider how much you wanted it."

Riley stirred the eggs he was scrambling. "I did. I've never wanted anyone more."

"Have you told him that?"

"What should I say? Hey, tonight's free of charge. Let's pretend it's a date."

"Riley, be serious."

"Nothing I can think to say sounds right. I'm not ready for that yet."

Marc made a noise of displeasure. "When will you be?"

"I don't know. I need to be sure he won't laugh at me."

"Do you think he will after this weekend?" Marc asked.

Riley slid the eggs onto a plate and started buttering his toast. "What if this is just a crush? What if it passes? I don't want to make a fool of myself."

"I've seen you crushing plenty of times, but I've never heard you talk about anyone like you talk about Thorne."

Marc was right, and Riley knew it, but he wished it were that simple, that the feelings would go away and he could get on with his life. "He asked me for another weekend."

"What did you say?"

Riley took his plate and coffee mug to the tiny table by the window and gazed out at the morning sky. "I said I'd do one night, not two. I can't do another whole weekend. I could barely make myself leave last night."

"You need to tell him. And then it either ends or it changes."

Marc was right. For all his flighty ways, he was absolutely right. But Riley wasn't ready to risk ending things with Thorne. "I'll go back this weekend and then maybe—"

"Riley."

"I know. I asked for your help, and now I'm not listening."

Marc laughed. "Sounds like we switched places."

"Yeah, it does." Riley took a sip of coffee. "How are things out there?"

"You're changing the subject."

Riley smiled. He'd known Marc would pick up on that. "Damn right I am."

"Things are weird."

Riley finished a bite of eggs. "Weird how?"

"Hamilton keeps wanting us to hook up with other guys, which is fine, but I'd like to have some time for just us. He's always going to LA, and when he's home he wants to go out. I must be getting old, but sometimes I just want to stay in, watch movies, hang out, like we used to do."

Like Riley wanted to do with Thorne. "That sounds like a bad scene. Don't you think you should—"

"No, I'm not going to run back to Atlanta, not yet anyway." Of course he wouldn't. Marc would wait until that asshole had completely broken his heart.

"You can have your old room back anytime."

"Thanks." Marc sounded sad, defeated, and Riley wanted to punch the bastard who'd done that to him.

"We're both fucked, aren't we?" Marc asked.

"Yeah, probably, but try to take care of yourself."

"You do the same."

Riley hung up and realized he wasn't all that hungry after all.

***

Several weeks later, as Dash and Thorne lay in bed on a Saturday morning, Thorne propped himself up on his elbow and looked at Dash, really looked at him, like he was seeing all the emotions Dash wanted to keep hidden. "I have something special planned for next week."

"You do?" Dash asked, heart pounding much too fast.

"Yes, if you can stay the night and most of Saturday. I'd love for you to stay longer."

Dash considered how to answer. He'd stayed overnight some weekends and others not, trying to fight what was becoming an addiction to Thorne's bed. "I can stay until Saturday evening."

Thorne smiled. "Then you should bring some clothes you don't mind getting wet."

Dash couldn't keep the surprise off his face. "We're going sailing?"

"If you'd like to."

"I'll stay the whole weekend." The words were out before Dash had made a conscious decision to say them. If Thorne was ready to share something that had been his passion, things were moving in the right direction. A relationship might be improbable, but not impossible, right?

"You will?" Thorne looked like he'd been certain Dash would say no. "I don't have to offer my ass this time?"

Dash smiled as he pulled on his shirt. "I have a feeling you'll be offering your ass even if you get nothing extra in return."

"I hate it when you're right."

But Dash knew Thorne didn't really mind at all, not when Dash was right about sex, anyway. He could see the outline of Thorne's hard cock under the sheet. *Get out of here before you're tempted to suck him off.*

"Of course you do." If only this wasn't a business transaction. What if he asked Thorne for it not to be? What if he suggested they went sailing off the clock? The words swam around in Dash's mouth, but he refused to let them out. He wanted to see Thorne on a boat, the one place he might relax, let go,

172

be himself for more than a few minutes. He wouldn't risk losing his chance by asking for something ridiculous. One more weekend and then something would have to give.

"I'll see you next Friday," he said, gathering the last of his things.

"I'll be waiting."

Chapter Fifteen

Dash studied the sailboat Thorne had rented. Maybe this was a mistake. He had zero experience with boats beyond an ill-fated canoe trip he took with his friend Susan, Lilah, and Susan's now-ex husband. He'd been eighteen, and he'd spent most of the weekend soaking wet. But Thorne obviously knew what he was doing as he scurried around the deck, checking out the various ropes. Were they called rigging? He suddenly imagined Thorne racing up a rope to look out from the crow's nest, but sexy as the idea was, Thorne wasn't actually a pirate. This was just a small sailboat, boating for the rich and idle, not risking life and limb on the high seas.

Heat filled his cheeks when he remembered what he'd said about playing pirate and captive. Why the fuck was he blushing? Rent boys didn't blush.

"Come aboard, we're all set," Thorne called.

Dash held out the picnic basket, afraid the rocking of the boat would make him drop it. Once the basket was safe in the boat, Dash gingerly placed one foot on the deck, pausing with his arms out for balance as the boat rocked. Why did everyone look so agile doing this in movies?

Thorne took his hand. "You don't have to be that careful. You aren't going to tip her over."

Dash took the next step and he was on board, the boat swaying gently under his feet. The wind was strong enough to ruffle even Thorne's short hair. He assumed that meant it was a good day for sailing.

"Don't lean too far over the side, listen to me if I tell you to shift your weight, and duck if I say so or the boom might try to take your head off." Thorne patted the long pole supporting the bottom of the larger sail. That must be the boom.

"I think I can remember that."

"Then you'll be fine." Thorne gestured toward one of the benches lining the sides of the boat. "Have a seat."

The seats didn't look very comfortable. Was Thorne serious about fucking in this thing? Dash had been with men in a hell of a lot of different places, including full-on ass sex in a MINI Cooper, and he still wasn't sure sex in a sailboat would be practical.

"I didn't realize it would be this small."

Thorne laughed. "It's a sailboat, not a yacht. And a small sailboat at that. The one I owned was several feet longer. This one's only a fifteen-foot daysailer."

"I guess I really don't know much about boats."

Thorne smiled at him, obviously pleased to be the one in the know. "Just relax and trust me."

He did trust Thorne when it came to most things, boats included. He just didn't trust him enough to admit what he really wanted. Maybe that night if the day on the water went as well as he hoped.

"You *can* swim, right?" Thorne asked.

"Yes." Dash hoped he wouldn't end up in the water, though.

"Good. I haven't sailed in a while, but we're on a lake, not the ocean. I doubt we'll be testing your swimming skills.

175

"See that little island out there?" He pointed to what looked like nothing more than a rock and a small tree far out into the lake.

Dash nodded.

"We're going to head for it and then anchor close by. It's barely big enough to spread our picnic blanket on, but no one will disturb us there."

Dash liked that idea. A lot. He was ready to get his hands on Thorne. "Aye, aye, captain."

Thorne raised a brow. "Pirate play starting already?"

"Mutiny plans are underway." Dash deliberately glanced toward the coils of rope on the deck.

"Sounds intriguing."

As Thorne worked, Dash tried to convince himself he wasn't going to be spilled into the water. Or worse, get seasick. He had a good stomach for roller coasters and such, and he could read in a car, so he had high hopes. But it wasn't the internal pep talk that made his nervousness dissolve. It was watching Thorne move around on the boat, the muscles in his arms flexing as he tightened ropes, the view of his gorgeous ass as he checked the sails and familiarized himself with all the craft's workings. The shorts he wore had ragged cuffs and his T-shirt was a bit too tight. He hadn't bothered to shave that morning, and the stubble looked good on him.

"You're fucking gorgeous like this, you know? All dressed down and scruffy."

Thorne looked at Dash, and Dash's chest tightened. The look of open admiration on Thorne's face did unnerving things to Dash's insides. "Thanks."

"How does it feel to be in a boat again?"

Thorne smiled. "Wonderful."

LATER THAT MORNING, with the boat anchored off the tiny island, Thorne and Dash lay on a blanket, looking up at the cloudless sky.

"When did you realize you liked men?" Thorne had wanted to ask that question for weeks now.

Dash chewed on his lip as he considered the question. "I think I've always known. When friends were salivating over actresses, it was always the hot actors that made me feel funny inside. When I first started jerking off, it was never to thoughts of boobs and always to the thought of some hot athlete or even a guy I'd seen at school. Male bodies were what did it for me. I hated that at first. I didn't want to feel different from all my friends, but I knew I was. I never went out with a girl other than as a friend. By the time I was seventeen, I was ready to admit exactly what I wanted and go for it. I didn't go quite so far as to take a boy to prom, but I sure as hell fucked one afterward."

Thorne laughed with him.

"So what about you?" Dash asked.

Thorne should have known that question was coming. He'd asked Dash, so it was only fair for him to reveal a little about himself, though the real answer to that question was one he'd never told anyone.

"I guess the feelings had been there for me all along too, but I hid them, pushed them down so deep I occasionally forgot they existed. I dated girls in high school and college. I slept with them and enjoyed it, but something always seemed to be missing from those encounters." He paused and looked at Dash.

Dash reached up and ran his thumb over Thorne's cheekbone. "Tell me more." His voice was low and compelling. Thorne did as he asked.

"One night when I was twenty, I got drunk with a guy I was friends with. We made out, and it was better than any sex I'd ever had. He never spoke to me again. But after that, I occasionally gave in and went to a gay club, where I'd pick up a guy, fuck him and then pretend it meant nothing. I kept dating women, because that was what I was supposed to do."

Thorne paused, not sure he should go on. Was he really going to let Dash in on a secret he'd kept for sixteen years? Had it really been that long? For the first few months, he kept thinking someone would find out, some clue would give him away, but if anyone figured it out, they never mentioned it.

"I met Clint when he hired me to work at Symthson Associates. He was…" Thorne took a slow breath, needing a moment to focus so he didn't get lost in the memories. "I've never told anyone about him."

Dash laid a hand on his leg. "I'm here to listen if you want to tell me. If not, that's okay too. Whatever feels right."

"I've never wanted to talk about it until now, but with you…I think it's time."

Dash nodded. "Go as slow as you need to. I'll be here."

Thorne rolled over on his side and propped his head on his elbow so he was looking down at Dash. "Clint was married. He was so fucking conflicted about cheating. He didn't want to hurt his wife or leave his kids, but he knew he was gay. From the moment I met him I thought about him constantly, fantasized about him fucking me. Then one day we were the last ones leaving the office. He asked me to join him for a drink. We were in the bar long enough to take a sip, maybe two, before we headed to a hotel." Thorne glanced at Dash. He didn't look phased. He'd probably heard far worse.

As if reading his mind, Dash took his hand and squeezed it. "I've slept with plenty of married men. I'm certainly not going to judge you."

Thorne should have realized Dash would have married clients. Maybe he hadn't thought about it because he didn't like thinking of Dash with other men at all. "I knew Clint's wife and his kids, saw them at company picnics, had to pretend…" He paused as tears stung his eyes. He hadn't even cried when Clint died. He'd been too shocked, too much in denial. And then he'd been shut out. He'd focused on work, on simply keeping moving.

Dash rose up and kissed him softly. He was tempted to lose himself in Dash, but if he didn't finish his story now, he never would. "We were together such as it was for two years and then Clint had a heart attack. He died a few hours later. I never got to say good-bye and then I couldn't grieve for him like I needed to, because I had to hide what he meant to me. Someone from the office had to travel to see a client on the day of the funeral. I scheduled myself to do it because I knew I couldn't hold myself together." The tears came then, hot and fast. "So now you can see why I'm so fucked up about relationships."

Thorne let himself be pulled down to lie on

Dash's chest. "I'm right here," Dash said. "You don't have to hold back anymore."

Thorne was grateful for the warmth and tenderness. And as his tears slowed, he realized that while the pain of losing Clint so suddenly was still there, it had eased. Telling Dash had been the right thing to do.

"I never tried dating after that. Once I moved up to senior partner, I started paying for what I wanted. It was so much simpler."

"I hear that a lot, that paying for sex makes it simple," Dash said. "It can, but it can also—"

"Complicate things." Thorne finished the statement for him, certain Dash could feel his heart pounding heavily against his chest. He wanted to explain just how complex his feelings for Dash had become, but he didn't have the nerve. Once said, the words couldn't be taken back. They would change everything.

"Is this the first time you let yourself mourn him?" Dash asked as he stroked Thorne's hair.

"Yes. At first I was afraid if I did, I'd never come back to myself, that I'd let grief take me. Now the pain has dulled, but it's still there."

"How could it not be? You lost someone you loved."

"Who knows what would have happened, whether he would ever have left his wife. I was probably a fool to believe he would but…yeah, I did love him."

Dash held him, and Thorne let more tears fall. What was the point in fighting them? When the storm of his emotions quieted, Dash slipped out from under him. "Stay there. I'll be right back."

What was Dash up to? Thorne propped himself on his arms so he could see. When Dash stepped into the boat and then out again with a coil of rope, a shudder of lust ran through Thorne.

"Raise your hands over your head," Dash said, his voice low, commanding but not harsh.

Thorne's cock hardened as Dash wrapped the rope around the thin trunk of the tree and then his wrists and secured it. Dash left the bonds loose, which was good since the rope was scratchy. Thorne could free himself if he wanted to, but he didn't.

Dash shoved Thorne's shirt up and lavished kisses over his chest. He teased Thorne's nipples to hard nubs, sucking, licking, biting. Thorne arched up, wanting more. Dash kissed his way down Thorne's torso as he unfastened his shorts. Then finally, he drew Thorne's cock deep into his mouth. Thorne thrust into that inviting warmth as he fought the urge to tug his hands free so he could keep Dash right where he wanted him. Dash sucked him until Thorne was sure he was going to shoot in Dash's mouth, but Dash stopped just in time.

Thorne watched as he pulled a condom from his pocket. He expected Dash to put it on himself, but he rolled it slowly down Thorne's dick, the touch of his hands bringing Thorne right back to the edge.

When Thorne was covered, Dash stood and shucked his bathing trunks. He sucked on his fingers until they were slick with spit and then began to open himself up. Thorne bit his lip to hold in a moan. He needed to be inside Dash right that second. "Don't make me wait. I don't give a fuck about your

181

anticipation theories right now."

Dash laughed. "Neither do I. I don't remember where I put the lube, and I don't want to search for it." He leaned over Thorne and dribbled spit onto his cock.

"Oh, fuck. Are you sure about this?" Thorne hoped he was.

Dash answered by straddling Thorne and sinking slowly onto his cock. His ass was so fucking tight. Thorne wasn't sure he could take much more. Dash didn't stop moving until he was fully seated. His eyes were shut tight, and his thighs were rock hard with tension.

"Dash?"

"Gimme a sec, okay?"

When Dash opened his eyes, the predatory hunger in them made Thorne shudder.

"I'm going to ride you until you lose your mind," Dash said. "I'm going to make you forget everything but my ass squeezing your cock. You got that? But I'm going to do it at my own speed."

Thorne struggled against the ropes. "Need to touch you. Need—"

"Not yet."

Dash rose up and then drove back down, making Thorne cry out. Thorne was grateful there wasn't anyone close by, not that he really cared at this point. *Let them watch.* It wasn't like anyone could fail to be mesmerized by Dash like this, all hot and commanding.

Dash rose again, moving even more slowly this time. "I wonder how long you think I can keep this up."

Professional Distance

Thorne was done with waiting. "Fuck. Me. Now."

"No, I think this is all you need." He kept up the maddeningly slow rhythm.

Thorne fumbled with the ropes, working them loose so he could slip his hands out. "When I get these ropes loose—"

Dash had the nerve to laugh. "You don't really want to free yourself."

"What makes you so fucking sure?"

"Because if you do, I'll stop and you won't get to come."

That was so not happening. "What if I make myself come?"

"You won't, because I'm in charge, and you're going to do what I say."

Just like that, Thorne stopped fighting. Dash was right. He needed Dash controlling him so he could let go.

Dash ran a hand down his chest. "That's more like it."

"You can't go slow forever," Thorne challenged. He immediately realized his words would only make Dash try harder to do just that.

"I could with anyone else, but with you... What you do to me, Thorne, it's ..." Dash let his head fall back and sucked in a sharp breath. If Thorne guessed right, his cock had just brushed Dash's prostate.

Dash didn't say any more, but he did pick up the pace. Thorne worked his hips as much as he could with Dash on top. He longed to turn him over and thrust deep, but he also wanted Dash in charge.

Sweat ran down Dash's face and chest, dripping

onto Thorne, mingling with his own. The sun beat down on them, lighting them up outside the way Dash fucking him was lighting Thorne up inside.

"Thorne. God, Thorne. I can't hold back," Dash cried.

"Then come. Please."

"Yes!" Dash grabbed his cock, jacking himself until he shuddered and cum splattered Thorne's chest. The sight sent Thorne over the edge. He bucked so hard he nearly unseated Dash. His orgasm went on and on. When he was wrung dry, he collapsed, head hitting the ground with a *thunk*.

The next thing he was aware of was Dash untying his hands and rubbing his wrists. "Are you okay?"

"I think you scrambled my brains."

"Seriously Thorne?" Dash looked truly worried.

"I'm fine. Just floating."

Dash stretched out next to Thorne and put his head on Thorne's chest. "I wish…"

"What? Tell me." Did he want to know?

"I wish we could just stay here."

"We can," Thorne said. "I could rent a cabin."

"No, I mean… Never mind."

"Stay here away from the world, cocooned like this, fucking, drinking, sailing, no responsibilities, no one else intruding," Thorne suggested.

"Yeah, like that."

"Me too."

Neither of them said anything else for a long time.

Chapter Sixteen

Dash liked having a plan for his appointments with clients, especially Thorne, since he could hardly think, much less devise an erotic scenario once Thorne started kissing him. But one week after their sailing trip, he showed up at Thorne's apartment with nothing in mind other than not making a fool of himself and not letting Thorne talk him into staying the night. He was helping Susan the next day, and he needed some distance. He was forgetting exactly what the nature of his relationship with Thorne was far too often.

As it turned out, he didn't need a plan. Thorne grabbed him as soon as he stepped in the door, pushed him up against the wall and kissed him, hard and desperate. They didn't slow down until Dash had come hard enough to see stars. He lay there, thinking he should get dressed and leave before he talked himself into staying the night or Thorne did.

Thorne rolled over to face him. "I have a favor to ask."

Dash tried to hide his concern. "What is it?"

"Don't look so apprehensive, it's nothing bad. At least, I don't think it is."

"I'm not—"

Thorne's expression made it clear he didn't believe Dash. "I've asked a lot of you."

And you've paid me very well. Dash kept that

thought to himself, considering how weird things had gotten the last time he'd called attention to the fact that he was only Thorne's rent boy. Did Thorne want him to be more? No. He was just uncomfortable about paying him for anything more than sex. That had to be it.

"There's an art opening next Friday. My company is one of the top sponsors. I'd like you to go with me."

"*With you* with you? Like as an escort? Won't that be an indication that you're not as straight as people think you are?"

Thorne considered the question for a moment. "As my friend."

That was a disaster waiting to happen. "You really think no one's going to guess what's up?"

Thorne waved away his concern. "They can guess all they want."

"So you'll just talk casually with me, remember not to touch me, and—"

"Forget it."

The intensely hurt expression on Thorne's face surprised Dash. He laid his hand on top of Thorne's. "I don't want you to out yourself if you're not ready."

Thorne closed his eyes, and Dash watched his chest rise and fall. "I'm not ready to stand up and make a big speech about who I take to bed, but I'm beyond caring about starting rumors."

Dash caressed the back of Thorne's hand. "Are you, really?"

"Yes." Thorne looked at him, his eyes filled with a mix of desire and something so painful Dash almost looked away.

"Then I'll go." Dash couldn't say no. He'd gone to plenty of similar affairs as an escort: sometimes men—or women—hired him solely for that purpose with no sex after. Except, when he thought about pretending to be Thorne's date, his pulse sped up so fast he wondered if his heart would give out. "Is this a black-tie affair? Should I rent a tux?"

"I'll get you one. Don't worry," Thorne said. His enigmatic smile unsettled Dash.

"Won't I need to be fitted?"

Thorne shook his head. "I know your size."

"Is that some secret hidden talent? You look at a man and instantly know his measurements?"

Thorne laughed. "Hardly, though my tailor apparently has superpowers."

"You actually have a fucking tailor?" Of course he did.

"I do." Obviously unwilling to reveal more, Thorne pulled Dash to him for a kiss, one that was soft, sweet, and filled with emotion.

Dash needed to get out of there. He pulled away and slid from the bed.

"Do you really have to go?" Thorne asked.

Don't give in. Don't let him seduce you. "I do."

"So next Friday then. You'll need to come a few hours earlier than usual."

***

THORNE REMOVED THE garment bag protecting the tux he'd had altered for Dash. He'd simply shown Darius, his tailor, a picture of Dash and described him, but he was confident it would fit. The man was fucking brilliant.

Thorne hung the tux next to his own and

wondered for at least the tenth time that day if he'd lost his mind asking Dash to the opening. No way in hell could he go the whole night without touching Dash, and he doubted he'd be able to take his eyes off Dash for more than a few seconds at a time. It wasn't just that he was relentlessly horny around Dash, now he could feel himself go all moony when he looked at him. How could Dash not see it? Maybe he did and was ignoring it. Clients probably fell for him all the time.

He looks at you the same way.
No, that's just wishful thinking.

Thorne ran his hand down the tux, imagining Dash in it. He was going to look so fucking perfect. Everyone at the museum would watch him when he walked by, admiring how he was well-spoken, soft, and boyish, and yet strong and in control. They'd be drawn by his beautiful skin, twinkling eyes, plump lips. Men and women would attempt to coax him into their beds. Thorne always had known how to hire the best.

Dash was his hired companion, nothing more. That thought had him reaching for some antacids. How had he gotten so screwed up when it came to his personal life?

You lost the only other man you've cared for, and no one even knew it.

Other people lose things and don't…

No. Thorne had to shut down this line of thinking if he were going to make it through the night.

Dash arrived a few minutes later, looking less confident than usual. No self-assured seductive swagger. No sense that he might order Thorne to his knees or tell him to bend over the back of the couch. "Don't tell me you're nervous about tonight."

Dash scowled at him. "How well do you know the people who will be there?"

Thorne considered the guest list. "Some of them I don't know at all, but several people from my office will be there and others who are business connections of one type or another. I know all the museum board members since I've served on it, off and on, for years."

"And you told me all you did was work," Dash scoffed.

"Work and the occasional charitable activity. I admitted to that."

Dash smiled. "You did, but I still don't think this is a good idea."

Thorne waved away his concern. "I don't care."

"About what I think?"

Thorne shook his head. "About what anyone thinks."

Dash started to say something, but he froze. Thorne realized he was staring at the tuxes hanging from Thorne's closet door. His eyes widened as he approached the garments. "Those don't look like any tuxes I've ever rented."

Thorne smiled. "That's because they aren't made of ill-fitting polyester."

Dash fingered the jacket. "This might actually be comfortable."

"It's yours, by the way."

"You mean, for the night?"

"No, for always."

Dash stared at him like he'd lost his mind. "You

bought it?"

"I could hardly have it altered otherwise."

"Nobody owns tuxedos."

"I do."

"Why would you—" Dash looked truly perplexed.

"Because I wanted to; now go put it on so we can see how it fits."

"And what will we do if it's not right?"

Thorne shrugged. "Fix it."

"Is everything that simple for you?"

"Everything that can be fixed with money."

Dash shook his head, but he was smiling. He grabbed the tux and headed toward the bathroom.

"Where are you going?"

"To the bathroom. To change."

The bathroom? "Sudden case of modesty?"

Dash laughed. "No, I want to make an entrance."

Several minutes later Thorne resorted to pacing. What was Dash doing in there? It didn't take that long to get dressed. Did the tux not fit after all?

He was about to go knock on the bathroom door when Dash opened it. Any complaints about how long he took to change died when Thorne saw him. He was fucking stunning. "You…I…wow."

Dash grinned. "Thanks. Your tailor must practice some dark brand of magic. This fits like it was made for me."

"Now, aren't you glad I didn't rent you some uncomfortable sack?"

"I…thank you. Sorry it took so long, I had to look up a video on how to tie a bowtie."

Thorne couldn't help but laugh. "You did an

excellent job."

"Thank you."

Thorne glanced at the clock on his bedside table. "Damn. I was hoping there would be time to get you out of it again."

"Not until the party is over. Go put yours on, and I'll pour you a drink. How about that?"

Thorne looked at Dash longingly, taking in his beauty a few seconds longer. "Okay." There would be time later to peel him out of the tux, slowly, carefully, revealing every inch of him.

THE ROOM GLOWED softly from the strings of lights circling the ceiling and snaking around the potted trees positioned along the wall between groups of paintings. There was a low murmur of talking, clinking glass, and a whirl of exceptionally well-dressed people. Dash was dizzied by it all, but the art was beautiful. He hadn't been sure what to expect—modern nonsense that was nothing but a splash of color on the canvas, desolate, depressing images that made a point too esoteric for him to grasp. Instead, the room was filled with a series of amazingly lifelike landscapes that captured the sun's rays in a way that Dash wouldn't have thought possible outside of a photograph. He was seriously impressed.

Thorne had wandered off to schmooze a lucrative client, and Dash was taking the opportunity to circle the room and enjoy the art. He was studying Sea at Sunrise when someone stepped up beside him, much too close to be polite.

When he saw who it was, nausea closed his throat, and a sick sweat broke out on his neck. This man was a former client. One he'd turned down for a second appointment because he'd been too rough, rushing things that didn't need to be rushed and making sure to tell Dash how little he was worth. In all the time he'd spent worrying that Thorne's colleagues would realize he was more than Thorne's friend, or that he'd have nothing to say when one of them asked him how he'd met Thorne, he'd never considered the likelihood of running into one of his own clients. He should have known better. These were exactly the kind of men who patronized Sheila's service.

"How did you end up here?" The man's tone made it clear that someone as lowly as Dash had no business in an art museum.

"I like art."

The asshole snorted. "At the price of these tickets you must have liked it enough to give a blowjob or two."

Anger rushed through Dash, and he clenched his fists. He would not make a scene.

"I suppose you're here with someone. Who's the lucky man who bid high enough for you?"

"I hope you have a lovely evening. I'm going to look at some of the other paintings." Dash turned to go.

The man seized his arm. "How much to do me in the bathroom while your client waits?"

"I would never treat a client with such disrespect."

"Ha! You fuck people for money. What do you care how many? Maybe I could convince him that we should tag-team you."

"I don't know how to make this any more clear," Dash said. "I am not interested in being with you, personally or professionally."

"What is your fucking problem? You think I—" The man paused, looking over Dash's shoulder. Then he smiled. "Oh, is this the one? I didn't even know he was gay."

"Let go of him." Thorne's voice had an edge to it that made even Dash wary.

"Are you going to make me?"

"I'm going to have you thrown out on your ass, barred from the museum, and possibly charged with assault if you don't walk away right now."

The man stepped back, but he gestured toward Dash. "You know what he is, don't you?"

"Yes, he's my friend, and he asked you to leave him alone."

"He's a fucking whore."

Thorne punched him, fist connecting with his jaw, causing a sickening crack. The man fell back, hitting the polished wood floor hard enough to bounce. Before he could get back on his feet, two security guards arrived.

"How did you know to call them?" Dash asked.

Thorne scowled. "I know what that man is. I didn't know if it would escalate like this, but I wasn't taking any chances."

Thorne winced as he flexed and shook his hand.

"Are you okay?"

He nodded. "I'm fine. I'll get some ice in a minute."

"Sir, can you explain what happened here?" one of the security guards asked.

Thorne nodded. "This asshole was harassing my friend."

"Is this true, sir?" the man asked Dash.

"Yes."

"He's a fucking whore," the asshole yelled as he finally pulled himself up off the floor. "That's all he is."

"Get him out of here," Thorne ordered.

The other guards began dragging the man out. He shook them off and straightened his suit. "I'm going," he announced as if he had a choice. The guards followed him toward the door.

When Dash looked away from the asshole, he saw the museum director rushing toward Thorne. "Are you all right, Mr. Shipton?"

No one seemed to care that Thorne had punched the man, and neither the guards nor the director appeared to give any credence to what the asshole said. Thorne had power, and people did what he said. Dash had to admit it was a hell of a turn-on, that and the fact that Thorne had once again defended Dash. Maybe he truly did see Dash as more than an employee.

"Sir, are you okay?" the director asked.

Dash nodded. "I'm fine."

"You weren't injured? You're certain?"

"No, he only threatened me. I'm truly fine."

"This isn't the first time he's caused trouble here. I regret that I allowed him to return."

"Apology accepted," Thorne said, before Dash had a chance to respond.

"If you two are truly all right, I'll do my best to minimize the interest in this incident and continue with our evening."

Dash smiled at her. "By all means. The last thing I'd want to do is take away from the art. These paintings are exquisite."

"Thank you, sir. We're proud to have them."

Thorne leaned closer to Dash as she walked away. "Would you like one?"

Dash was still trying to sort out what had just happened. "Would I… What?"

"Want a painting?"

The least expensive one Dash had seen cost several hundred thousand dollars. "You can't buy me a painting."

"I assure you I can."

"No, I mean I won't let you."

"Then pick out one for my apartment."

He'd still be buying it for Dash though, wouldn't he? "Thorne?"

He narrowed his eyes. "Do it."

His body reacted to Thorne's tone. Thorne high on his own power was way too sexy. He glanced to the side and saw Lauren, Thorne's assistant, watching them. Dash stepped back. "I think we're being obvious."

"I think I don't care."

"I think you've had a lot of champagne."

Thorne waved dismissively. "I'm going to buy a painting and take you home before anyone else makes me so mad I want to rip someone's fucking head off."

Dash laid a hand on Thorne's arm. "I'm fine, really."

"No one has the right to treat you like you're property. You provide a service for money. So do I."

Did Thorne have to make Dash fall even harder for him? "It's different."

"It shouldn't be."

"Thank you for being so enlightened."

"Anytime, my dear." Thorne sketched a bow.

"People are watching."

Thorne shook his head. "Lauren is watching. If she hasn't figured us out by now, she's not the woman I think she is."

Thorne was far too gorgeous when he smiled. "Go buy a painting."

"This one?" Thorne gestured toward the seascape in front of them.

Dash shook his head. "No, the one with the sailboat on the lake." Dash pointed across the room.

"Sold," Thorne declared.

Chapter Seventeen

After discarding jackets, vests, bowties, and shoes—the most comfortable dress shoes Dash had ever owned—Thorne and Dash reclined on Thorne's couch with glasses of whiskey. Dash agreed to abandon his usual rule of not drinking while working as long as Thorne didn't want anything kinky.

Thorne pouted. "I was hoping we could play pirate mutiny. But instead of walking the plank…"

Dash shook his head. "You're really drunk."

Thorne giggled, proving Dash's point. "Peggy's a very wise woman."

Dash tried to follow Thorne's line of thinking. "Peggy? The museum director?"

He nodded. "She buys good champagne, so everyone drinks. Drunk people buy paintings. They often regret it later, but returns aren't accepted." He laughed so hard he actually gripped his sides, but a few seconds later, he looked up at Dash, expression far more serious.

"Was Collins a former client?"

"The man you punched?" Dash had never known his name.

Thorne nodded.

"I only saw him once."

"Did he hurt you?"

"Not seriously, but he…wasn't kind."

The fire that had been in Thorne's eyes when

he'd punched Collins returned. "I have connections. I could get him disbarred."

As much as Thorne's protectiveness turned him on, Dash didn't want him to do that. "I'm not a princess in need of a knight."

Thorne fingered one of his shirt buttons. "You sure as hell could pass for a prince all dressed up like this."

It was a bad sign that Dash loved Thorne's drunken flattery. "Kiss me."

Thorne did, soft and sweet, taking his time, touching Dash so gently it was more a caress of lips than a kiss. There was no wild rush of passion, yet when Thorne pulled back, Dash wanted nothing more than to be fucked by him. No, that wasn't right. He wanted Thorne to make love to him because that would erase the ugliness of the night. Dash rarely hated what he did, but that night, that odious bastard Collins had made him ashamed. Thorne could erase the feeling.

Thorne brushed the back of his hand over Dash's cheek. "Don't let that son of a bitch make you feel bad."

"Make me feel good instead." Dash's voice cracked. Thorne was seeing him at his worst.

"There's nothing I want more." Thorne's breath was warm against his ear.

Dash's embarrassment dissipated because Thorne understood what he needed. It was what Thorne himself often needed.

Dash remembered for a moment that Thorne was a client and Dash was there to pleasure him. "Are you sure? If you'd rather—"

"There's nothing I'd rather do than please you. Forget why you're really here. Your only job right now is to feel."

Dash did feel, so keenly it hurt. Would he survive this?

"Let's go to bed," Thorne said.

Dash stood on shaky legs. Thorne took hold of his shoulders and turned him around.

"Move. I need to spread you out and open you up. I can't do that on the fucking couch."

Dash's mouth went dry, and his cock tried to push through the snug pants of his new tux. Somehow, he managed to walk across the room, hurried along by Thorne.

"Strip," Thorne demanded when they were standing at the end of the bed.

Dash turned and studied Thorne as he rubbed his thumb over Thorne's lower lip. He needed to feel that fullness, so he rose up and ran his tongue across it.

Thorne gasped, grabbed Dash's waistband, and hauled him up against his firm body. "If you're going to tease me, I'll strip you myself."

"Don't damage this thing getting it off me," Dash insisted. "I've never owned anything like this."

"I'll buy you another one."

"The fuck you will."

Thorne shoved Dash's pants and briefs to his feet, and Dash kicked them off. Then Thorne lifted each of Dash's arms, removing the cufflinks and tossing them—with surprisingly good aim—into a bowl on his dresser. When he started work on Dash's buttons, Dash could feel his impatience. He was going to rip the fucking shirt.

"Let me." But Dash's hands were no quicker. They were shaking from anticipation, need, and a hint of embarrassment at how unnerved he was.

Thorne batted his hands away, undid the first two buttons and then tugged on his wrists to indicate that he should lift his arms. Thorne pulled the shirt off and tossed it onto a chair. Then he put a hand in the middle of Dash's chest and pushed. "Lie down, spread for me, and let me do the work."

Dash stretched out on his back and watched as Thorne undressed himself more efficiently than he had Dash. He kept his briefs on, and Dash raised a brow.

"If I don't have some kind of barrier between us, I'll be inside you before I get halfway through what I have planned."

Dash grinned and licked his lips with deliberate slowness. "I'm not sure I care."

"I do. You deserve this."

Dash didn't want Thorne to feel that way. Not unless… "Thorne, you don't—"

"Yes, I do."

There was no talking for a while after that. Thorne touched Dash everywhere, his mouth following his hands. He nuzzled Dash's cock, but refused to take it in his mouth. Dash reached for him to force the issue, but Thorne pinned his hands to the mattress and kept going, licking his balls, nibbling his inner thighs, driving him out of his fucking mind.

"Fuck, Thorne. Don't tease me."

"What happened to anticipation being the best thing ever?" Thorne asked.

"Shut up!"

Thorne chuckled. "Turn over."

"You'll have to let go of my wrists first."

"That's too bad. I liked you struggling under me."

Dash gave him a mock scowl. "Is this payback?"

"No." Thorne's tone was serious now. "I don't need to get revenge. You knew just what I needed, and now I want to do the same for you."

Dash shuddered as he turned onto his stomach. Thorne's words were dangerous. Thorne had always been an amazing lover, never one to demand his money's worth and give nothing in return. But this was still just sex, wasn't it?

Thorne started at Dash's feet, rubbing them and then massaging his calf muscles. Dash was in an odd state of utterly relaxed and horny as fuck. His legs felt boneless, weights against the mattress. But his cock was hard as a rock. He couldn't help shifting against the bed, trying to get more friction.

"Hold still and let me love you," Thorne complained.

Love? This did feel like love.

Thorne's firm touch eased tight muscles all the way up Dash's body. By the time Thorne reached his shoulders, Dash was utterly under his spell, floating as if Thorne had taken him to another place.

"Pull you knees under you. It's time to open you up."

"Fuck." The word came out as a whisper.

"Yes…eventually."

Dash couldn't quite remember how to control his body. Finally, he managed to wake enough from his massage-induced daze to do as Thorne said.

Thorne reached under him and gave his cock a single stroke. "So fucking hard for me," he murmured.

Dash bit down on his lower lip to keep from whimpering and begging for more.

"You will not come until I say so, understand?"

"Thorne." Dash hated the whine in his voice.

Thorne laid a hand at the base of Dash's spine. Firm pressure, nothing truly sexual, but as far as Dash was concerned, Thorne might as well be stroking his cock again.

"Please," Dash begged, not even sure what he was asking.

"Relax."

"Isn't that my line?" Dash meant it to be humorous, but the words sounded desperate, confused.

"Tell me to stop if there's anything you don't like. Otherwise, relax and enjoy." Thorne was utterly serious.

"O-okay."

Thorne pulled Dash's ass cheeks apart and groaned. The sound ran through Dash like a current, lighting up every part of him that wasn't already restless.

"We're taking this slow." Thorne's face was so close to his hole Dash could feel his breath there. He squirmed, trying to free himself, but Thorne dug his fingers into Dash's ass.

Then he licked Dash's hole; fucking licked it.

"Th-Thorne?"

"I said I was going to open you up." His tone was calm, casual, not at all appropriate for what was happening.

"Oh my fucking God!"

Thorne circled Dash's entrance with his tongue and then pushed at the tight muscle.

Dash jerked, the sensation beyond intense. Just the thought of Thorne rimming him could probably make him come. No client had ever done that.

"Breathe," Thorne reminded him.

"Please." Dash needed more, so much more.

"Please what?"

"Please. Your tongue. Fuck me." He'd lost the ability to be coherent.

Thorne speared Dash's ass. Pushing deeper, tongue splitting him open. Dash was going to come apart. He couldn't hold back, couldn't take it.

Thorne clamped a hand around the base of Dash's shaft and squeezed hard, holding him back.

"Thorne!"

"Yes?" His voice was low, ridiculously calm.

"I need…"

"Yes?" The bastard laughed.

"Stop fucking around."

"You don't like this?"

"I fucking love it and you know that, but I'm going to lose my fucking mind if you don't give me more," Dash shouted.

"More? Okay."

Thorne thrust his tongue back in and worked it in and out, getting Dash slicked up and ending all resistance.

"Fuck, Thorne. Fuck!"

Thorne squeezed Dash's cock harder. "Not yet."

Dash laid his head on his arms. He was dripping

sweat and his whole body seemed to vibrate, his skin buzzing as if electrified. "Thorne?" He heard the sound of a condom wrapper tearing. *Thank fuck.*

Thorne moved behind him again, but he didn't enter him. Instead he lay over him, fitting his cock into the crack of Dash's ass. "Turn over," he said, right against Dash's ear. "I want to see you when you come."

Dash considered protesting, unsure if he could do what Thorne asked. Thorne would be able to see into Dash's soul when he was like this. Thorne hadn't been kidding about opening him up. Dash didn't think he had any barriers left after what Thorne had done. He turned over anyway, because he also wanted to see Thorne, wanted to watch his eyes light up when he pushed inside Dash.

Thorne pressed against the back of Dash's thighs, doubling his legs on his chest. He gazed down at Dash, his pupils huge. "So fucking perfect. All ready for my cock."

Dash nodded frantically. He was more than ready.

"Stay just like this. Open wide for me."

Dash held his legs, pinned in place by the force of Thorne's gaze and by his own need. But his mind screamed for him to shut down, to keep Thorne from seeing into him like this, because his ass wasn't the only thing open for Thorne. His heart was open too, and while he might feel the intensity of this fuck for days, he didn't think the wounds Thorne might inflict on his heart would ever heal.

This was it. Dash could still run. If he stayed, he risked losing himself in Thorne. But his heart was already damaged. *If you run, do you really think you could just forget him?*

He wouldn't, but having Thorne inside him after he'd stuck his fucking tongue in Dash's ass was going to be more dangerous to Dash than anything he'd done before. Even the sweet, soft kisses.

"Thorne. Thorne, I…"

Thorne looked up from where he was lining up his cock. His eyes widened at Dash's expression. "Are you okay?"

"I'm…" What the fuck was he supposed to say? That he was scared? That sounded absurd, and he wasn't sure Thorne would understand. Why would he be afraid? He'd bottomed for Thorne plenty of times. But he'd been in control. This was Thorne truly taking him.

"No. Just. I…need you." He wasn't going to run.

"I need you too, baby." Thorne pushed forward then, breaching Dash's ass. Dash wrapped his arms around Thorne's neck and his legs around Thorne's back, holding him close as Thorne drove into him, his rhythm fast but not punishing, just rough enough to keep Dash from overthinking. Thorne was loving him. It was physical and beautiful, but Dash wanted more.

He buried his face in Thorne's shoulder to hide the tears in his eyes.

"Harder," he whispered, hoping Thorne would think his voice was rough because of lust not sadness.

Thorne fucked him harder, faster. "Thorne, please!" He needed to come because Thorne inside him felt so good he couldn't stand it. He was literally crying for more.

"Dash! Oh God. This is so good. So fucking good. I don't want to stop. Don't want this to end but—"

He brushed Dash's prostate and Dash cried out, bucking against Thorne, desperate to come, but needing just a little more to go over. He reached between their bodies so he could jack himself off, and Thorne sat back, drawing Dash's legs over his shoulders. Thorne pushed his hand away and jacked his cock for him, holding him tight, moving his hand fast and twisting it over the top. Dash bucked, squirmed, struggled, needing more. And then suddenly he was there. Hot cum shooting from his cock, splashing all the way to his neck. It was truly a release that seemed to drain him of everything. Tension leached from his body, and he collapsed, no longer aware of anything but Thorne's harsh, quick breaths. Had he come too?

Thorne pulled out, still hard. Maybe he hadn't. He rolled the condom off his dick. "I want to come on you."

Dash sucked in his breath, not sure why that was so fucking hot. "Please."

Thorne rose over him and gripped his cock. Dash shifted so his arms were over his head. He couldn't take his eyes off Thorne's hand. Dash felt his own cock twitch as Thorne's cock grew redder, his balls high and tight. He was so close. So ready.

"Cover me in cum, Thorne. I want to fucking bathe in it."

"Fuck!" Thorne came then, thick ropes of spunk joining Dash's own on his chest and abdomen.

When Thorne finished, he remained still, hanging

over Dash, eyes closed, head bowed. "That was…"

Dash ran his hand over his sticky torso and held it up to Thorne. Thorne sucked each finger one by one. Then he lapped at Dash's palm. "So good. Almost enough to make me ready again."

Dash's cock was all for that, but he didn't say it, because his need was as painful as it was pleasurable. "We should take a break."

"Yeah, I guess so." Thorne rolled onto his back, and they both stared at the ceiling. Dash longed to know what Thorne was thinking. If only his thoughts were the same as Dash's. That they belonged together.

THORNE WOKE TO the smell of pancakes and coffee and the clatter of pans in the kitchen. He rolled over and smiled as his muscles twinged from the previous evening's exertions. As he kicked off the covers, he glanced at the time. Dash would go soon. After the intensity of what he'd felt the night before, he couldn't let Dash leave without making him an offer. Dash wasn't taking any more clients if Thorne could prevent it.

He pulled on his robe and wandered to the bathroom where he relieved himself and brushed his teeth so Dash would enjoy the first kiss of the day. He looked in the mirror. Too little sleep and too much fucking made every one of his years visible in the early morning light. Maybe a shower first?

"Thorne, are you up?" Dash called.

"Yes."

"Good. I'm making pancakes; come tell me what kind you want."

Thorne's heart pounded. "I'll be there in a second."

Walk out that door and ask him.

Thorne walked out the door. Dash stood in the kitchen in boxer-briefs and an apron, his hair standing up, flour on his face. He looked young, painfully young, and happy and energetic. *I can always ask him after breakfast.*

Thorne poured himself a cup of coffee, took a few sips, wrapped his arms around Dash from behind and checked out the batter he was stirring.

"Mmm. Good morning," Dash said, turning to give Thorne a light kiss.

"Yes, I think it will be." Holding Dash like this, things felt right again. They were no different than they'd been last night, when they were so close, so connected. Maybe Dash would say yes.

"I can make banana, blueberry, chocolate chip, or plain. What do you want?"

"Wow, I haven't had chocolate chip pancakes since…I don't know…college."

Dash shook his head. "That's a crime. You're going to have some right now."

He reached into a canvas market bag on the counter and pulled out a bag of chips. Thorne watched, arms still around him, as he opened them and poured them into a dish, which he set next to the stove.

"Do you want to learn the art of pancake making?" Dash asked.

"No, I just can't stop touching you." Thorne moved in closer, nuzzling Dash's neck and breathing deeply of his scent.

Dash slapped playfully at his hands. "Watch if you want, but no way in hell can I concentrate with you so close."

Thorne smiled. "Fair enough." If things went well, he wouldn't have to wait a week to touch Dash again.

Ask him.

After breakfast.

Coward.

I'm just hungry.

"Go. Sit." Dash gestured toward the barstools on the opposite side of the counter.

Thorne took his coffee and sat. He watched Dash sprinkle water on the griddle. The droplets sizzled and danced around.

"What was that for?" Thorne asked.

"To see if it was hot enough. You really don't know how to make pancakes?"

"I understand the basic theory but…no, not ones you'd want to eat," Thorne confessed.

"I really should teach you some basics."

Thorne shook his head. "I'm hopeless. Besides, it's more fun to watch you do it."

Dash gave him a mock scowl and poured out batter on the griddle. When there were six perfect circles there, he sprinkled each with chocolate chips.

Thorne glanced at his tablet, which was charging at the end of the bar. He should at least check his work e-mail. A few months ago he would have been up early, e-mailing, typing reports, checking in on different projects no matter that it was the weekend. His time with Dash had helped him break those habits, and now, he didn't even want to see those messages, didn't want to take any chances that some crisis might rob them of their time together. He'd begun to see the world differently, to want things he hadn't thought he'd ever want. There was so much more to life than his job. How the fuck had he let himself forget that?

He needed to go sailing again. Hell, he needed to look into buying a boat.

A few moments later, Dash served the pancakes, and Thorne couldn't resist taking a bite immediately. They were fluffy and perfect with just the right amount of chocolate chips to make them extra decadent but not so many that they took away from the buttery perfection of the pancake itself. "These may be the best pancakes I've ever eaten."

Dash settled into his chair and placed a bowl of fruit salad next to Thorne's plate. "I'm glad you like them." Dash took a bite and smiled as he chewed. "These did turn out really well."

"Have you ever cooked anything that didn't?"

Dash laughed. "Trust me, I've had my share of disasters. There's a learning curve for everything, but I'm proud of what I can do in the kitchen now."

"I feel privileged to have you share it with me."

"I love cooking for someone as appreciative as you." Dash gave him that sparkling grin, the one that always did him in.

This is a great time to segue into your offer. "Dash?"

Dash looked up and set his fork down. The look in his eyes concern, fear. Fuck, how could Thorne keep going now?

"I've been thinking about our arrangement

and…"

"Yes?" Less fear showed in Dash's eyes now. Was that a good sign?

"I hate it when you leave. I wish I could see more of you, and…"

Dash motioned for him to go on. He was leaning forward. Tense. Intent.

Thorne swallowed. *Say it.* "I was wondering if you'd like to work for me full time."

Dash jumped as if startled. His hand knocked into his juice glass, and it turned over. Orange juice ran all over the table and poured off the side. Neither of them moved.

Thorne knew he had said the wrong thing. He frantically thought how to take the look of horror off Dash's face. "Let me explain. I want you to cook for me, not just—"

"Shut up!" Dash pushed back from the table. The look of devastation on his face made Thorne sick. The pancake lay in his stomach, weighing him down.

"Please, I—"

"Just stop. You've said e-fucking-nough. I can't believe this. I thought… You're actually offering to *hire* me full time. To be… Oh my God."

Dash ran to the bedroom. Thorne followed, watching him grab his bag and toss it on the bed. He grabbed Dash's arm, but Dash wrenched free. "Don't touch me."

Oh God. How had he screwed up so badly? "Dash, please."

Dash ignored him, continuing to pack his things, even the things he'd started leaving at Thorne's place.

Thorne had to get his attention. "Riley."

Dash turned around, and for a moment Thorne braced for a punch. "Don't you dare call me that. You've just made it very clear that you never thought of me that way. I'm nothing but an employee, and my working name is Dash. Don't worry, though. You won't need to call me anything. I won't be coming back."

Thorne had to do something. The look of shock and pain on Dash's face was killing him. "I made a mistake."

"Yeah, maybe your biggest one ever."

"Look, I didn't mean—"

"You really thought I'd agree to let you hide me away here? To be your 24/7 dirty secret?" Dash shook his head. "I actually thought… Fuck!"

"Dash, I didn't explain things right. Please just listen to me."

"No. That's where I went wrong to start with. Listening to you, believing you, not so much what you said, but what you didn't say, what you… Oh fuck." He slammed his fist against the top of Thorne's dresser. "I actually thought you were going to ask me to stay because you wanted me for me."

"I do."

"No, you want to own me," Dash snarled.

"That's not—"

"You want me to work for you."

Was this about him not being out? "Dash, I don't know if I can give you what you want, but at least talk to me about it."

"You could give me everything, but you won't."

Could he? What *did* Dash want? "I… Let me explain."

"No, I'm done being an idiot."

"You know I care for you. That I've never—"

Dash pushed Thorne out of his way and headed toward the door. "I don't want to hear anymore. I don't just care for you. I love you, or at least I did."

"You…what?" Thorne couldn't believe it. His head spun. Dash…loved him? Oh, fuck. He'd ruined everything.

Dash turned to face him. "I love you. Are you happy? Does it make your heart sing that you conquered me, that you succeeded in owning one more thing?"

Tears burned behind Thorne's eyes. If he'd had any idea Dash's feelings went that deep, that he truly… "Dash, I never—"

"Right, that's why you just offered to keep me here as your trophy."

"No, that's not it. I thought if you didn't need to work for Sheila, then we could have a chance to be togeth—"

"Together? Seriously? What bullshit. If I worked for you, there would be no together, just business."

"Then what the fuck has been going on for the last few months?"

Dash shook his head. "I thought I'd figured that out, but you just made it very clear that I was wrong."

Dash walked out then, slamming the door behind him.

Thorne almost chased after him, but what would be the point? Dash hated him. What chance did he have now?

You knew better. You son of a bitch, you knew better. Hiring him? What did you think he'd say?

I should have phrased it differently, made it more clear what I was actually asking him to do.
You didn't want him enough to do that.
I did. I wanted him more than anything.

Thorne sank onto the couch and buried his head in his hands. Sobs wracked his body until he couldn't cry anymore. Then he lay down and covered himself with a blanket, hoping he could sleep forever.

Chapter Eighteen

Thorne heard something outside his door. The doorman hadn't alerted him that he had a guest. The locking mechanism lit up green, and the knob turned. Dash? Had he come back? He still had Thorne's key, though he never used it.

Thorne's sister, Kathryn, opened the door and stepped in, closing it firmly behind her.

"What the hell are you doing here?" He didn't want to talk to anyone.

"You haven't been answering your phone. Yesterday you left Lauren a cryptic message about being sick, and today you just didn't show up. She was worried."

Was it Tuesday already? "I screwed up everything." He hadn't meant to say that out loud.

"Thorne, what are you talking about? Something at work?"

He shook his head. "Not work."

She frowned. "But work *is* your everything."

"Yeah, that's part of the problem."

Kathryn studied him, looking as worried as he'd ever seen her. How bad did he look?

"Jesus, Thorne, what happened to you?"

Pretty damn bad, apparently. He gestured to the half-empty decanter of bourbon on the coffee table. "You might want a drink before I explain. You can refill mine while you're at it."

She took the glass he held out. "You do realize it's ten in the morning, right?"

"I don't fucking care."

Probably knowing it was pointless to argue with him in this state, she got herself a glass from the sideboard and poured a heavy measure of bourbon for each of them.

After Thorne downed most of his in one go, he leaned his head back against the sofa and closed his eyes. "I'm gay."

Kathryn sputtered and sat her glass down. "What?"

"You heard me."

She tossed back about half the liquid in her glass. "Wow. When you said I should sit down…"

"I really meant it."

She took another sip, a smaller one, and set her glass down. "How long have you known?"

"That I liked men?"

She nodded.

"Since college."

"No one at work knows?"

He nodded to confirm and then polished off the rest of his drink. He needed fortification after his confession. At least she wasn't ranting at him.

"And this…" She waved her hand to indicate the blanket, the bourbon, his unkempt appearance.

"A complete breakdown."

"If you're admitting to it, then it's worse than I thought. What the fuck happened?" His sister rarely cussed. He must have seriously shocked her.

"I fell in love."

"With a man?"

"With a man I hired."

"Hired? For…?"

He gave her a withering look.

"Ah." She studied him for a few seconds. "The drink seems to have done you some good. You look more like yourself now."

"My real self is an ass according to Dash."

"Is that the man you fell for?"

Thorne nodded. "God. This… I didn't mean to tell you all this. What do you think of me now?"

"I think you're hurting worse than I've seen you since high school."

"High school was never this bad."

Kathryn moved to the couch, settled beside him, and put a comforting hand on his shoulder. "So, what are we going to do about it?"

"*We* aren't going to do anything. You're going to leave and let me wallow in misery."

"What about work?"

"What about it?"

"Thorne, despite the fact that I've been telling you to take some time off for approximately a decade, you have a job. You can't just ignore it."

"I actually could. I'm owed several months off. I'm going to take some time."

"First, you have to at least call the office and put people on your projects. You can't just disappear and… Wow, this man has really changed you, hasn't he?"

"You like the new me? Unwashed, undressed, and drunk at ten a.m."

"No, but there's something under all that, something good. I can hear it in your voice."

217

"It was good, but he's gone, and I'm worse off now than if…"

Kathryn shook her head. "I don't think so."

Thorne scowled at her.

"Eventually—the sooner the better if we're going to fix this situation—you need to tell me what happened in more detail, and—"

"I hired him to fuck me. Then, instead of telling him I'd fallen in love with him, I offered to hire him full time."

"To *hire* him full time?"

"Yeah, that's basically what he said but with more colorful language."

"Oh, Thorne."

How could he explain without sounding even stupider than he already did? "I thought…"

"I'm sure you did. You might not be very wise when it comes to relationships, but you aren't cruel."

"Just because you have a perfect marriage to the perfect man doesn't mean the rest of us have your powers."

Kathryn snorted. "My marriage is far from perfect."

"The fuck it isn't."

She poured herself another drink. He'd always had this effect on her. "Thorne, no marriage is perfect. And even if mine was, that doesn't mean you and Dash don't deserve a chance to be happy."

"He's young. Did I mention that? Very young. And he does deserve happiness, but he'll have a better chance of finding it without me."

Kathryn ignored his self-deprecation. "How young is he?"

"Twenty-two. That's partly why I didn't think he'd want to date me."

"Whew! That is young."

Thorne wasn't sure he liked how readily she agreed with him. "Not a lot of old guys working for escort services. And it's not what you're thinking. We'd joked about him being my personal chef. I was going to hire him to cook for me."

"Did he understand what you were hiring him for?"

"I thought so, but now I'm not sure."

Kathryn sighed. "Have you tried to contact him?"

Thorne laughed, the sound brittle. "I called him—I don't know—ten or twenty times over the weekend, like a fucking stalker. Then yesterday morning, he called me and told me he wanted to hate me, but he couldn't. I started to hope… But then he asked me to stop calling."

"Did you?" Kathryn asked.

"I did, but I deposited a 'tip' into his account with the service."

"How much?" Kathryn frowned like she knew he'd done something else idiotic. It was the same look she'd given him every time he fucked up as a kid.

"Sixty-five thousand dollars."

"Oh my God." Kathryn downed the rest of her drink.

"It's enough for his baking and pastry arts degree. That's why he's working as an escort, to earn money for school. He refused it, though. The woman who runs the service called me and explained that the tip was being refunded."

"Thorne…" Kathryn shook her head.

"I screwed up again, right?"

"Did you really think he was going to take your money after you insulted him?"

Thorne poured himself another drink, though he wanted to give up and just take a swig from the decanter. "I didn't mean to insult him. All I wanted was to take care of him."

She nodded. "Possibly he understands that, but his pride took a hit, and—" She gestured toward the half-empty bourbon bottle. "So did yours."

"My pride could handle it."

Kathryn raised her brows, obviously questioning his assessment.

"It hurts so bad. Losing someone." Not even losing Clint had made him this desperate to crawl under the covers and never come out.

She sighed. "Give him some time. Work on yourself."

"Me? What's the point?"

Kathryn narrowed her eyes. "If you can't answer that, there's no hope of getting him back."

"You're taking all this rather well. Your brother is gay. He hires prostitutes. He's an idiot."

"The last I knew. The first I suspected, and the second... Well, there are worse things, and it's not like you hired Dash off the street. I think a hell of a lot more men and women pay for it than we think."

Apparently, based on what had happened at the art opening. "Maybe they do. By work on myself, do you mean come out?"

"Possibly, but there are other things you could do, like find something you care about other than work and—" She frowned. "Sex."

Thorne held up his hand. "We are so not discussing that."

Kathryn smiled. "I won't say it again."

"You do realize I have clients who won't accept an openly gay consultant."

"Fuck 'em."

"Oh my God. Did you really just say that?"

"I did. Also, there's a difference between hiding and announcing you're gay to everyone you meet. Tell Lauren and the other senior partners and quit worrying what everyone else knows or thinks."

"Lauren probably knows. I brought Dash to the art opening. If she didn't know before that, I'm fairly certain she did afterward."

Kathryn nodded. "I bet she does, but knowing and being told are not the same. She deserves to be in your confidence, considering what she puts up with from you."

Thorne couldn't argue with that.

"Start there. When you're ready," Kathryn said.

"I'll think about it."

"That will have to do for now. That and getting off the couch, eating instead of drinking your meals, and generally acting like a grown-up with a job."

Thorne flipped her off.

***

Despite Kathryn's encouragement, Thorne barely got off the couch for the next two days, continuing the fiction that he was sick, and he was, just not with the flu or whatever people at work imagined. If it hadn't been for Kathryn bringing food by, he might not have eaten either. But on Thursday night, he realized he couldn't hide forever. Kathryn was right, damn her; if he was going to take time off—and he was—he had to do it like a grown-up.

He showed up at work on Friday morning, groomed, sober, well fed—he'd grabbed an egg-and-cheese wrap on the way to work in deference to Dash's insistence on the importance of breakfast. As soon as he'd made the decision the night before to start being a functioning adult again, he'd sent an e-mail calling a meeting of the senior partners. Then he'd stayed up until three working, which was easy since he'd done nothing but doze for days. First, he'd strategized how to delegate his workload for the next two weeks. Then he'd gotten online and rented a lakeside cabin in the Blue Ridge mountains. As soon as he wrapped up his meeting, he'd be looking into sailboat rentals. Hell, maybe he'd just buy one while he was up there.

Lauren rose from her desk as he approached. "Are you okay? What happened?"

He inclined his head toward his office door. "Let's talk in there."

Once inside, he shut the door and leaned against his desk.

Lauren studied him. "You weren't really sick, were you? What's going on?"

"Have a seat." His legs no longer wanted to hold him up, but he managed to circle his desk before crashing into his chair. He'd thought this part would be easy, but Lauren's opinion mattered more than he'd realized. Over the last several years, he'd come to rely on her more than anyone else in his life, even Kathryn. The thought of her looking at him in disgust made him ill. But she deserved to know, didn't she…?

"Are you okay?" she asked.

"I'm fine. Physically at least. Although if anyone asks, tell them I was hit with a serious case of food poisoning." He'd rather he had been.

"O-kaaay."

He couldn't keep her guessing any longer. "I'm assuming you've noticed that I've been different for a while now."

"You mean how you haven't e-mailed me ten times over the weekend or asked if I could come in at six a.m. to go over notes for a meeting? That sort of different?"

Had he really been that bad? "Yes, that."

"You've been looking more relaxed too, at least until today."

"I'd never expected to change like this. I'd never had anything in my life more important than this job, never let myself care about anything else until I couldn't help it." He paused and stared out the window.

"Wait. Are you trying to say you fell in love?"

He nodded, a short, sharp movement.

"With the young man you brought to the opening? The one you defended?"

He sagged back against his chair, relieved he didn't have to say it. "So you did know."

"That you were gay?"

He nodded.

"I wasn't sure if you were gay or bi, but I knew you weren't simply friends with that young man."

Thorne turned away, looking out the window. He forced himself to ignore the tightness of his chest and the burning behind his eyes. He had to keep it together. "Now we're not anything at all."

"Oh, I'm sorry." Her voice was low and soft, like she was unsure whether to speak at all.

"So am I. I need some time to…process. I'm taking two weeks off."

"T-two weeks? I don't think you've ever taken more than a day except when your mother was in the hospital."

"When my sister had her first baby, I took…two days."

"Yes, but you checked in every few minutes."

He had. "I'm ready to make some serious changes in my life."

"Does that include coming out?"

He nodded. "It does."

"So this early meeting with the senior partners…?"

"I'm going to tell them. I don't feel like I owe that to anyone here but you. However, if I'm going to stop hiding, word will get around. I'd rather tell them than deal with rumors."

Lauren nodded. "Good decision."

"Thank you. I'll leave shortly after the meeting and be back in the office two weeks from Monday. I've worked out the best way to divide my workload and rescheduled my trip to New York."

"I saw that when I got in this morning," Lauren said.

"I'll e-mail you everything else you need along with a number where I can be reached in an emergency. Kathryn will also be able to get in touch with me, but no one else."

"Where are you heading?"

"A lake near Bryson City, North Carolina. I'm going sailing."

Her eyes widened. "Sailing? Like on a sailboat?"

"Don't look so shocked. I used to own a boat."

She narrowed her eyes. "I'm struggling to imagine you doing something so…outdoorsy."

He wanted to be offended, but he couldn't. "I enjoy the water. I don't always wear suits, you know."

"I'd wondered."

Thorne gave her a mock glare.

She was undaunted. "I like this new you."

"Thank you. Maybe…well, hopefully this trip will be good for me."

Lauren smiled. "It will. I'm sure of it."

He finished his coffee and glanced at the time.

"You have a meeting to get to," Lauren said. "Should I join you?"

Thorne wanted to say yes, but if anything did turn ugly, he didn't want her there. "No, thank you. I'm going to do this alone."

Thorne had told himself the meeting would go smoothly. A few conservative clients were the ones he was worried about, the ones who might refuse to work with him. His senior partners already knew him well, they weren't going to care who he was fucking as long as he got it together and did his job. But as he opened the conference room door and faced them, he realized that was all bullshit. His mouth went dry, his pulse sped up, and he was sorry he'd eaten breakfast.

Five curious faces stared back at him as Thorne fought to hide his nerves. If only Dash were there to hold his hand. Before Thorne had screwed everything up, he would've come if Thorne had asked.

"So what's up?" Dan, the next most senior team member asked. He was always anxious for meetings to end so he could get moving.

"I need, uncharacteristically, to discuss a personal matter. I'm choosing to tell you rather than having you hear it through gossip and because there's the potential for it to"—How to phrase it?—"disturb clients." Dan was frowning. Sandra looked concerned. The others looked a combination of annoyed and curious. Why had he thought this was a good idea?

Just do it. "I'm gay."

The words hung in the air, thick and heavy.

Thorne started breathing again when Lisa smiled. "Thank you for telling us. I wish I could say it won't cause any issues. It's sad that you still have to be concerned." She glanced toward Dan as if expecting him to say something. He didn't look particularly surprised or concerned. In fact, his expression said he thought Thorne was wasting his time with such trivia.

"I know of a few clients who won't be thrilled, but I doubt most of them will care," Sandra said. She'd shown a touch of shock but no malice.

"I don't plan to announce my sexuality or anything about my personal life to clients, but they may find out anyway, especially those whom I see socially."

Sandra and Dan nodded.

Bob looked like he was working through a difficult puzzle. "How long… No, that's none of my business. But I just can't see it." He shook his head.

"It doesn't matter though. I mean, you don't work with your dick."

Bob had always had a way with words. How he managed to turn his filters on and win over clients, Thorne still didn't know. At least he was being supportive in his own way.

Jack stared at Thorne and then glanced around the room as if confused. When his gaze landed back on Thorne, he spoke. "This is a joke, right? It's like April Fool's Day or something and I forgot."

Thorne scowled. "I assure you I'm not joking."

"So I'm just supposed to be okay with this?"

"If by okay you mean continuing to work with me in the same way you have before, then yes."

"Wow, that's just…wow." Jack looked around the room again. "So I'm the only one who has a problem with Shipton being a…?" The word "fag" hovered in the air, though he didn't say it.

"Who the hell cares who he sleeps with?" Dan asked.

"Clients who don't want to work with a fucking fairy." So much for holding back on name-calling.

Jack grabbed his briefcase and stormed out.

Sandra stood as if ready to go after him, but Thorne held up his hand.

"Let him go. He'll either come to terms with who I am, or I'll give him a reference for another job. I'm not looking for approval. I'm giving information and expecting the same job from you that you were doing yesterday."

Dan nodded. "Not a problem for me."

"Me either," Bob said.

Thorne took a slow breath and tried to adjust to

what had happened. He'd never have guessed Jack would be the one to reject him. He'd been far more concerned about Bob or Dan. Bob had predictably been crude, but he didn't seem truly bothered. Dan was unfazed, supportive even. Maybe he didn't know his partners as well as he thought he did.

"One more announcement." He could feel the tension in the room. "I'm also going to be taking two weeks off—"

"Wait, what?" Now Lisa was shocked. "You? Time off?"

"Yes. Me. Time off."

"Well, this is a day of revelation." Bob rolled his chair over to the window and gazed out. "Hmm, no signs of the apocalypse yet."

Thorne gave a halfhearted laugh. "So far."

"You're truly not coming into the office for two entire weeks?" Sandra asked.

"Or e-mailing us about work?" Bob added.

"Or working at one a.m. on a Sunday?" Dan apparently needed to get in on this too.

"That's right. I will not be working for the next two weeks."

"Is this like a midlife crisis or something?" Bob asked.

"No. I've always been gay."

Bob rolled his eyes. "I meant the time off thing."

"Oh." Once again he'd misjudged, expecting to be challenged. "Possibly. It's time I made some changes."

Dan nodded. "I'm assuming you have assignments for us while you're gone."

Now that was normal. Dan wanting him to get to

the point. "I do."

He explained how they could handle the clients he'd been working with while he was gone. Fortunately, there weren't any projects needing a final briefing during the next two weeks. "Ask Lauren if you need anything. She knows how to get in touch with me if there's an emergency."

"Wait—" Lisa held up a hand. "Tell me you're not going to be out in the wilderness with no cell phone or internet. Because if you are, I'm going to stage an intervention." She looked truly horrified.

"Nothing quite that uncivilized, but I won't be taking my work phone." He tapped the phone he'd laid on the table.

"Are you sure you're all right?" Sandra asked.

"Very sure. More all right than I've been in a long time."

Bob frowned. "You don't look it." Ah yes, blunt as ever.

"Maybe I will in two weeks."

Dan, Bob, and Lisa packed up their things and left the room, but Sandra lingered. "What you just did was very brave. I'm assuming you're not making announcements to anyone else."

Thorne nodded. "That's right, but word will get around. I felt like I owed my top people this courtesy in case it does change things with clients."

"It sucks that there's even a chance of that."

It did. "I've got to be realistic."

She nodded. "Call me if you need anything or just someone to talk to."

Thorne shouldn't have been surprised by her concern, but he wasn't used to people wanting to take care of him. "Thank you. That means a lot. I don't show how much I appreciate you and the other partners nearly enough."

"If you started getting too complimentary, we'd be sure something was wrong."

He smiled. "I could do better, though."

"Maybe, but you're a good man. I think most of us know that." Thorne hadn't realized how much her approval mattered until she said that.

"Thank you." He barely got the words out with a steady voice.

Sandra smiled. "See you in two weeks."

He waved to her as she exited the room.

Chapter Nineteen

A week. A whole week had passed since Riley had walked out on Thorne, and he'd felt like he'd been asleep for most of it. Leaves were turning and beginning to fall off the trees. But instead of enjoying the brilliant colors like he usually did, Riley thought about how he felt as brittle and dead as the mass of brown leaves piling up on the ground.

He'd quit working for Sheila. How could he work for another client when all he thought about was Thorne? He couldn't imagine ever wanting anyone else, and he resented that. Resented that he couldn't stop loving Thorne when he wanted to hate him. But his earnings in the months he worked for Thorne had added so much to his bank account that he could start school in January if he was careful about money until then. He'd cook with Susan, and that would be enough.

He was much more worried about his emotional state than his financial one. He'd heal eventually, wouldn't he?

Susan assured him he would. She'd been incredibly supportive, but he'd grown tired of her bashing Thorne. Yes, Thorne had been an ass, an idiot. But had Thorne truly meant to hurt him? After days of reflection, Riley didn't think so. Of course, that didn't mean Thorne was in love with him. But what if…

No. If he let himself run with those thoughts, he'd call Thorne. And then he'd be right back where he'd been before—in love with a man who only appreciated what Riley could do for him. Or at least, Thorne wouldn't admit to more. That was not what Riley needed.

Calling Thorne was a terrible idea, but he needed to call Marc. He'd been avoiding his friend because he knew he'd have a breakdown if he started talking about Thorne. He'd sobbed all over Susan and then eaten three quarters of a devil's food cake the day Thorne had made his business proposition. Marc had warned him. And he wouldn't hesitate to point that out; that was just how Marc was. And as much as Riley was tired of Susan insisting that Thorne was, if not Satan himself, his top minion, he also wasn't ready for Marc to remind him that there was fault on both sides. Marc would see right through him. Riley still believed Thorne was more at fault, but he could have handled things differently himself.

His phone buzzed, interrupting his nightly pity party. Marc's smiling face showed on the screen. Speak of the devil. Marc had called twice the day before. Both times he'd left a message asking Riley to call him back. The second time he'd sounded uncharacteristically upset. Was he worried that he hadn't heard from Riley in so long?

He accepted the call. "Hey, Marc."

"Where the fuck have you been?"

"I—"

"Never mind. I'm coming home. My overnight flight leaves in three hours, and I'm hoping you'll pick me up."

Marc's despondent tone told Riley he wasn't just coming for a spontaneous visit. "How long will you be here?"

"I'm moving back."

Apparently the last week hadn't gone any better for Marc than it had for him. "Oh, fuck."

"Yeah, he ended it. I was counting on making it through the holidays at least. January is a good time to be alone, shivering in a blanket, drinking cocoa, and having movie marathons. Fall is a time for dating."

That was so Marc. "Do you need a place to stay?"

"Yes, I was hoping—"

"Please move back in. I could use the help with rent. Thorne asked me to *work* for him full time. I stormed out, quit Sheila's, and I've basically been hiding for the past week."

"Wow, we'll make cheerful companions, won't we?"

"What's your airline and flight number?" Riley asked.

Marc gave him the info.

"I'll be there."

Marc moved back in with Riley the next day, and they spent several weeks drinking, crying, watching sad movies, and generally hiding from the world.

***

THORNE'S TWO WEEKS of vacation were a mix of grieving, restless energy, and sailing. Once Thorne got over thinking constantly of the last time he'd been in a boat—and the things Dash had done to him on that tiny island—he managed to relax and take in the cool air, the breeze, the freedom he felt. He was on the water for hours every day except the few when rain poured down. He spent those days feeling sorry for himself and jerking off to thoughts of Dash.

By the time he returned to work, he was far from healed, but he no longer thought the weight of his need for Dash would crush him. Jack told Thorne he was "considering other options," but he managed to keep his personal issues out of the office. Thorne got a few stares from junior partners and assistants, but for the most part things were just like they'd always been. But Thorne wasn't; he would never be the same.

On Friday morning, nearly six weeks after Dash had walked out the door, Thorne hit snooze on the alarm and rolled over. Fridays were the worst. He hadn't been sober on a Friday night yet. He also hadn't eaten a pancake, or cake of any sort, and he didn't know if he'd ever go to Bavaria Haus again. Fuck, when would this get easier? When would he be okay again?

Never.

At least most of the changes Dash had wrought in his life were good. The rest... He'd just have to keep praying that would pass. Maybe...no, he wasn't ready for that, or was he?

Would getting laid exorcise his Friday demons? He hadn't wanted any man but Dash in months, but he couldn't stay celibate forever. He could go to the sort of club where sexual need hung in the air, where there was no doubt what everyone was there for. Maybe he could at least forget the ache he still felt every day for a few hot, sweaty moments.

He dragged himself out of bed and dressed for work, not yet decided about what the night would entail. He picked up coffee from a cart. Then, as he passed the door of a restaurant, the sweet smell of pancakes and syrup hit him, and his stomach clenched. He tossed his coffee in the trash. He'd regret that later when a caffeine headache rendered him useless, but he couldn't possibly swallow anything right then. The smell of pancakes had made him sick ever since that horrible morning five weeks and six days ago.

He'd managed to push himself through work each day, robotically going through the motions but lacking the spark that had once made him a great consultant. He'd gone sailing almost every Saturday, and the time on the water was the highlight of the week, though it would have been so much better with Dash at his side. He pretended he was happy, hoping that eventually he'd convince himself of it. But as soon as he smelled chocolate or heard a voice that reminded him of Dash, or saw a young man with blond curly hair, all the pain came back. Thinking of Dash still had the weight to crush him. His sister and Lauren had both made suggestions for things that might take his mind off Dash. But those were, at best, temporary fixes. He began working longer hours again, because even relaxing reminded him of Dash.

He'd watched *Say Anything* about twenty times since Dash left, and he'd cried every fucking time. He'd also watched *The Breakfast Club* and *Sixteen Candles* and *Some Kind of Wonderful*. He was turning into a fucking sap. That was going to end tonight. He would find a man and fuck him until he begged for mercy. Hell, maybe he'd even try a threesome.

Chapter Twenty

Almost six weeks post-Thorne, on a Friday afternoon, Riley entered his apartment covered in flour. He'd been making tarts with Susan and all he wanted now was to take a shower and spend the night watching sad movies and moping, same as every Friday night since his non-relationship with Thorne had ended.

Marc looked up from his tablet and announced, "We're going out tonight."

"What? No, I'm not ready."

"You're never going to feel ready, but we've cried enough. It's time to get out there and fuck those assholes out of our systems."

That was how Marc had always handled breakups, and unlike Riley, he'd had his share. The fact that it had been weeks since he'd been with another man showed Riley just how much Marc had felt for Hamilton, the son of a bitch who'd lured him to California so he'd have a convenient lay, not to mention a housekeeper, until he found someone out there. Hamilton made Thorne look like a saint, a mixed-up, closeted, arrogant, privileged saint, but still.

"I don't *want* to fuck anyone," Riley confessed, sounding far whinier than he'd meant to.

Marc arched a brow.

How did Marc always know exactly what he was

thinking? "Fine. I don't want to fuck anyone but Thorne."

"Are you going to be celibate for the rest of your life?"

Riley glared at him.

"Either call him or come out with me."

Riley frowned. "Call him? You actually think I should?"

"You're the one who said—"

Riley didn't let him finish. "No, I'm not calling him."

"Then how long are you going to wait to get back out there?"

Riley sighed. Marc was right. He needed to at least try to see if anyone else appealed to him. He'd never know if he stayed home.

"All right. I'll go. I don't promise to do anything but window-shop, but you're right. I need to get out of the house."

"Enough tequila and you'll be raring to go with some young stud."

Any man he hooked up with would have to be young, since he immediately compared all older men to Thorne. "Enough tequila and I'll be on the floor with a limp dick."

"Bullshit, you've never been unable to get it up."

True. Alcohol rarely affected him that way. But no way was he drinking while Marc was on the prowl, because if he got drunk and Marc wasn't there to stop him, Riley just might give in to the urge to call Thorne.

***

THORNE FLIPPED THROUGH the clothes in

his closet, frowning at everything he saw. He could wear something that made him look like he was trying to appear ten—if not twenty—years younger. Or, he could wear something that screamed sugar daddy. Maybe his lack of appropriate clothing was a sign that going to a club at his age was a terrible idea, but he chose to ignore it. Eventually, he settled on a black turtleneck sweater and some dark jeans that were tight enough to show off his ass but not so tight they looked obscene.

When the car service pulled up to the club he'd chosen, the driver looked at him curiously. "You're sure this is the place?"

"I'm sure."

"Okay, then. What time should I be back?"

"I'll call."

"Yes, sir."

Music from the club vibrated in Thorne's chest even from the curb. He was truly too old for this.

Don't turn back now. You can't put this off forever.

He wouldn't put off sex forever, but he didn't have to prowl around a club, looking for an anonymous fuck. He was out of the closet now. Shouldn't he be looking for something a little less dark and suspicious?

He frowned at the surroundings once he was inside, even more certain he'd made a mistake. It didn't look like it had been cleaned in weeks. The barstool he chose was sticky on the side. He did not want to think about that. There was a small, artificial Christmas tree behind the bar. Now that it was right in front of him, he realized it was covered in penis lights. Yep, this was definitely a mistake.

But Thorne's need to finish anything he started forced him to stay where he was and order a bourbon on the rocks. It was an old man's drink, but he sure as hell wasn't going to drink some of the cocktails he saw in the hands of the younger men. They looked like they were radioactive.

Thorne took a sip of his reliable drink and scanned the crowd. Most of the men looked Dash's age or even younger. No doubt many of them probably were there on false IDs. Several of them had bodies that were true works of art. Before he'd met Dash, he would have been more than happy to take one of them home, but now all he did was compare them. Not a single one measured up. Apparently, Dash hadn't been kidding when he'd promised to ruin Thorne for other men. If he knew how well he'd done his job, Dash would have a good laugh at his perfect revenge.

"Hi, Daddy, you looking for a boy?" A skinny redhead in leather pants slithered onto the stool next to Thorne, moving in a way that made him appear boneless. He also appeared to be about eighteen.

Thorne shook his head. "I'm not the man you're looking for."

"You could be. You want a sample?"

"No thank y—" He froze mid-sentence. Marc and Dash had just walked in the door. It had never occurred to him that he'd see Dash there. And what the hell was Marc doing back in town? He should go before one of them noticed him. But he was paralyzed, unable to stop watching Dash.

"You with them?" Skinny Boy asked, following

his stare. "They're fucking hot."

"No, but I'd like to be, with one of them, anyway." Why the hell had Thorne told a stranger that?

"Good luck." The boy oozed back off the stool and sauntered off.

Thorne watched Marc and Dash approach the bar.

Leave. Turn around.

But he was too late.

Marc sat on the recently vacated stool next to him, while Dash remained standing. "I never expected to see you slumming it here," Marc said.

Thorne glanced at Dash. His eyes were wide, and he held himself as though ready to flee.

"I've never been here before, thought I'd give it a try." Thorne wasn't sure how he forced the words out. Having Dash so close made it hard to breathe, much less speak.

"Not paying for it these days?" Marc asked.

"No, I decided that wasn't working out for me." He looked at Dash as he spoke, and Dash pretended to see right through him.

"I see." Marc turned to Dash. "Can I get you a drink?"

"Yeah. Anything that's fucking strong."

"You got it." Marc headed to the far end of the bar, a better spot to catch the bartender's attention.

After Marc departed, Thorne inclined his head toward the empty stool beside him. With obvious reluctance, Dash sat down.

"I'm sorry," Thorne said, not knowing what else to do.

He thought Dash might pretend he couldn't hear. Instead, he gave Thorne a curt nod.

Say something. "Do you want to dance?"

"No."

That had been stupid. "Dash, I never meant—"

"To hurt me. To insult me. I want to believe that, but even if I do, I can't see you again. I just fucking can't…" He walked away into the crowd.

Marc returned holding two bright-green drinks. "Where's Riley?"

Thorne motioned toward the dance floor where Dash was now sandwiched between a beautiful man with dark skin and dreadlocks and the twink who'd hit on Thorne.

"You hurt him," Marc said, settling on the stool next to Thorne.

"I know."

"You still want him?"

Thorne nodded, unable to deny it.

"Then don't give up."

Marc walked away before Thorne could ask him what he meant by that. Thorne had seen pain in Dash's eyes. Marc might think he knew what he was talking about, but Thorne didn't see Dash forgiving him anytime soon, not before it was too late. It wouldn't take Dash long to meet someone more suited to him than Thorne.

Thorne drained his bourbon, tossed some money on the bar, and walked out, alone. Was that how he would live the rest of his life? Alone? Maybe that was what he deserved.

***

Thorne came out to his parents at Thanksgiving,

or as his mother saw it, he "ruined" Thanksgiving. From his perspective, it was one of the best family holidays ever.

The next day, Friday, he phoned Sheila and scheduled a companion for the night. He was going to conquer his obsession with Dash.

Lachlan, the dark-haired man who showed up at his door, was beautiful. Thorne invited him in for coffee, and they talked. He found out Lachlan was majoring in business, and they had a lovely discussion about management techniques. Then Thorne paid him, sent him on his way, and jacked off to memories of Dash, once in bed and once in the shower.

***

Two weeks after Thanksgiving, Thorne donned his tux and prepared to attend the Arts Council's holiday party. Memories of Dash in the tux Thorne had bought assaulted him. He'd been gorgeous, perfect. And yet Thorne had forced him to pretend to be Thorne's friend, not his lover. If he could do that over, if he could have Dash at his side now...

He slammed the mirrored door of his closet and turned away. He didn't want to do this. The party was at the art museum, and he'd think of nothing but that final night with Dash. He couldn't cancel though. Peggy had asked him to say a few words to the other donors. And Kathryn would be there. They'd been spending a lot more time together, and he'd managed to convince her to do some work for the membership committee. She would help him get through the night.

Thorne glanced at the clock. Time to go. When he got to the lobby, he remembered that he hadn't checked his mail the night before. There was a card in his box. The envelope was red, making him think it was a holiday card, but it had no return address. He was about to stash it in his jacket pocket when something made him change his mind and open it. On the front was a picture of three camels crossing the desert, presumably carrying the three wise men. Inside, there was a holiday message, but he ignored it and read the words written in an angular scrawl. "End his dry spell before Susan or I kill him. He deserves a Merry Christmas." It was signed Marc.

Thorne's heart pounded so hard he feared he might keel over. There was no question who "he" was. Holy fuck! Marc was telling Thorne to go after Dash. But it had been less than a month since he'd seen Dash at the club, and Dash had said he couldn't be around Thorne.

His eyes said something different.

No. Thorne was going to respect what he said. He tore the card and threw it in the trashcan by the lobby doors. The little pieces fluttered, some catching on the rim. Thorne immediately began to reconsider. Dry spell? Did that truly mean Dash hadn't been with anyone else? He'd assumed Dash had taken someone home from the club the night they saw each other, that he'd been hooking up routinely. If he hadn't, then was he hurting too? Could they heal each other?

***

Christmas piano music filled the reception hall with its tinkly joy. Smiling, glittering people moved around one another, talking animatedly. But Thorne sat by himself. He'd talked no more that evening than social obligation dictated. More than once he'd been asked if he was feeling okay. After dismissing Peggy's concerns with a flippant answer about possibly coming down with something, he'd given his speech, hoping it didn't sound as flat as he felt. Then he'd wandered the room, halfheartedly looking for Kathryn in the crowd. When he couldn't locate her, he settled on a bench near the spot where he and Dash had stood after he'd punched the shit out of Collins; that had felt so good. The painting Dash had picked out had arrived a few days after he'd left, and it still sat in Thorne's guest room, wrapped up, waiting.

I want him back.

The thought startled Thorne, not the sentiment—he'd wanted Dash back since the moment he'd walked out the door—but the fact that for the first time, he considered actually fighting for him.

Kathryn found him a few moments later. He patted the space beside him, and she sat. "Are you okay?"

"Yes. No. If you had to win Derek back, what would you do?"

"Win him back?"

Thorne's mind was moving too fast to stop for a long explanation. "Just say, God forbid, something happened and you split up."

"Are you finally ready to fight for Dash?"

"Maybe. Yes."

"Hmm." Kathryn pondered the question. "I'd recreate some important memory, like our first date or the trip we took on our tenth anniversary."

"We didn't have a first date or really any dates but…special moments. We had plenty of those." Thorne thought about the time he'd spent with Dash.

It was only a few months, but it felt like so much longer. Sailing together. That had been special. "It's too cold to go sailing," he mused.

Kathryn nodded in agreement.

They hadn't been out that many times. They'd spent much more time inside, lying around, watching movies.

Suddenly, he knew exactly what he should do. *Please let this work.*

Chapter Twenty-One

Marc gave Riley a confused look. "Is that…"

"Peter Gabriel," Riley and Marc said in unison.

They raced to the window, and Marc jerked the cord to raise the blinds, tangling them as they rushed upward.

Thorne stood beside his sleek Mercedes, wearing a dark suit and a beard that looked damn good on him. He was also holding his phone and Bluetooth speakers in the air, blasting "In Your Eyes" louder than speakers that small should go. Of course he'd have the best tech.

Why am I thinking about tech? My former lover—former client—is re-enacting Say Anything *in front of my apartment.*

"Oh my fucking God!" Marc said, never taking his eyes from Thorne.

"I…" Riley couldn't speak. He could hardly breathe. His heart was pounding, and it felt like it was in his throat.

"Dude, you've got to go down there."

"I…"

Marc waved at Thorne and then grabbed Riley by the arm and dragged him toward the door. "Go down there and talk to him right now."

Riley's feet wouldn't work. "I can't."

"Yes. You can. I don't care if you tell him it's over for good, but you've got to say something. If nothing else, the guy has balls."

The swirl of confusing thoughts in his head dizzied Riley. "We watched it together. He'd never seen it even though he was in high school when it came out, and he never… I'm babbling."

"Go!" Marc practically shoved him down the stairs.

Riley caught himself against the wall and kept moving. By the time he reached the bottom of the stairs he was running.

Thorne turned when he saw him, the music continued to play, but he set the speakers on the roof of his car.

"Wh-what are you doing?"

Thorne raised a brow, that damn sardonic look he was so good at. "I did hope you would remember."

Riley gestured toward the speakers. "Of course I remember. But why?"

"Why do you think? Because I made a terrible mistake, and I needed to get your attention so I could apologize and see if…" He took a slow breath, and Riley watched his chest rise and fall. "If there is truly no chance, or if there's some amount of hope left for us."

"Us?"

"Yes, us; you and me. I was a fool, and I hurt you. I know you may never be able to forgive me, but I'm here to say what I should have said back then. I don't want to be a client to you. I want to be so much more."

"Are you sure? Because two months ago it sounded like you just wanted to own me."

Thorne winced and glanced around. They'd

acquired quite a collection of onlookers. He tapped his phone, silencing the music. "Could we take this inside?"

"In the lobby at least," Riley said, not yet sure he wanted Thorne in his home. And even more uncertain whether he wanted Thorne in his life.

"I never wanted to own you," Thorne said as the door closed behind them.

Riley raised his brows.

"I can be an arrogant son of a bitch. That's true enough, and yes, I like getting my way. But what I really wanted was to spend every day with you. To wake up with you. To know you weren't sleeping with anyone else. To know that when you looked at me like you cared, like it was more than a job, that look was sincere."

Riley frowned. "Of course it was sincere. How the fuck could you doubt that?"

"Because I was scared. Scared if I asked for more than a business arrangement, you would walk away and I'd never see you again. I couldn't fathom why you would want to be in a relationship with me."

"What?" Riley couldn't believe what he was hearing. "You thought I didn't want you?"

"I thought you wouldn't want to date me. We have a few differences you know, like twenty years of them."

"I don't give a fuck about that," Riley snapped.

"You don't?"

"No, but I sure as hell never thought you'd want an actual relationship with *me*, a kid, a prostitute."

Thorne shook his head. "I never thought of you as—"

"You tried to make me a full-time employee, one whose job was to fuck you."

"And cook for me."

"God, Thorne, do you hear yourself?"

He held up a hand. "I'm sorry. It was a solution I could offer that would let me see you every day. I thought it was the best option to get what I wanted."

So typical of Thorne, maneuvering to get what he wanted. "What about what I wanted?"

"It doesn't matter what I say. You aren't going to believe I was thinking of you, of the best way for you to make money for school, to have a job while you were still in school that didn't involve working nights or seeing assholes like Collins."

"Fuck Collins. I can handle myself, Thorne. I don't need a sugar daddy." Had Thorne always been this fucking infuriating?

"I wanted to offer you some security."

"You wanted me to warm your bed," Riley countered.

"I did, but it was because…because I…"

The panicked look on Thorne's face made Riley feel a little bit sorry for him. "You still can't say it, can you?"

"No, I'm still scared, but…" Thorne stroked his well-trimmed beard. "This isn't the only change I've made."

"Really?" Why did that surprise Riley more than anything else that had happened so far that night? Maybe because Thorne only did things his way.

"If you'd have dinner with me, or lunch—lunch is a nice, neutral, nondate-like meal—I'll tell you. No pressure, no expectations. Just talking."

"You mean this, don't you? You really wanted us to be together for more than just sex."

Thorne nodded. "I wanted you any way I could have you, but the best case scenario was that you would be my partner, that you would be with me because it was what you wanted rather than a job."

"Why didn't you say that?"

"I thought you'd laugh at me."

Was he fucking kidding? "How could you not see how I felt about you? Every time I came to see you, I worried about how transparent I was. I might as well have put on a sign that said: I've fallen in love. I'm fragile. I'm dying inside because I want you and I can't have you. Then I thought you were going to suggest exactly what I'd been hoping, that we drop the client/escort relationship and actually go out. When you asked me to work for you, it was like being punched."

Thorne looked ill, his face pale, his eyes dull. "My God, Dash. I thought the same thing. That you'd see through me, that you'd realize I'd started thinking of you as my lover. I wish I could go back and redo everything. I was an arrogant ass, but I was desperate. I couldn't stand the thought of you with other clients. It was selfish and stupid, okay? You've always enjoyed me admitting I was wrong. Well, you've been right about everything."

Riley shook his head. "No, not even close."

Thorne frowned. "What do you mean?"

"I should've told you how I felt. I almost did so many times. I wanted to keep seeing you, but as a lover, not as a client. I could never work up the courage to say it, though, because I didn't think

251

someone so successful, so—not old—but so far down the road from where I was, could ever want me on my own terms."

Thorne ran a hand over his hair. He glanced away and then back. "I did want you. I…do. I want anything you're willing to give."

"So you would've said yes if I'd asked?"

Thorne nodded.

"But you said you hadn't been on a date in years, that you thought sex was much better when it was paid for."

Thorne groaned and leaned against the wall as if unable to hold himself up anymore. "I didn't know you then. I couldn't imagine a man worth the upheaval in my life, but you are that man. I know it might be too late. If so, just tell me, and I won't bother you again. But if there's any chance…"

Riley stared into Thorne's eyes; there was pain there, but also hope, and it was infectious. "I…yeah, there's a chance."

"Where do we go from here? Your call." Thorne's soft smile lit up the shadowy entryway.

"You're not planning to keep serenading me every night?" Riley asked, finally letting himself smile too.

Thorne laughed. "No, that was a one-time thing. I'm sure I looked quite ridiculous."

Riley shook his head. "You looked romantic and forlorn. I don't think anything else would've gotten me to listen to you. But the fact that you remembered…" Riley had to stop speaking when his voice broke. He took a breath, trying to recover his cool. "That was brave of you and…" He smiled. "Just fucking awesome."

"Thanks." Thorne was actually blushing, and it looked damn good on him. "So, lunch?"

"Yes, when?" Riley asked.

"Soon, but maybe not tomorrow."

Riley frowned. "Why not?"

"It's Friday. We need a new pattern."

Riley grinned. "I wouldn't have taken you for the superstitious type."

"I was hurt too, Dash, even if it was my fault. I haven't been sober on a Friday in a long time."

Riley was stunned and slightly gratified.

Thorne continued. "I'm spending the weekend at the lake with my sister and her family so—"

"You're what?" Riley couldn't have heard that right.

"I told you I'd made changes. So what about Monday at noon?"

Riley didn't have to stop and consider. He had to find out if there was still a chance for them. "Yes."

"I'll send a car to pick you up."

Riley shook his head. "I'll meet you. Just tell me where."

"There's an Italian place, Molto Bella, down the street from my office."

"Is this your kind of place? Should I wear a suit?"

Thorne smiled. "No. It's unpretentious but excellent."

"I'll be there."

Riley studied Thorne for a few moments, allowing himself to truly take in the sight of him now that they were potentially moving forward. "You look good. I like this." He reached up and stroked Thorne's beard, but as soon as he felt the rasp of hair, he pulled his hand back, realizing he shouldn't be touching Thorne.

"I don't mind," Thorne said.

"It's not fair to you, though. I can't tease you when I don't know what I want."

Thorne smiled. "I know what I want."

There was the Thorne he remembered. "Thank you for telling me, for showing up here. I was too chicken to call you."

Thorne's eyes widened. "You wanted to call me?"

"Every fucking day."

The emotion in Thorne's eyes was strong enough to knock Riley over.

Thorne turned to go to his car. One slow step. Then another. Then another.

Riley didn't want him to leave, not yet. "Thorne?"

"Yes?" He stopped but didn't turn around.

"There's a twenty-four-hour doughnut place down the street. They actually have really good coffee. Would you—?"

He spun to face Riley. "Yes!"

"Okay, let me just tell Marc. I'll be right back."

THORNE LET DASH pay for their coffee and doughnuts though it wasn't an easy concession. He'd gone with Dash's recommendation of a cinnamon cake doughnut, but he wasn't sure he could actually eat. What if he said the wrong thing? This might well be his last chance with Dash.

Dash gestured toward a corner booth, and Thorne headed in that direction. Once they were seated, an awkward silence settled over them. The walk to the shop had been short, and traffic made the street loud even at that time of night, so they hadn't really had to talk until now. Obviously, neither of them knew what to say.

After staring at his coffee for far too long, Thorne blurted out. "I came out at work."

Dash looked up, his eyes wide. "You did?"

"I did. And I told my family too."

Dash whistled. "How'd that go?"

Thorne smiled at the memory, no point in letting it get him down. "Yeah, it was a fun Thanksgiving."

Dash's mouth dropped open. "You told them at Thanksgiving?"

"Yes. I'm an ass, aren't I?"

Dash snorted. "That's hardly news."

"Do you want to hear the story?"

"If you… Yes." Dash nodded.

"I told my sister first. Right after you…after we… She wasn't surprised. My parents on the other hand… I told them at Thanksgiving, because I'm an asshole. Dad stomped out. Mom had a fit. But I got through it. I also took two weeks off."

"Two whole weeks?"

Thorne laughed. "Yes, the senior partners were equally shocked."

"Did you go sailing?"

He nodded.

"Did you buy a boat?"

"No. I…" *Wanted to wait for you.* "Might get one in the spring."

"I've made changes too," Dash said. "I quit my job."

"Really? I… I'm sorry if I…" As much as Thorne had wanted him to quit, he didn't want to be responsible for Dash being unemployed.

"No. It was time. I've got enough saved."

He'd have more if he'd taken the money Thorne wanted to give him. "Dash, are you sure… I—"

"Do not bring up the money you tried to give me. That was… What made you think that was okay?"

"You deserve to go to school, and I wanted to help."

Dash lowered his head into his hands and ruffled his hair. "You don't get it, do you?"

Thorne hadn't until Kathryn had talked to him. "I insulted you."

"I'm not working for you, and I'm not taking your 'gift.'" Thorne heard the sarcastic air quotes.

"What if I said it was a scholarship?"

"Thorne." He was pushing it, and he had to stop.

"Fine; I felt terrible after you left; guilty, stupid, ashamed. I wanted to make it better, but I ended up doing something stupid again. I get that, but I just wanted you to be able to follow your dream without having to work anymore."

"You didn't want me to see any other clients, even if I was no longer seeing you."

Heat rushed to Thorne's face. He wasn't going to deny it. "Yes, that too."

Dash's expression softened. "I didn't want to see any more clients. The job had been fun, but it wasn't anymore unless I was with you."

"Could we start over? Try dating? I can go

slow."

Dash closed his eyes. And Thorne measured off the seconds by tapping his fingers against the cup he'd yet to take a sip from. Neither of them had touched their doughnuts.

"I want to say yes, but I'm…"

"Scared? Because I am too. But I'm just as scared not to try, because I can't stop thinking about you. You changed me. I eat breakfast now, and I never work on Saturday afternoons, and—"

Dash laughed. "I think about you all the time too. I watch a movie and think whether you'd like it. I see paintings and wonder if you'd enjoy them."

"Just have lunch with me, like we agreed. No pressure, just talking, friendship."

Dash frowned. "Is that all you want?"

"No. It's far from all I want. Because what I want is…everything. But it's a beginning."

Dash chewed his lower lip. Thorne's cock responded to the sight of Dash's tongue. Could he go slow? Yes, he had to. Anticipation was sweet, right?

Dash raised his coffee cup. "To beginnings." They tapped their cups together, laughing. It felt good to laugh with Dash again.

"Now try your doughnut," Dash encouraged.

Thorne picked up the pastry, but Dash shook his head. "Not like that. You've got to dunk it in the coffee. They were made for each other."

Thorne looked around in case his mother or the manners police were watching. He'd already made a fool of himself in front of Dash's neighbors. Why was he worried about a little doughnut dunking?

"Mmm," he said as he bit into the now coffee-flavored pastry. "You have great taste."

Dash looked him up and down, seeming to relax for the first time since they'd sat down. "Yeah, maybe I do."

The quirk of his lips—God, how Thorne had always loved that smug little smile—made Thorne's pulse accelerate and warmth spread through his chest. He wanted Dash, needed him. *Please let me say the right things this time.*

They finished their doughnuts and coffee and walked back to Dash's apartment. Halfway there, Dash reached for Thorne's hand and intertwined their fingers. It was the first time Thorne had ever walked down the street holding hands with a man. He glanced around, wondering if they'd be noticed.

"It's fine here. Trust me."

Thorne nodded.

When they got to Dash's building, Dash didn't stop at Thorne's car, so Thorne followed him into the lobby. As soon as he was through the door, Dash pushed him up against the wall of mailboxes.

Thorne stared into Dash's eyes, not daring to breathe. Lust blazed there, and Thorne had to force himself to swallow.

Dash leaned in until his mouth was by Thorne's ear. "Tell me there hasn't been anyone since me. Lie to me if you need to."

Thorne laughed, a deep sound of happiness. "I don't have to lie. No one measures up to you."

"Damn right they don't. Did you jerk off thinking of me? Because I thought of you, of your ass ready for my cock."

"Fuck, Dash, I thought we were taking things

slow."

Dash laughed. "We are."

It didn't feel slow to Thorne as Dash kissed him, his hard cock pressed against Thorne's hip. But a few seconds later, Dash pulled back and released him. "Are you going to call me Riley, now?"

"You said—"

"Things are different now, I want to be real with you, to be myself. Dash is me too, though, a wilder, more confident side of me."

"I want to know all of you, Dash, Riley, and any other parts of you hiding in there." They both laughed, nerves coming out as mirth. Then Thorne drew in a slow breath, choosing his words carefully. "I've spent so long trying *not* to call you Riley I'm not sure if I can, but if that's what you want, I'll try."

"I… I don't know what I want. Let's see what feels right, but if you want to call me Riley, I won't… It's okay."

Thorne nodded, afraid his voice would shake if he spoke.

"Lunch. Monday," Dash said.

"Yes."

"Go home now, Thorne." The implication was that Dash—*Riley*—was going to fuck him in the lobby if he didn't.

A bit of exhibitionism didn't sound so bad right then, but Thorne forced himself to put one foot in front of the other.

Chapter Twenty-Two

Lunch at Molto Bella was delicious. Riley had forgotten just how much he loved eggplant parmesan. And garlic rolls. God, the garlic rolls were heavenly. But the company was even better. He and Thorne talked about the positive things they'd done in the last couple of months, keeping the conversation light, letting it flow. Riley shared that he was signed up for school in January and Susan was considering opening her own bakery. Thorne said he hoped to land a new client in the next few weeks. What they didn't mention was Christmas. It would be here in less than two weeks. Did Riley want to spend it with Thorne?

When the waitress brought the check, Riley realized they'd been there for over an hour and Thorne hadn't mentioned any need to get back to work. Would wonders never cease?

"I'll get this," Riley said, trying to grab the check before Thorne did.

"We'll split it."

Riley noticed the tension in Thorne's jaw. He hated not paying for both of them, but Riley needed them on equal ground even if Thorne could have bought everything on the menu and never noticed the expense.

After they paid, they exited the restaurant together and walked toward Thorne's office. The atmosphere was more awkward than it had been the night before, possibly because it felt like they were both holding their breaths, unsure where to go from there. Riley shivered as cold wind seemed to cut right through his coat. His phone buzzed in his pocket as he neared the spot where he would have to let Thorne go with so many things still unsaid. He pulled it out and saw a text from Marc. *Lunch over? Needing a Rudolph fix? Bring your man.*

As much as Riley loved the idea of curling up on the couch watching *Rudolph*—or any Christmas special for that matter—with Thorne, he knew Thorne had to get back to work. He also knew Marc had ulterior motives. Since the *Say Anything* evening, he was all for Thorne and Riley getting back together.

Riley shoved the phone back in his pocket. They were across the street from Thorne's office now. He only had a few seconds to decide what to do.

"So, do we keep going slow?" Thorne asked.

Was that what Riley wanted? No, he wanted to shove Thorne up against the tree behind him and take him rough and hard, but that was clearly out of the question. "That's probably best."

Thorne nodded. He glanced around as if checking out the environment. "I would kiss you good-bye but…" He shrugged and leaned in to give Riley a quick brush of his lips across his cheek. Riley moaned as Thorne pulled back, needing more.

At that moment, he realized snow had begun to fall, tiny flakes that glittered in the weak sunshine. "It's snowing."

Thorne smiled. "I didn't believe it would."

December snow was rare in Atlanta. Riley had a crazy thought that it was a sign. "I know you're supposed to be at work, but do you want to come back to my apartment and watch *Rudolph*?"

Thorne frowned. "The Christmas special or does that imply something kinky I'm not aware of?"

He laughed. "No. Marc and I are suckers for Christmas shows. He asked if I wanted to watch one this afternoon and, well…"

Thorne pulled his phone from his pocket and held up a finger, silently asking Riley to wait. He tapped the screen and brought it to his ear. "Lauren, please cancel my meetings for the afternoon…Yes, I know he'll be pissed. Send Jack."

Riley continued to listen to the one-sided conversation.

"Right, that's a terrible idea. Send Sandra…Something vital's come up…No, I'm fine…Really, very fine…I'll stop by around five, so you can brief me on anything then. Don't disturb me for the next few hours unless the building is burning down."

Riley stared at him when he ended the call. Had he really just cancelled an afternoon of meetings?

"I didn't think you'd say yes."

"For you, I'll always say yes. You're the one who taught me that some things matter more than business. A lot of things, actually, but people I care about in particular."

Riley smiled. "Come on, let's go."

MARC HAD THE DVD cued up when they arrived. "Hey, Thorne."

"Hello, Marc." Thorne's voice was formal, reserved. How did Thorne feel about Marc being there? Was he wondering if Marc and Riley… But Riley had sworn there'd been no one, and Thorne wouldn't doubt him, would he?

Riley and Thorne settled on the couch, and Marc sprawled in a comfy chair, legs flung over one of the arms. He spent as much time watching them as he did the TV. And the look on his face said he thought they were the cutest fucking thing he'd ever seen.

Riley finally threw a pillow at him. "Pay attention. Hermey's about to do his pig impression. It's your favorite part."

Thorne laughed. "His acting skills are unparalleled."

Marc's mouth fell open, and Riley turned to Thorne.

Thorne arched a brow. "Did you seriously think I never watched this?"

"I figured you'd seen it as a kid, but not that you'd have a favorite part."

Thorne shrugged. "I like Christmas."

"You like working," Marc said.

Thorne smiled and glanced at Riley. "Not as much now."

Riley wrapped an arm around Thorne and snuggled closer. Thorne sighed, relaxing against him. Riley knew then that he wasn't going to let Thorne go. He assumed Thorne would spend Christmas Day with his family, and Riley had promised to have dinner at Susan's on Christmas Eve, but he wanted to spend at least part of the holiday with Thorne, watching cartoons, eating too much and… Could he really wait five more days to be inside Thorne again?

Yes, because he wasn't going to rush things. He

needed Thorne, but that need was deeper than lust, deeper than anything he'd felt before. Thorne had screwed up, but Riley still loved him. It was the season of forgiveness, and he was ready.

The end credits rolled, and Riley turned off the TV. Thorne lifted his head from Riley's shoulder and smiled at him. Riley shivered at the sight of the longing in Thorne's eyes. Thorne cupped Riley's cheek in his hand, thumb lightly stroking him.

"Umm…I guess I'll be heading out now," Marc said.

Thorne nodded, but he didn't look away from Riley.

"Maybe I'll go see a movie or something."

Riley waved in Marc's direction. "Bye."

A few moments later the door shut, and Thorne kissed Riley, his touch soft, gentle. When Riley had all the gentleness he could take, he sank his teeth into Thorne's lower lip and sucked on the plump flesh. Thorne opened for him, letting him explore, taste, revel in him. Oh, how Riley had missed the intensity of his reactions.

"Riley," Thorne groaned. The sound of his given name buzzed through Riley, making him even more desperate for contact.

As if sensing what he wanted, Thorne shifted, straddling Riley. He didn't seem the least bit concerned that he was rumpling his suit pants. Riley slid his hands into Thorne's hair, holding him in place as they kissed so frantically they seemed to be trying to consume each other. Thorne ground against him, and Riley arched up, trying to get more contact. Finally Thorne pulled back and stared down at Riley, panting.

Riley's pulse whooshed in his ears, and the room spun. "Fuck."

"Yeah."

"I meant to go slow," Riley confessed.

Thorne climbed off Riley and stood. "We never were very good at that."

Riley fought the urge to reach for him as Thorne gathered his suit jacket and long wool coat from the chair where he'd deposited them.

"I need to get back to work, and if this goes any further…I'll be trading slow for fast and hard."

Riley almost ordered him to get on his knees and to hell with slow, but he forced the words back down. "Okay. I can wait until next time."

Thorne studied him for a moment, seeming to look right into him. Did he know how much Riley wanted him? "Next time? You mean—"

"I want to see you for Christmas." The words burst from him.

"I have to go to my parents' for lunch on Christmas Day, but I haven't made any other plans. I'd wanted us to be together, but I didn't dare hope."

"I want to see you, very much."

"I'd bring you with me to meet my parents if you wanted me to."

Riley sucked in a breath, shocked. "You would?"

"I would. I'm not ashamed of our relationship, if that's what this is now. I would tell the world that I…that…"

Riley smiled. Thorne might not be quite ready to say those little words, but Thorne loved him. He was certain of it now.

"But my parents wouldn't treat you with respect, and I won't subject you to that."

"How much do they know about me?" Riley asked, afraid of the answer.

"Nothing. I would never tell them how I met you. They simply wouldn't respect any man I brought to their house as my lover. My sister Kathryn knows, but she doesn't care how we ended up together. She encouraged me to find out if you'd give me another chance. I'll introduce you any time you're ready. If you want to meet her that is."

Riley smiled at Thorne's nervousness. "I do."

The look of pure joy on his face made Riley reconsider the whole waiting idea once again.

"Can you come over on Christmas Eve? I'd love to spend the evening with you."

Riley nodded. "I'm having dinner with Susan, but I'll come over right afterward. I'll even bring leftovers."

"Perfect." Thorne glanced at the door and then back at Riley. "If we're truly waiting, I should go."

Riley wasn't feeling very patient, but he was determined. "Christmas is only five days away."

"And I'll be more eager than most kids for it to get here," Thorne said as he slipped on his coat.

Riley smiled as he closed the door behind him. If things went well, this would be a very merry Christmas indeed.

Chapter Twenty-Three

Thorne had never cared about holiday presents. Lauren had done his shopping in recent years, but for Riley, he'd need a perfect gift, and it couldn't be expensive. Nothing too lavish. Of course he had every intention of giving Riley the painting he'd bought for him, or at least having Riley help him hang it. He'd agonized about a present since the night he'd stood in front of Riley's apartment feeling ridiculous and praying his gesture would be enough. Like many risks he'd taken in his life, it had paid off. That was a good sign, right?

But what could he get Riley that he would believe was sincere? Thorne had considered a set of Brat Pack movies, but Riley probably owned most of them already. Then Thorne had hit upon an idea. It had seemed brilliant at the time; now it seemed absurd. Riley loved food and cooking; and every Christmas when Thorne was little his grandmother had made tiramisu. Just the smell of it meant Christmas to him. His mom hadn't been much of a baker, so she'd bought the holiday desserts after Thorne's grandmother died. But Kathryn had their grandmother's recipes, so he'd called her.

"I need Grandma's recipe for tiramisu, the one she made every Christmas."

"Is Riley going to make it for you?" Kathryn asked.

"No, I'm going to make it for him."

It had taken Kathryn quite a while to recover from her laughing fit.

"What's that Italian place you love? Why don't you get some there?"

He wasn't going to be talked out of this. "No. This is his present."

"Thorne—"

"Just send me the damn recipe."

"Okay. Let me know how it turns out." She could barely get the words out through her giggles.

Despite his sister's reaction and what he'd told Riley about his cooking skills, Thorne had been confident that if he studied hard enough, he could make anything. He'd watched tutorials, read the recipe over and over again, and googled something about almost every step.

It was a disaster. What the hell was the deal with custard anyway? How did anyone make it without getting little bits of cooked egg in it or having it scorch on the bottom of the pan or…any of the other nasty things that he'd done to it? His apartment smelled like burned sugar, and he'd been forced to open some windows despite the fact that it was freezing out.

Finally, he'd given up and made a cheaters' version, using instant pudding. At the last second, on Christmas Eve afternoon, he'd begged Salvadora at Molto Bella to sell him a pan of her tiramisu. After he showed Riley his pitiful effort, they could eat the good stuff.

Now Riley would be there any minute. Thorne paced his apartment. He fucking hated being so nervous. Had he done the right thing by not buying him an expensive gift? If he'd thought Riley would have accepted them, he would have showered him with an endless line of presents. Relationships were fucking hard.

The intercom buzzed, making him jump. "Mr. Dashwood is here."

"Thank you. Send him up."

Thorne took a long, slow breath and wiped his sweaty hands on his pants. *Don't screw this up*. He had the sense this was a make-or-break moment. Either he and Riley moved forward or they didn't.

Knock! Knock! Riley's two sharp raps. Thorne walked to the door. *Stay calm.*

He opened the door and stared. Riley was holding a large paper bag, and he had a tote slung over his shoulder, but Thorne barely spared a second to wonder what he'd brought with him, because Riley was wearing a battered leather jacket and a shirt under it that clung to his body. His jeans were Thorne's favorite ones, worn and so tight they hugged right up against Riley's balls.

He swept his gaze back up Riley's body and swallowed. "You look amazing."

Riley grinned. "Thanks, I was hoping this wasn't a dress-up affair."

"No dressing up necessary." *No clothes necessary at all*. Thorne almost said those words out loud but stopped himself. "Come in," he said, stepping back.

Riley walked past him and set the paper bag on the kitchen counter. "I brought some leftovers from Susan's since you never have food."

"I've gotten better." Not much, but a little.

He set the other bag down on the floor by the bar. "What's in that one?" Thorne asked.

"Something for later." Riley's wicked smile made Thorne wonder if he'd brought some toys like he used to.

"Would you like coffee?"

"Sure. I'll make some."

Thorne held up his hand. "No. I'll make it. You have a seat."

"You make coffee now? You *have* changed."

Thorne smiled. "Yes, I have."

After Thorne got the coffee started, he joined Riley on the couch. A wrapped box sat on the table in front of him. Riley must have gotten it from his bag while Thorne was busy.

"This is for you," Riley said, his voice slightly shaky.

Thorne hadn't expected Riley to bring him anything. "You didn't—"

"I wanted to."

"Should I open it now?"

"Yes. If you want to."

Thorne took the box. He caressed the shiny silver paper. He knew that no other present he received that year—or possibly any other—would mean as much as whatever was in this box.

He pulled the paper away carefully.

"I should have known you wouldn't rip the paper."

Thorne smiled. "No, not even as a child. You tear right into gifts, though, don't you?"

Riley laughed. "I do. I like to get into things as

fast as I can."

Thorne's cock responded to those words as if they were talking about far more than gifts. Thorne opened the box. A T-shirt lay on top. There was a picture of a sailboat on the front and the words *Work like a captain, Play like a pirate*. He lifted it and held it up to himself. "Oh my God, I love it."

"You said you thought you'd buy a boat next spring so…"

"Riley, this is awesome. Where did you find it?"

"One of Susan's friend's sails, and she directed me to a shop that has sailing equipment and gifts." He gestured toward the box. "There's something else in there."

Riley had really put a lot of thought into his gift. Thorne should have done more than make shitty tiramisu. He reached into the box and pulled out something wrapped in tissue paper. He unwrapped it, but he wasn't sure what it was other than two bow shackles with a leather strips attached.

"It's a bracelet," Riley said. "I thought it was fun and possibly…useful."

Thorne stared at the loop of leather and imagined the uses Riley had in mind. He swallowed and glanced up. "Useful? Yes, it could be."

Riley beamed at him. The coffee pot gave two long beeps, signaling that it was ready.

"Coffee?" Thorne asked.

"Yes."

"I…um…I have something for you, but you're probably stuffed from dinner at Susan's." Why hadn't he thought of that? Why hadn't he just bought a gift? There *was* still the painting.

"We ate early, kind of a lunch/dinner combo, so I'm… You got food for us?"

"In a way." Thorne rose from the table. "Just wait here, okay?"

Riley eyed him curiously, but he stayed put.

Thorne's heart pounded as he took the messy pan of tiramisu he'd made from the fridge. He cut two pieces and put them on plates, then poured coffee and put everything they needed on a tray. His hands shook as he carried it to the coffee table. Dishes rattled, giving Riley a clue how nervous he was. When he set the tray down, he said, "I wanted to make something for you."

"Y-you made this?"

"I tried to follow my grandmother's recipe—she made tiramisu every Christmas—but it didn't work, so I had to use something simpler." Heat filled Thorne's cheeks. This was not going well. "Whenever you cooked for me, I liked how it made me feel cared for, and I wanted to do that for you because…" Thorne drew in a deep breath. "I love you."

"Oh, Thorne." Riley stood and pulled Thorne into his arms, burying his face into Thorne's shoulder. "I love you too."

Thorne sank to his knees in front of Riley, wrapped his arms around him, and laid his head against his stomach. "I love you so much it hurts. I thought I'd never make it without you."

Riley slid his hands into Thorne's hair and tilted his head up. "I never stopped caring for you. I was just hurt and angry. I understand now. You thought—"

"I was an arrogant ass."

Riley smiled. "Of course you were, but that's just who you are."

Thorne laughed, and Riley tugged on him. "Get up here." He stood, and Riley kissed him, just a soft touch of lips. "I can't get carried away yet. I need to taste this tiramisu."

They both sat, and Thorne took a sip of coffee, needing something to do with his hands. "If it's awful, I have backup from Cafe Molto Bella."

"I don't want backup. I want the one you made," Riley insisted.

Thorne watched Riley take a bite, sliding his mouth along the fork, eyes closed. "Perfect."

Thorne snorted. "It is not. I used…" He leaned in close, hand against his mouth and spoke in a dramatic whisper. "Instant pudding."

Riley rolled his eyes. "Custard is very challenging. And I don't care what you used; you made this for me. That's special."

Thorne tasted it then. "Hmm, it's not too bad after all. Not like Grandma's, but better than I expected."

"Do you remember the black forest cake?" Riley's voice had changed to the low, sexy purr that drove Thorne mad.

"Yes," Thorne said, heart pounding.

"I think this tiramisu would taste even better eaten the same way."

"You do realize tiramisu always makes me think of Christmas at Grandma's, right?"

Riley gave a sly grin. "Christmas changes when you're all grown up."

Thorne groaned. It sure as hell did. "Does that mean we're done with slow, because—"

"Fuck slow. I've been so horny today, fantasizing about how I'd be coming over here and fucking you tonight, that I could hardly think."

And Thorne had thought he'd have to seduce Riley. "So you've known all day that you were…that we were going to…"

"I've known since the last time I saw you. What do you think is in the other bag?"

Thorne swallowed hard. "I…"

"I wanted to take you in the lobby of my building that night, right there up against the wall. And the other day on the couch. I don't know how I stopped myself."

"Riley, I—"

"Stop talking," Dash—no *Riley*—demanded. Thorne couldn't help thinking of him as Dash when he got that commanding tone.

Thorne had never been happier to be bossed around.

Riley spread tiramisu over Thorne's lips and then proceeded to lick it off, very slowly. Thorne dug his fingers into his thighs to keep from reaching for him.

When Thorne's lips were thoroughly cleaned, Riley sat back and gave Thorne a once-over, his eyes dark with lust. "Maybe we should put those new bracelets to use tonight."

"Fuck, yes. I've missed this, Riley. I want you to… I need…"

Riley smiled. "I know." He tugged at Thorne's shirt. "Off."

Thorne yanked it over his head and tossed it

aside. Riley took more cream and rubbed it onto
Thorne's nipples. "Don't move," he whispered as he
leaned down, mouth inches from tasting Thorne.

Thorne wasn't sure he could obey as Riley
sucked and licked and nibbled. He nearly bit through
his bottom lip, trying to hold in the pathetic whimpers
threatening to escape.

Riley looked up and gave him an evil grin.
"We're definitely using the bracelets later." He
paused and swiped his tongue across Thorne's nipple,
making him shudder. "I've got plans for you."

"Please!" Thorne didn't know if he was begging
for more or for mercy.

"Tell me what you want, Thorne."

"I want you to use me. Take me any way you
want. I just…need you."

"Mmm. That's just what I wanted to hear."

Riley nibbled his way down Thorne's torso,
stopping at his waistband. "Lose the pants," he
demanded as he rose to his feet.

Thorne wasn't sure his legs would hold him up if
he stood, so he unfastened his pants while sitting and
lifted his hips just enough to wiggle out of them.

Riley jerked them off his legs. "Lie back, one leg
over the arm of the couch. Hands underneath you."

Fuck. His commanding tone was the sexiest thing
ever.

Thorne spread himself for Riley. He knew what
was coming, and he was afraid he might burst into
flames, but it would be a good way to go.

Riley dipped his finger into the tiramisu. But
instead of smearing it on Thorne's cock, he sucked it
off his finger. "I want cock with no added flavor

tonight."

Thorne stared, not believing he'd said that.

Riley licked his cock then, little flicks of his tongue down the length of his shaft that had Thorne lifting his hips and begging for more.

"So eager," Riley purred.

"It's been too long."

"Did you jerk off thinking of this?"

Thorne groaned. "God yes. I thought about you, your mouth, your cock."

Riley grinned. Then he teased Thorne's cockhead, pushing his tongue into the slit.

"Stop fucking teasing me."

Riley sucked him in then, taking him deep, swallowing until his face brushed Thorne's pubic bone. He was going to fucking come any second. Then Riley pulled back and looked at Thorne with a teasing glint in his eyes. No way was Riley going to make things easy on him.

Without speaking, Riley stood and stripped. Thorne watched, eager to see his beautiful body again. When he freed his cock it sprung up red and needy, precum beaded on the tip. Thorne longed to lick it off. It had been so long since he'd tasted Riley.

But Dash—and he was definitely Dash to Thorne now—was in charge, and that wasn't what Dash wanted. "I want you behind the couch, bent over, hands together behind you."

"Are you going to…?"

"Restrain you? Yes."

"Fuck."

"Exactly. Hard and deep. You need that, don't you?" Dash asked.

"So much. So fucking much."

Thorne shivered when Dash wrapped the cool leather around his wrists. When he heard the click of the shackle, he couldn't keep himself from testing their strength. He tugged hard, harder. The bracelets were locked tight. He wasn't getting loose. "Dash? Um…Riley?"

"I'm right here." Dash laid a hand between his shoulder blades, gently encouraging him to lie back down. "And I think Dash is the man you need right now. He's the man who can bring you to your knees, no matter how stubborn you are. Call me anything you want, as long as you do exactly what I say."

Thorne turned and glared at him, bristling at how much he needed to be dominated.

Dash just smiled. "You remember how this works, right? If you say red, I'll stop and unfasten you. This is all about pleasure."

Thorne relaxed and let himself fold in two over the back of the couch. He trusted Dash.

"Remember the first time I had you like this?"

Thorne nodded.

"You struggled. You didn't want to submit."

He couldn't seem to form a coherent thought with Dash right there ready to take him, use him.

"Are you going to struggle tonight?"

"No. Yes. I don't know."

"I want you to, and I want you to know that I'm going to drive this into your ass no matter what." He brushed his cock over Thorne's hole. "You got that?"

"Yes."

"Good." Dash walked away, and Thorne turned his head and watched as Dash donned a condom and slicked himself up.

Thorne dropped his head back down when Dash moved behind him, gripped his ass cheeks, and pulled them apart.

"Look at that ass," Dash said, sliding a finger inside him. "So ready for me. You need a cock in there so bad, don't you?"

Thorne tried to pull away as Dash finger-fucked him. He wanted to deny how right Dash was.

"But you don't like needing me like that, do you?"

"Bastard," Thorne murmured, but he pushed back against Dash, rubbing his ass on Dash's cock.

Thorne thought Dash would keep dragging things out, but he gripped Thorne's hips and thrust into him. Thorne gasped and struggled, fighting to get away while wanting more, wanting to be split in two.

Dash used a hand on Thorne's back to push him down, hold him, but otherwise he held still. "I… Fuck, I got carried away. Are you all right?"

"I'm fine," Thorne snarled.

Dash pushed deeper then. Fuck, he was big.

"Still fucking fine now?" he asked, the worry gone from his voice.

Thorne shoved himself back, taking Dash deeper. "Yes, you son of a bitch. I want it all."

Dash gave it to him. Driving in until he was buried to the balls and then pulling back and doing it again, never giving Thorne time to catch his breath. Thorne's ass burned, and he tried in vain to break out of his bonds, but he'd never been happier. He wanted more, wanted to be owned. "Fuck me, Dash. I want to come."

Dash grabbed his wrists and tugged, almost lifting him off the couch. "I say when, not you."

Thorne struggled, trying his best to break free of the bracelet. "I can't... I—"

Dash reached around and stroked Thorne's cock. "Yes, you can. I'm close and so are you, and you're going to come exactly. When. I. Tell. You. To." Dash punctuated each word with a hard thrust.

Thorne stopped fighting him then, giving in to his true desire to do anything to please Dash. "Yes!"

Dash fucked him over and over, finding the perfect angle to hit his sweet spot and light him up. Dash's hand on Thorne's cock matched the rhythm of his thrusts. Faster. So close. So...

"Come. Now."

Thorne did. Dash's words pushed him right over. His body jerked, and he shot over Dash's hand. Dash kept working him, his slick spunk making it easier. Then Dash shouted, bucked against him, and rode out his own release.

"Fuck," Dash exhaled as he collapsed against Thorne's back.

"That was amazing." Thorne's heart seemed ready to burst from his chest.

A few moments later, Dash rose up. "I missed you."

"I missed you too." Thorne winced when Dash pulled out. Damn, he was going to be sore.

Dash released his hands and rubbed his wrists. They were going to be sore too and maybe bruised, but he didn't care. "Are you okay?"

Thorne had never been better, never thought he'd feel this good again. Dash, Riley, it didn't matter.

This was the man he belonged with. "Completely. For the first time in months."

Riley tugged on his arm. "Let me help you get cleaned up."

Thorne wasn't sure he could stand, but with Riley's help he got to his feet, steadying himself on the back of the couch.

Riley wrapped an arm around his waist. "Lean on me."

Thorne did. When they reached the bathroom, Riley let go of Thorne, and he sank down to the fluffy white carpet in front of the sink.

"Are you sure you're okay?" Riley asked, handing him a glass of water.

Thorne took a few sips before answering. His head spun, but he knew that would pass. "I'm fine. Really. I love how intensely you fuck me."

Riley grinned. "Good. Let's take a cool shower so you won't overheat."

Thorne nodded.

Riley managed to get him cleaned and dried and in bed, and they fell asleep wrapped up in each other. At some point Thorne woke to Riley kissing his way down his chest. "I need more," Riley said.

"Yes. More. Never gonna get enough of you," he murmured.

***

Hours later, Thorne woke to weak winter sun poking its way through the window. He stretched and rubbed his eyes.

"Merry Christmas."

The voice startled him. He turned over to see Riley watching him. He was really there, in bed with

Thorne. The night before hadn't been a dream.

"Merry Christmas." Thorne's voice was scratchy.

Riley snuggled against him. "I've missed this, waking up next to you. Seeing you all mussed from sleep rather than the polished businessman from the night before."

"Do I hold my polish while my ass is spread and begging for your cock?"

Riley laughed. "No matter how much you beg, you still want to control things. But like this, you're all soft, sweet."

Thorne wasn't sure whether to be offended or not.

"You ready to get up? We could have tiramisu for breakfast."

"The same way you had it last night?" Thorne asked.

Riley appeared to consider his options. "Maybe not at first."

"What happened to getting veggies and fruit in me?"

"It's Christmas."

Thorne rolled over. "Do you think Santa left us something?"

"Have you been a good boy?"

Thorne laughed. "No, but if you reach under the covers, I've got a present for you."

Ignoring him, Riley slid from the bed. "Breakfast first."

"I can't get enough of you, you know that, right?"

"I do. We have hours until you have to leave."

Thorne forced himself to look at the clock. It was

only eight. "We do, but I have a project for us."

"What kind of project?"

"Feed me and I'll tell you about it."

After they'd eaten—tiramisu and fruit salad Riley had brought from Susan's—Thorne told Riley to close his eyes. He retrieved the painting from the spare bedroom, unwrapped it, and carried it back to where he'd left Riley at the table. "Okay, open your eyes."

Riley did. "Oh my God, that's the painting, the one from the art opening. You bought it."

"I did. It was delivered a few days after you…left."

"And you never put it up."

"I wanted us to hang it together. I wanted it to be for you."

Riley looked like he was going to protest, but then he simply said, "Thank you."

"So where should we put it?"

Riley turned, looking around the apartment. "Here." He pointed to the wall behind the table. "The light is perfect."

Thorne smiled. "I agree, and every time you cook for me, we'll see it." As soon as the words were out, he worried he'd said the wrong thing. "If you want to cook for me, that is. No pressure."

"I do. I want to spend a lot of time here, with you."

"You're always welcome."

"I'll remember that."

"I'm serious; you could even…" Move in. Thorne wanted to say it, but it was too early. He knew that.

"What?"

"Nothing."

"Thorne." Riley's tone said he'd keep asking until Thorne told him.

"I was going to say move in, but I shouldn't ask that now. I'm trying to be good and not demand too much."

"I'll think about it."

Thorne couldn't believe it. He'd expected to be scolded. "You will?"

"Yes, and in the meantime, I'll keep making sure you remember that sometimes, I'm the one who makes the demands."

Thorne thought about being bent over the couch the night before. "I like it when you're demanding."

Riley smiled. "On occasion, I like you that way too."

"I'm sorry for hurting you."

Riley wrapped his arms around Thorne and pulled him close. "I know. I forgive you."

Thorne sucked in his breath. How could those simple words mean so much? He felt lighter, happier even than he'd been the night before. "Thank you."

"Thank *you* for not giving up on me, for risking yourself. If you hadn't…"

"I couldn't let you go."

"Merry Christmas," Riley murmured, pulling Thorne down for a kiss.

Merry Christmas. Thorne merely thought the words as Riley's lips met his and everything in his world brightened. This was joy. This was love. And somehow, he'd been lucky enough to find it.

Dear Reader,

Thank you for purchasing *Professional Distance*. I hope you enjoyed it. *Thorne and Dash Books 2 and 3* will be published in 2016. If you like erotic gay romance, you may also enjoy the *Fitting In* series. I offer a free book to anyone who joins my mailing list. To learn more, go to silviaviolet.com/newsletter.

Please consider leaving a review where you purchased this ebook or on Goodreads. Reviews and word-of-mouth recommendations are vital to independent authors.

I love hearing from readers. You can email me at silviaviolet@gmail.com. To read excerpts from all of my titles, visit my website: silviaviolet.com.

Silvia Violet

Author Bio

Silvia Violet writes erotic romance in a variety of genres including paranormal, contemporary, and historical. She can be found haunting coffee shops looking for the darkest, strongest cup of coffee she can find. Once equipped with the needed fuel, she can happily sit for hours pounding away at her laptop. Silvia typically leaves home disguised as a suburban stay-at-home-mom, and other coffee shop patrons tend to ask her hilarious questions like "Do you write children's books?" She loves watching the looks on their faces when they learn what she's actually up to. When not writing, Silvia enjoys baking sinfully delicious treats, exploring new styles of cooking, and reading to her incorrigible offspring.

Website: http://silviaviolet.com

Facebook: http://facebook.com/silvia.violet

Twitter: http://twitter.com/Silvia_Violet

Pinterest: http://www.pinterest.com/silviaviolet/

Tumblr: http://silviaviolet.tumblr.com/

Titles by Silvia Violet

Coming Clean
If Wishes Were Horses
Needing A Little Christmas
One Kiss

Fitting In
Fitting In
Sorting Out
Burning Up

Unexpected
Unexpected Rescue
Unexpected Trust
Unexpected Engagement

Wild R Farm
Finding Release
Arresting Love
Embracing Need
Taming Tristan
Willing Hands
Shifting Hearts
Wild R Christmas

Galactic Betrayal
Abandoned
Deceived

Available from Dreamspinner Press
Denying Yourself
Pressure Points

Available from Changeling Press
Savage Wolf
Sex on the Hoof
Paws on Me
Hoofin' it to the Altar

Available from Loose Id
Astronomical
Meteor Strike

28104015R00161

Made in the USA
Middletown, DE
02 January 2016